True Image

A Novel

Susan Statham

True Image
Copyright © 2024 Susan Statham
All rights reserved
Published by Blue Denim Press Inc.
First Edition
ISBN -978-1-998494-03-3

This is a work of fiction. Any resemblance to real people is unintentional and co-incidental.

Cover Image—Susan Statham
Cover Design—Shane Joseph

Library and Archives Canada Cataloguing in Publication

Title: True image : a novel / Susan Statham.
Names: Statham, Susan, 1951- author
Description: First edition.
Identifiers: Canadiana (print) 20240415965 | Canadiana (ebook) 20240415973 | ISBN 9781998494033 (softcover) | ISBN 9781998494040 (Kindle) | ISBN 9781998494057 (EPUB) | ISBN 9781998494064 (IngramSpark EPUB)
Subjects: LCGFT: Detective and mystery fiction. | LCGFT: Novels.
Classification: LCC PS8637.T375 T78 2024 | DDC C813/.6—dc23

Dedication

For Joy

Previous Books by Susan Statham

The Painter's Craft (Book 1 featuring Maud Gibbons)

Chapter 1

Damn it. Lost again. Good navigators have instant recognition of left and right but I'm not a good navigator. It was 2003 and I didn't have GPS or a smartphone. What I did have, thanks to my agent, was a hand-drawn map and easing my new car onto the gravel shoulder, I checked it again. When I saw the error of my ways, I made an illegal U-turn and, in less time than it takes to read a compass, found the sign for Cherry Hill Road.

Two weeks before my road trip into the Ontario countryside, I got a call from my agent, Mr. Evelyn Baer, aka Ted. He invited me to his office to discuss a commission, and I was there before he hung up the phone. I wouldn't have been quite so eager had he told me the client's name.

As owners of Barrington Pharmaceuticals, Veronica and Alton Barrington, were part of Toronto's elite. Learning Mrs. Veronica Barrington had selected me to paint her portrait raised both awe and suspicion. Had every portrait artist in the city, if not the country, turned it down? Or was I just that good? Neither seemed true nor were they.

Ted insisted I had been chosen from many, but admitted the field was reduced by Veronica's conditions.

"Conditions?"

"Don't look so worried, Maud. You got the first one handled. She wants a female artist."

I liked the idea of a client who supported women artists.

"Her second stipulation could be considered unusual by today's standards." He paused just long enough for my imagination to take me to places of maximum discomfort.

"Oh, yes?" I asked.

"The thing is, Veronica wants to be painted from life."

"Really?" Since most clients barely sat still long enough for a few good reference photos, I had to know why.

Using air quotes and a slightly higher voice, he said, "To sit for one's portrait is to participate in its creation."

"Surely Mrs. Barrington doesn't want to help with the painting—does she?" I envisioned her taking my brush and adding a flourish. "I can't paint someone who's going to monitor my every brush stroke."

"Maud, don't look so worried. I'm sure Veronica simply feels by showing up each day and taking the pose, she's participating in the process. She also understands this is an unusual request and because of that, you will be financially compensated."

Financial compensation sounded good, but at what cost? I was used to working from photographs, alone, in the quiet of my studio. Painting the live model would be like going back to school except in that scenario, I paid for the privilege. In this one, I'd be getting paid. I might even be willing to work in a garret and survive on a daily crust of bread—provided the lighting was good.

"There's one more thing," my agent confessed. "Veronica resides at her country estate during the summer, so you'll be expected to paint the portrait there."

"And commute?" It would be the end of my old car, probably with me in it.

"No, no, of course not. You'll stay there. It's a lovely old place, and since Veronica doesn't want a complicated background, it shouldn't take more than a couple of weeks." He handed me the cheque. "If you accept the commission, this is half. You'll receive the balance upon completion."

I stared at the digits. Wow, this was serious compensation. "Where is this place?" I asked, envisioning a windswept, isolated island rife with a murder of angry crows.

"Just a couple of hours east of the city. It's not actually on the lake but there is a pool and I think you told me you liked to swim."

"I do."

"Great. You can think of it as a busman's holiday."

"So, Mrs. Veronica Barrington, she's not Attila the Hun's sister, is she?"

"Maybe." He smirked and patted my shoulder. "Just kidding. I think you'll find Veronica a very interesting woman."

Interesting? Now there's a word to describe a blind date memorable for all the wrong reasons. I looked at the cheque. This was the down payment on a used car and one that wouldn't inhale water every time I drove through a puddle. It was also the smile of pride on my uncle's face, a high-stress adventure and my first truly lucrative portrait commission. I thought of Pietro Annigoni painting Queen Elizabeth at Buckingham Palace. "Okay," I said and put the cheque in my purse. "Now, how do I get there?"

"It's an easy drive," he said, with the casual detachment of someone seldom misplaced and never lost. I almost believed him.

Chapter 2

Turning north on Cherry Hill Road, I felt confident that, barring any more wrong turns, I might get to the Barrington Estate at the appointed hour, eleven a.m. According to Mrs. Barrington's instructions, it would give me time to unpack and get my bearings before lunch at noon sharp.

As I approached the expected fork in the road, my map told me to look for the sign pointing to the house. I stopped the car and looked to the north and south, or east and west depending on the direction I was facing. I saw nothing but bristling shrubs and optimistic saplings.

I was reaching once more for the map when a rap on the driver's window sent my heart into my throat and my skull into the headrest. Turning only my eyes, I glimpsed a face of wrinkled leather and slowly raised my left elbow to surreptitiously push down the lock on my door. Senseless behaviour, I know, because if I truly believed he was a homicidal maniac, why worry about insulting him with the suggestion that he couldn't be trusted? Another tap on the window and I lowered it a few centimetres. A blast of summer heat accompanied a voice as rough as his skin. "You Ms. Gibbons?"

I nodded.

He dipped his head. "Caleb Moses, handyman for Mrs. Barrington."

I let my shoulders and the window drop. I even managed a smile. "Nice to meet you. I was looking for the sign." I waved my paper map.

"Sorry, Miss. I should have come up here earlier to clear away these bushes." He pointed to the road on my left. "You follow along there. You'll come to the house soon enough."

I did as instructed and found myself in a tunnel of leaves provided by the lush trees growing on either side of the road. As the dirt road transformed into a white-pebbled drive, carpeted on either side with an emerald lawn, I saw my first view of the Barrington summer home.

Built on higher ground, the house soared above me, its brick the colour of dried blood, and its third story defended by a steep black roof. Less intimidating were the green and white striped awnings hanging like heavy eyelids over the first-floor windows. And around the border of a stone patio, danced a healthy bed of red and white petunias.

At the side of the house, I parked in the shade of a towering oak, exited the car, and breathed in the floral-scented air. Standing on one of the rolling hills of Northumberland, the view took me across acres of land and down to shimmering blue where Lake Ontario merged with the sky.

Gradually aware of the swoosh-squeal of rhythmic metal, I turned to see a young girl held captive on a chain-link swing. I waved and called hello, but she didn't respond.

"Don't waste your breath." Standing behind me on a large wooden porch was one of van Gogh's peasant women. "You must be Miss Gibbons." She carried her considerable weight down four steps to the paving stones. "Thought you were comin' at eleven."

I checked my watch. It was 11:10. "I made a wrong turn—"

"Ya look kinda young." Her eyes narrowed.

"Oh, well, thank you Ms …" I extended my hand and she wiped her palms on the skirt of a floral apron before grazing my fingertips.

"Mrs. Fleeten. I'm the housekeeper and cook. You can call me Dinah, everyone else does." Her tone suggested she'd rather they didn't.

"I had a school friend named Jessica Fleeten. Could you be related?"

"Nope. Born a Corday. Do you have much luggage?" She made a visor with her hand and scanned the area. "Caleb should have cleared those bushes by now. Talk about closin' the barn door after the horses have left." She made another quick scan of the driveway. "Well, come on then. I'll help ya. Where're your bags?"

I held the remote toward the trunk and pressed a button. The alarm was deafening. "Sorry," I yelled over the din, fiddling with what was suddenly a complex piece of equipment. Finally, I hit a button that silenced the horn. "I just bought this car. I'm not used to the remote."

"So it would seem. You gonna try again?" Dinah took a step backward.

This time the trunk popped open. She leaned in, ignored all the art equipment and pulled out my suitcase. "Mercy," she muttered before grunting and dragging the case and herself toward the side door. I followed with my gym bag, paintbox and portable aluminum easel.

At the porch landing, Dinah turned toward the girl on the swing. "Get yourselves to the garden," she bellowed and to me said, "Penelope never listens but her minder's lurking around there somewhere." She pushed open the heavy wooden door. "Watch your step."

Chapter 3

We entered a hallway paved with Vermeer's beautiful black and white tiles. While Dinah lingered at the open door, likely looking for the handyman, I set down my case and flattened my palm against the smooth, cool marble.

"Men, I tell ya," Dinah grumbled. "How long does it take to clear a few bushes?" She slammed the door and I scrambled to my feet as she pushed past me. "Course we mustn't paint all men with the same brush."

"No, of course not," I said, as if I was somehow complicit in the denigration of all men.

"My Mr. Fleeten was a fine man—gone too soon. Not that I'm questionin' the good Lord's decisions. When one door closes another one opens and he sent me my dear Beau. You'll be meetin' him soon enough."

"That's nice," I mumbled, distracted by a view of the kitchen. The appliances gleamed expensively and dark granite countertops sliced between well-appointed cupboards. It was, however, half the size of my expectations.

"My kitchen is state-of-the-art," Dinah said, reaching around me to close the door.

Kitchen disappointment evaporated when we reached the living room—the high ceiling, wooden beams and walls the colour of vintage lace seemed the perfect accent for gleaming oak floors and a rich Persian carpet. Three leather sofas formed a U in front of the most incredible fireplace I'd ever seen.

Dinah followed my gaze. "Like that, eh?"

"I do." I ran my fingers over the large, smooth stones. "I wonder if they got these locally. Do you know when the house was built?"

"Nineteen thirteen, and it's full of surprises. There's a whole wing just for guests, and we got a titanic swimmin' pool."

"It must have been built for a big family."

"Nope. Built by some rich gent from Toronto for his ailin' daughter. She died."

"In the pool?"

"No, in her bed." Dinah tilted her head toward the back of the house. "Up the road, there's a coach house where me and Mr. Fleeten lived as year-round caretakers. Now Caleb's got it."

I wasn't sure if she was seeking my sympathy or my outrage, but I ceased to care when I noticed the painting above the mantel. "Wow. Is that a—"

"Hey, this case ain't gettin' any lighter." Like a plump border collie, Dinah began herding me toward a grand staircase. Carpeted in stippled wool fibres of grey and blue, it was a gentle waterfall.

"My God, is this real?" I asked, pausing in front of a small drawing at the top of the stairs.

"Course it's real. It's hangin' there ain't it?"

"What I meant was ..."

Dinah huffed, mumbling something about her employer's questionable decision to put me in Rex's room. "He's the middle son and in Europe with his father so he's got no say in the matter, not that he'd complain. He's a nice young man, even if he's not a patch on my boy." Halfway down the broad hall, Dinah paused at a closed door. "This is my Beau's room." I half-expected her to bow in homage.

Many more steps down the hall and on the opposite side, she stopped, dropped my case and released one of those sighs my mother uses when she wants appreciation. I obliged, adding "so much" to my "thank you," and she opened the door.

Anxious to get rid of the weight, I dropped my heavy gym bag on the queen-sized bed. Dinah, surprisingly nimble on her short chubby legs, immediately pulled the bag to the floor, clicking her tongue as she swept a hand across the tartan bedspread.

"Do you know where I'll be working?" I asked, still clutching my easel and paintbox.

"Working?" The word dripped disdain.

"Yes," I said, pulling back my shoulders. "Painting Mrs. Barrington's portrait."

"Oh, that." Dinah rubbed her hand across the dust-free maple dresser, a gesture that signified what she considered real work. "I'm sure her ladyship has taken care of it."

Setting the paintbox on the floor next to the dresser, I leaned the easel against the wall.

"Well," Dinah clapped her hands together. "I gotta go. Caleb will be waitin' and I need to make sure Miss Conlin got the girl off that dang swing. She's the kid's minder." Hesitating at the doorway she added, "Did ya know she's peculiar?"

"Miss Conlin?"

"No, no—the daughter, Penelope. She's got that autism thing." Dinah tapped her temple. "Not all there, if you get my meaning. Needs a firm hand."

"When I was a girl, we had a neighbour whose son was on the autism spectrum. He was—"

"Okay, I gotta go. Don't dawdle. We run on schedules here, breakfast at eight-thirty, lunch at noon and supper at five-thirty. Should be six but the girl can't wait."

Dinah yanked the door closed and my easel, like nails scratching a blackboard, clawed down the wall, its thick metal hasp gouging a thin, yet distinct, groove. Damn it.

Chapter 4

The chime of my cell phone reminded me of a promised call to my uncle. It was on its fourth ring by the time I dug it out of my purse. "Hi, Uncle Sid, I just got here."

"And how is it?"

"Impressive and intimidating. The property's huge, the house is grand and there's a Bateman in my room, a Picasso drawing hanging in the hall, and a Thomson oil over the fireplace. Gosh, I hope they don't use it—the fireplace that is."

"Sounds like they appreciate good art."

"I know. How can I compete?"

"Now Maudie, don't think like that. After all, these are people with the luxury of choices and they chose you."

Uncle Sid has always been my biggest fan. He and my Aunt Emma gave me a home when my parents moved west. After my aunt died, he supported me through art college, eventually giving me a job at his detective agency.

"You're right, Uncle Sid. I'm sure it'll be fine," I forced a confidence I didn't feel and switched the subject to Sherlock. "Does he miss me?"

"Of course, he does and like any bloodhound he's been trying to find you. In fact, he got so tired sniffing every inch of the office, he's having a little snooze. Now, tell me about your client?"

"I haven't met her yet. I only met the cook."

"They have a cook?" He snorted. "Of course they do. What about an armed guard for those pricey paintings?"

"I know you're only half joking, but I don't think a thief could find this place. It's hidden away in the countryside."

My uncle reminded me what Sherlock, the detective, not our dog, had said about houses in the country. "Consider their isolation and the impunity with which crime may be committed there. So, keep your new cell phone charged and handy. And to do that, you need to get the charger out of your suitcase."

I hadn't wanted the interruptions or the hassle of a mobile phone, but after we ended the call, and before I unpacked most of my clothes, I dutifully retrieved and plugged in the charger. Scanning the room for something to hide the scratch on the wall, I chose a small upholstered chair and dragged it into position.

On my way back to my car, I noticed a drawing of totem poles and was only mildly surprised by the signature—how quickly one's expectations adjust. At the kitchen door, I pushed it open to ask Dinah where I should leave my car. She was at the sink but before I could say a word, she spun around like a startled cat, raised her wet palms and pushed at the air. "Out you go! Out you go!"

Her outburst propelled me backwards and I collided with someone unable to get out of my way. A loud crack made us awkward tap dancers as a small plastic case skidded down the hall.

"Is your phone, okay?" I asked the young woman who scooped it up.

"Should be. I got a new heavy-duty case." She held it out for me to have a look.

"Nice. Maybe I should get one." This, from someone who hadn't even wanted a cell phone.

After securing the phone in the pocket of her cargo pants, she reached for my hand. "You must be Maud, the artist. I'm really, really glad you're here."

"Really? Well, thank you, Ms. ..."

"Jamie, Jamie Conlin."

Dinah hadn't described her, but I'd imagined a cross between Mr. Chips and Nurse Ratched. Certainly not Sargent's Lady Agnew in a baseball cap.

"Are you all settled in?"

"More or less." I mentioned the few things remaining in my car and Jamie offered to help, eagerly following me out the side door.

"Hey, nice car."

I beamed as if I'd built it myself. "Thanks, it's not new, just new to me." I'm not sure why I felt the need for explanation but at least this time I had no problem opening the trunk. Jamie grabbed my drawing board, camera bag, and tripod. I reached in for the large carryall I'd stuffed with all the supplies I might need and many I probably wouldn't. "Do you know if it's okay to leave my car here?" I must have sounded like a worried mother.

"I'd say sure, but you might want to ask Dinah."

"I tried."

"And she threw you out of the kitchen, right?"

"Technically, no. I never actually got in."

"Don't take it personally," Jamie whispered, as we passed the kitchen door. "She can be a tyrant but you'll forgive her when you taste her cooking and if you do need to visit her kitchen kingdom, knock first. She'll either crack open the door and ask what you want or yell at you to go away. There's only one person who's always welcome."

"And would that person be Beau?" I asked.

Jamie laughed. "You must have spent at least two minutes talking to Dinah."

"Yeah, she greeted me when I got here and showed me to my room." As Jamie and I climbed the stairs to the second floor, I recounted bits of Dinah's conversation, including her mention of Penelope's autism and the need for what she called a minder.

"I'm a special ed teacher at Penny's school, hired for the summer. I also studied nursing for long enough to know it wasn't for me. Both areas are useful when working with children as challenged as Penelope. Of course, if you ask the eccentric Mrs. Barrington, she'll tell you I'm her daughter's personal assistant."

"Eccentric?" I led the way into my room, indicating a spot next to the dresser for the art supplies.

"Hmm, maybe obsessive-compulsive is a better description."

Neither option sounded promising. "Anything else I should know about her?" I perched on the side of the bed.

Momentarily distracted, Jamie said, "Gee, that's a funny place for a chair," and glanced around the room before taking a seat. "Anyway, you were asking about Mrs. Barrington. I'd have to say the woman has a few issues." Seeing the look on my face, Jamie added, "Don't worry, she's not an axe murderer or anything. She's just not what you might call, um, nice."

I wanted to ask if she was what you might call interesting, but sensed Jamie had other words to describe the woman.

"She's a retired lawyer and a snob who likes to lecture, possibly because she's always the smartest person in the room. Or at least she thinks she is. Fortunately for me, she spends a lot of time in her own room working on some secret project."

"Does it involve a pentagram and a broom?"

Jamie giggled. "Maybe, though I've never seen the broom. Usually, she's just working at her desk. Perhaps the Queen B is writing a book or keeping a scandalous diary."

"The Queen B?"

Jamie's face reddened like a kid caught stealing candy. "Please don't repeat that. She hates nicknames and has no sense of humour. During my job interview, she asked me what 'Jamie' was short for. I told her my parents thought they were having a boy and had chosen the name James but she was convinced they'd called me Jemima. Good for you with Maud. Do you know what it means?"

"Thanks, but I can't take any credit and I was named after my father's favourite aunt."

"Mrs. Barrington will probably figure that out, then she'll give you a history lesson. At least it's a name no one can morph into a nickname. I mean, you couldn't be called Mau or Ud or Mad."

"How about Mud?" I suggested, eliciting shared laughter.

"Well," Jamie rose to her feet, "my name will be Mudd if I don't retrieve the darling daughter before her mother gets home. She's with Caleb and Steady. Want to meet the crew?"

Closing the bedroom door behind us I told Jamie I'd met Caleb at the fork in the road. "Who's Steady?"

"Oh, that's not his real name. According to Dinah, it's Tosh, like the Jamaican singer. Can't say I've heard of him."

"Me neither but how did Tosh become Steady?"

"When Caleb was teaching him to walk on a lead, he didn't say 'heel,' he said 'steady.'"

I stopped at the top of the stairs. "You're talking about a dog, aren't you?"

"Yeah, didn't I say? He's a retriever with a little shepherd and maybe border collie or is it poodle?" She chewed her bottom lip. "Anyway, he arrived a few years ago and Penny bonded with him almost immediately, rare for an autistic child. She insisted everyone call him Steady. Sadly, she no longer calls him anything at all."

"Why not?" I followed Jamie along another hallway and out an unfamiliar door to a well-trodden path.

"Penelope's language skills were always limited but one day last year, she simply stopped talking. Her parents brought in the usual cohort of specialists, and we did what we could at school but nothing made any difference. According to Dinah 'the girl' needs less of what she calls *special treatment* and more discipline. In her words, 'She'd talk for herself if ya all didn't talk for her.'

"Of course, Dinah thinks there's only one Barrington who deserves special treatment and the thing is, I kind of agree with her." Jamie's face took on the glow of someone about to describe a saint and then she did. "Beau is pretty special. He's funny and fun and gorgeous. He's a Barrington, so tall and slim, but the only one with golden curls. Kinda like an angel's."

I anticipated a few words of poetry but her reverie broke as she looked toward the garden. "There's Penny," she said and I followed the direction of her outstretched hand. "Now, Maud, when you meet her, talk softly and avoid any sudden movement. She may look fragile but she's surprisingly strong."

Chapter 5

Penny stood on the perimeter of a kaleidoscope of blossoms while Caleb worked in the middle of the garden, cutting flowers and adding them to a large bouquet. As we approached, a big yellow dog galumphed across the grass toward us. With the crazy joie de vivre of happy canines, he zoomed in for a pet and a scratch behind the ears before running back to his master, leaving me with a longing for my own fur-faced boy.

Jamie slowed the pace as we got closer to the tall raw-boned girl in faded pink shorts and, despite the summer heat, a baggy pale blue sweater with sagging pockets. Her body stiffened noticeably when her teacher gently touched her shoulder.

"Penelope," Jamie slowly removed her hand, "I want you to meet Maud. Remember in your art books and jigsaw puzzles—all those paintings of faces? Maud is here to paint Mommy's portrait. Isn't that exciting?"

I greeted Penny with a soft hello and though I didn't expect a response, I also didn't expect her to fold like a pop-up card. As both arms wrapped around her waist, she tucked her head so tightly against her chest that her auburn hair closed like a curtain over her face. I knew it wasn't a total shutdown because, like something out of a horror movie, I could see her eyes staring at me through the thick strands. I gasped and when I did, Penny's forearm sprung out like an electric gate. She may have wanted to push me, hit me or shake my hand. Before she did anything, Steady was back nuzzling her for a pet and as her thin fingers disappeared into the dog's heavy fur, I remembered to breathe.

"Taking a little longer than usual Miss," Caleb called to Jamie. "Here's what we got so far." He raised the bouquet for inspection and Steady trotted back to his master.

Jamie signed a thumbs up, turned toward Penny and said, "Okay kiddo, lunchtime." Penny's robot-like gait was unexpectedly speedy. "Food is a great motivator for our Pen."

"Good to know," I muttered.

Back in the living room, Jamie pointed to an archway in the far wall. "Maud, you might as well go directly into the dining room. If the Queen B's not there, she will be shortly."

"Does she sting?" I asked.

"What?"

"The Queen B."

"Only if she thinks you're a queen bee too," said Jamie.

"I hope I'm safe. I have no intention of threatening her hive."

"Speaking of threatening, be sure to use the name Penelope in front of her mother. Now, I need to take Penny upstairs to convince her she could make her Momma happy if she wore her new sundress." Bending a little closer to my ear, Jamie whispered, "Actually, I've never seen the woman happy." With a sigh and a sympathetic smile, she wished me good luck.

Seemed I was going to need it. An unhappy, eccentric snob with a stinger and obsessive-compulsive tendencies sounded like someone impossible to please. I couldn't deny the urge to flee, but if I did a runner, it might as well be directly to the car dealership.

A good omen greeted me when I stepped into the dining room. The sunlight, streaming through a pair of stunning French doors refracted through a crystal vase of cut flowers and created a rainbow.

On a walnut dining table large enough to seat twelve, were four emerald green placements, like lily pads at the far end of a pond. I picked up one of the side plates and recognized my grandmother's *Country Rose* pattern. The memories of family get-togethers evaporated the moment someone said my name. She was a woman of surprising height and enviable posture.

"Hello. Yes, I'm Maud Gibbons." I gingerly replaced the plate and extended a hand she didn't bother to shake.

"I'm Veronica Barrington. Welcome to Altica." Before I could ask, she told me it was her husband, Alton's idea. "The first three letters of his name with the last three of mine." Her words were carefully enunciated. "I assume Dinah helped you settle in." She pulled back the chair at the head of the table, sat down and with her long thin fingers gestured, in no particular direction, for me to do the same. I chose the place to her right. "No not there, that's Jamie's seat. Have you met Miss Jamie Conlin?"

"Yes, and Penny too." I clamped my mouth shut but it was too late.

"Penny? She is not a copper coin. Her name is Penelope—like the wife of Odysseus. It means the weaver. Are you familiar with the story? And do sit down." The gold flecks in her hazel eyes were incandescent.

Shifting my weight from one foot to the other, my hand hovered over the chair next to Jamie's.

"Over here," said Mrs. Barrington, indicating the chair to her left.

I walked around the table just as Jamie trudged in looking like the dog who chewed the remote, at least until she caught sight of her employer. "Wow," she said, "you got your hair streaked."

"Not streaked," Mrs. Barrington corrected. "This is balayage, from the French *balayer* meaning to sweep." Her auburn hair glistened like mica. "The highlights are hand painted on the surface of the hair." She turned to me. "A wonderful look for my portrait, is it not?"

"Yes, I think—"

"Jamie, where is Penelope?" Mrs. Barrington asked, uninterested in my thoughts.

Jamie took one step to the left and revealed the girl hiding behind her. "I'm sorry Mrs. Barrington. I tried but she still won't wear any of her new clothes."

The Queen B, as Jamie so aptly referred to her, clicked her tongue in exasperation. "You simply cannot give in to these whims. She looks like one of Fagin's pickpockets." With strained patience, she leaned toward her daughter. "Penelope dear, I told you Maud was arriving today. I wanted you to wear your pink sundress. It's been waiting in your closet for weeks." She raised an eye to Jamie. "At the very least, you must convince her to abandon that shapeless old cardigan."

Hearing her mother's words, Penelope crossed her reed-thin arms and grabbed tightly to the sleeves of a sweater that was like a second skin. Poised for comment, Mrs. Barrington was interrupted when a door in the panelled wall behind her swung open to reveal Dinah. "I'll have yer food out there in two shakes of a goat's tail."

"Lamb's," said Mrs. Barrington.

The door had swung shut but was instantly reopened. "Are you wantin' lamb?" asked Dinah.

"No," said her employer. "We want what you've prepared. And Dinah, lunch should have been," the door swung shut, and Mrs. Barrington raised her voice "on the table five minutes ago."

Like game show contestants, Jamie and Penny remained standing behind their chairs. I had no idea what they were waiting for. Eventually, Mrs. Barrington gave Jamie a nod and in what appeared a well-practised routine, she coaxed Penny onto a chair and slipped onto the one next to her. Almost instantly, the young girl clenched her hands into tight fists, raised them to her shoulders and began to frantically pound the table.

Over the racket, Mrs. Barrington said, "Jamie, you should have waited. Call for Dinah."

She was hardly out of her chair when the cook appeared and set a tray on the table. The moment she placed a glass of milk, a sandwich and an apple, in front of Penelope, the pounding stopped. "There ya go, little lady. Dinah's here just in time with your favourite lunch."

"Hardly just in time," snapped Mrs. Barrington. "You know Penelope's food must precede her to the table."

"It wouldn't hurt for the girl to learn some patience," said Dinah, letting the door close behind her once again.

Chapter 6

Jamie was right about Dinah's culinary talent. Her flaws began to fade with every mouthful. The egg salad with Spanish onion and Boston lettuce on a fresh croissant was the perfect blend of smooth and perky. The prosciutto with watercress, alfalfa sprouts and parmesan cheese on whole wheat, brimmed with crunchy flavour.

"How does Dinah make a sandwich so … amazing?"

Jamie shrugged. "She'd never say. But the eggs come from chickens in a coop near the coach house and she makes almost all of the condiments from scratch, even the mustard."

"Our cook is a wonder," added Mrs. Barrington, her voice devoid of wonder. "Now my dear, is your name spelt with or without an 'e'?"

I admitted my lack of an 'e.'

"M-a-u-d. Uncommon and never popular. I suppose you were named for a grandmother or great-aunt. And do you know anything about its derivation?"

Jamie stifled a giggle and I confessed only to knowing about my father's favourite aunt. Mrs. Barrington straightened her already erect posture and cleared her throat. "Maud is a medieval form of the name Matilda. The Empress Maude was the granddaughter of William the Conqueror and as her father's only surviving heir to the throne of England, she was forced into a bloody civil war by her cousin. The name Maud with or without an 'e' means 'maiden in battle.'"

"Well, I've had my battles. None, fortunately, on the magnitude of a civil war."

"Hah," said Jamie. "When is war ever civil?"

"Yes, quite," agreed Mrs. Barrington. "Maud, has Jamie told you about Penelope's expertise in assembling jigsaw puzzles?" She might have been describing her daughter's latest research in astrophysics.

I shook my head, glancing at the young girl who, despite her continuous chewing, had only finished half a sandwich. She must expend more calories than she ingests.

"Penelope loves her puzzling but it's something you have to see to appreciate," said Jamie. "Come up after lunch. We're on the third floor."

"Following lunch," declared the Queen B, "I will be escorting Maud to her temporary studio in the library."

Jamie's shoulders drooped slightly and I quickly promised to pop up as soon as I could. When Dinah returned with a pot of tea and a plate of delicious-looking date squares, I told her how much I'd enjoyed her sandwiches. I didn't get a thank you but before she returned to the kitchen, Dinah nudged the plate a little closer to me.

"Did Dinah happen to mention that we will be celebrating my son Beau's birthday tomorrow?" asked Mrs. Barrington.

"No, but she did say I'd meet him soon and that he's a fine lad."

"That he is." Mrs. Barrington looked at Jamie. "Wouldn't you agree Miss Conlin?"

A blush flowed across Jamie's cheeks like a dab of crimson paint on wet watercolour paper. Penny, having finished her apple, began to fidget and with obvious relief, Jamie took the opportunity to escape.

"Jamie," Mrs. Barrington stopped her at the archway, "when you reach the loft, you'll find the latest acquisitions, van Gogh's *Starry Night* and Botticelli's *Birth of Venus*."

I munched on a date square and concluded that despite what I'd seen so far, my client had to be referring to jigsaw puzzles and not the actual paintings. I briefly considered asking for clarification when Mrs. Barrington rose from the table and told me to follow her. On the second floor, we walked past my designated room to the end of the hallway where she grabbed two ivory doorknobs on a set of double doors and pushed inward.

The room gave me a shiver of pleasure. A large rectangle with a wall of windows, it was flooded with light. All around me, oak bookcases supported hundreds of volumes and in one corner, an étagère displayed expensive-looking curios and sculptures. I stepped toward the gap between two of the bookcases and noticed a framed portrait reminiscent of William Shakespeare.

"Do you recognize that face, Maud?"

Without taking my eyes off the painting, I shook my head.

"It's a portrait of Dr. John Dee. A copy, of course, but a good copy. He once owned one of the greatest private libraries of 16th century England. Now if you'll have a look over here." She drew my attention to an area by the windows. "I had Caleb bring in two work tables and this nightstand, which I hope will make a suitable taboret. I know many artists choose to stand at the easel, not knowing your preference, I've provided a couple of chairs and a wooden stool."

My words of appreciation were brushed aside and she rushed me from the room to view the outfits she was considering for her portrait. A rabbit warren of hallways took us to another set of double doors. These opened to a large room with sky-blue walls and gauzy white curtains. Against the far wall, a royal blue duvet covered a king-sized bed and hanging above it, was a painting I once saw in the Louvre.

"Beautiful, isn't it? Another copy I'm afraid, however, Vermeer would approve. And now I want your opinion."

She waved toward four dresses facing outward from the rod in her walk-in closet. The complicated and time-consuming floral might have been worn by Mme. Moitessier in Ingres's portrait of the same name. Equally unfortunate was a tedious white taffeta with black polka-dots. I fingered the material and was told the dress was a replica of one worn by Marilyn Monroe. The dramatic arc of my client's eyebrows suggested she was almost as surprised as I was to see it had a home in her closet. "Alton gave it to me following a trip to Hollywood."

So, a walk down memory lane. As far as I was concerned, that's where it needed to stay. This left a stunning black evening gown and a beautifully cut linen suit. The gown was lovely but when she held it aloft, I thought of Sargent's *Madame X* and all that skin. I kept my focus on the linen suit. "The cut is very flattering," I told her. "And the subtle hues will bring out those beautiful highlights in your hair."

"Yes." She cupped the curve of her hair with an open palm. "One can't go wrong with Chanel but ..." She glanced at the taffeta.

"Perhaps you could accessorize the suit. Maybe something your husband gave you?"

From the top drawer of the dresser, she retrieved a deep green scarf. "Something like this?"

"Perfect," I said.

An outfit chosen, she released me to join Penelope and Jamie in the loft. "I'll let you know when I'm ready."

I turned back at the door. "Mrs. Barrington, you didn't say—what was the outcome of the war between the empress and her cousin?"

"Maude lost."

Chapter 7

Wandering the second-floor hallways and looking for a staircase to the third floor put me in mind of the many ways one can get lost—lost in battle, lost in translation, lost in thought, lost in time, lost in space. But in the words of my gym teacher, "You're only lost when you quit." Finally, it occurred to me that staircases are sometimes behind doors and I found it behind door number three.

After a steep and narrow climb, I fell into a William Waterhouse painting. Jamie, like the painting's subject, was standing in front of a stunning radius window. Holding a cell phone rather than a crystal ball, she saw me and slipped it into her pocket.

"Hey Maud, welcome to the loft." Waving me over to the window, she said, "We survey our kingdom from here, don't we, Sweet Pea?"

Penny was sitting at a long low table, head bent and eyes focused on her jigsaw puzzle. My greeting, as I squeezed by, was ignored while she picked and placed puzzle pieces.

Jamie tapped the glass. "We're facing south and that's Lake Ontario. It's lovely to look at but if you want to swim, follow that short path to the climate-controlled swimming pool."

Aquamarine tiles glistened through clear water. "What a luxury to start your day with an invigorating swim."

"Penny would disagree though she'd happily watch you from up here in her ivory tower."

"What's the building next to the pool?"

"They call it a cabana. Don't be fooled. It's more than just a place to change and shower. There's a kitchen, a lounge area and a couple of bedrooms."

"Wow, cool place to stay," I said.

"Posh, maybe. Cool? Not so much. There's no a/c." Jamie pulled out a kiddy chair. "Have a seat and check out our girl's progress on Van Gogh's *Starry Night.*"

I lowered myself onto the tiny chair. "Excuse the cramped quarters. Pen has outgrown this furniture but she won't give it up. Like most kids on the autism spectrum, she hates change. Same thing with her clothes. I'm grateful she only grows lengthwise."

"She seems tall for her age, but then you're all quite tall. I might have to come up here every day and sit on this chair just to feel like a grownup."

Jamie gripped my arm. "Please do."

I suddenly realized why Jamie welcomed my arrival with such enthusiasm. There were three other females in this house and no one to really talk to.

Shifting toward the puzzle, I watched Penny scan the pieces, choose one and pop it into place, over and over again. What would take me days, she could finish in hours. "Has she always been able to do this?"

Jamie shrugged. "I first noticed it at school. A bunch of donated puzzles quickly became Penny's obsession. We established limits. Different story here. Her mother buys her a new puzzle every time she goes into town and they're always more than a thousand pieces." Jamie pointed at the far wall. "Have a look at that shelving unit."

Stacks of clear plastic storage boxes filled the shelves. "Why aren't they in their original packaging?"

"The donated puzzles arrived in clear plastic boxes. We figured the original packaging had been damaged. Penny's need for the status quo meant all puzzles had to be in clear plastic boxes. The picture's gone, but our girl doesn't need it. Her mother labels each box. Then, of course, her daughter picks the labels off."

I read a few that survived her nimble fingers: Leonardo's *Mona Lisa*, Raphael's *Alba Madonna*, Vermeer's *Kitchen Maid*, and Monet's *Water Lilies*. "She's got some great art here."

"The Queen B justifies her daughter's obsession by having me develop a lesson—history, math, and art, from each puzzle. In the white bookcase by the far wall, you'll find some great reference material. I've learned a lot. Not sure I can say the same for Penelope. Her obsession is in the assembling."

I looked back at the radius window and imagined the moonlight streaming onto her puzzle table. "Is she ever compelled to get up at night and put a few tiles together?"

Jamie frowned. "No. Absolutely not allowed. The curtain is always drawn at bedtime, so it would be too dark anyway and I'd know if she pulled it open. Come see the rest of the loft and you'll understand why."

We crossed the room to a wide arched doorway. "The architect for this house certainly had a thing for arches."

Jamie agreed. "Mrs. B says they make a room appear more spacious." She rolled her eyes. "Like this place isn't big enough." We paused at the room on our left. "That's the bathroom. It's noteworthy for its enormous clawfoot bathtub. Gotta be sure not to overfill that baby. Penny could drown in there."

I peered over the edge feeling certain anyone could drown in there. Emerging from the bathroom, I noticed there was no door to Jamie's room.

"You can see why I would hear her. There used to be a door but this is a 24/7 job. My bit of privacy is the drapery." Two velvet curtains were tied back to metal knobs on either side of the opening. "The third floor was originally maids' quarters and a large storage area. Most of the interior walls were removed to create Penny's bedroom and playroom, and this section was partitioned for her caregiver." Jamie raised her eyebrows. "And she's had more than a few." A massive ornate wardrobe replaced a clothes closet.

"I don't suppose you've found a magical portal?" I asked, rubbing the old wood.

"No, but believe me, I've tried."

Spotting the Venetian lamp on her bedside table caused me to do a double-take. "Is that a Tiffany?"

Jamie shrugged. "I dunno. My lamp broke and Caleb found this in the storage area." She pointed to a door at the back of the room. "What makes a Tiffany so special?"

"Its uniqueness, history, workmanship, materials."

"Wow. Sounds pricey. What's it worth?"

"Ten thousand, maybe more."

"Double wow." Jamie reached out to caress the beautiful glass shade, only to pull her hand back like a shoplifter when we heard footsteps on the stairs. I followed the sound of laboured breathing and found Dinah on the landing, one hand over her heart and the other white-knuckled around the door jamb.

"Mercy it's hot up here." Her cheeks glowed like a neon Santa. "Yer wanted in the library," she told me, before turning toward the stairs.

"Shouldn't you rest for a minute?" I called, but she didn't stop. A quick thank you to Jamie, a promise to return, and I dashed after her. On the second floor, she pointed me in the right direction. I grabbed my camera and tripod from my room before joining Mrs. Barrington.

"Maud, what do you think of this?"

My client was sitting on a high-back chair, wearing the Chanel suit and the silk scarf. I wasn't sure if I was to consider the pose, her outfit or the chair until she stroked the baroque carving on the crest rail.

"Perhaps I should have a few curls in my hair to echo this pattern. As the artist, what do you think?"

I thought she didn't seem the type for curls. But then, she didn't seem the type to wear polka dots either. "Mrs. Barrington, I know you'll be posing for the portrait, but if you agree to a few photos, they'll help us decide on the best pose and whether you need those curls. Do you have a pose in mind?"

She slid forward on the chair and pressed one hand to her waist, elbow jutting defiantly. Resting the other elbow on the arm of the chair, she propped her chin on her cupped hand and stretched her mouth into a smile.

It was a pose that would soon collapse but I took a few pictures to humour her. As I expected, the jutting elbow quickly sagged, her head drooped, and the smile became a grimace.

"Mrs. Barrington, if I might make a suggestion?"

Her head popped up like a toupee in a strong wind. "What's wrong?"

I sat on the office chair to demonstrate. "Since you will be sitting for the portrait, it's best if you find your centre of gravity, and let the chair support your back. Then you can rest your hands in your lap or ..."

"Yes, Maud. You've made your point." She took a couple of deep breaths and while I attached the camera to the tripod, settled into a more natural pose.

"You certainly have a lovely place here, Mrs. Barrington, and the gardens are spectacular."

"Thank you, dear." She raised her chin, smugness replacing annoyance.

I took a few pictures at various angles, then asked her to think about her favourite vacation spot. A wistful expression provided better images. When it devolved into a toothy grin, I knew the session was over. Only Frans Hals successfully managed the full smile and even his subjects look crazed, if you stare at them long enough.

Scrolling through the images, I saw three or four with solid potential and shared them with my client. She barely took a glance. "They won't do."

"Are you sure, Mrs. Barrington? It's hard to judge when the images are so small. If I could use your printer—"

"I can see them well enough. It's the chair. Let's switch it out."

Another chair and more pictures but she was only marginally happier. Finally, my plea for prints got a nod.

"I don't have a printer here, but you can get them done in town. Dinah will give you directions." My client left the room before I disengaged my camera from the tripod.

Grateful to have left my car in a patch of cool shade, I had just placed Dinah's crude map on the passenger's seat when a cadmium yellow Miata roadster came racing toward the house. In a cloud of dust, it stopped within inches of the garage door and a golden-haired Adonis rose from the vehicle. I was sure his mother would welcome the early arrival of her son, for this must be Beau, but his companion, a scantily clad, long, lanky female with unnaturally large breasts and spiky orange hair would surely experience a very different reception.

Chapter 8

Within the hour, and after only a moment of directional indecision, I was travelling up the white-pebbled drive. Exiting my vehicle, I saw Jamie waving like an excited sports fan. Too impatient to wait by the swing, she charged up the path to meet me. "Maud, you won't believe it. Beau got here just after you left."

"I do believe it. He drove in while I was sitting in my car and, by the way, you're right about those curls."

Reflecting on Beau's hair gave her a few seconds of wistful pleasure before an abrupt return to the present. "Too bad he wasn't alone."

"I noticed that too."

"You saw her?" Jamie pulled me to a bench near Penny and the swing. "I don't get it. He's a day early and he brings home a stranger—emphasis on 'strange'. Who knew he even had a girlfriend? He introduced this one as his fiancée—his betrothed, intended, bride-to-be. Jesus, Mary and Joseph, tell me it can't last."

I offered a statistical reminder of the rate at which romantic relationships fall apart.

"You're right Maud, it'll be over by Sunday. Especially since she looks like a punkie-pole-dancing prostitute, not that there's anything wrong with that, but what can they possibly have in common?"

I offered a knowing look and a wink. Jamie's head rolled back. "Yeah, but after the hot and heavy becomes mundane and sticky, then what? And they won't get any familial support. You should have seen the Queen B. She went so pale she could have been standing in a puddle of her own blood."

"What do you think is going on? Is Beau the rebellious type?"

"Rebelling from what? He's got a sweet deal here, a job with the family business if he wants it and plenty of money for school in New York if he doesn't."

"So why bring home a fiancée guaranteed to mess with his plans?"

Jamie shook her head. "I don't know. Maybe she's like a foundling. Dinah told me when he was a kid, Beau used to bring home strays and needy friends."

"Was he allowed to keep those strays?"

Her eyes lit up. "No, not even a kitten."

Dinah, the drill sergeant, interrupted us with a call for dinner and I looked longingly toward my car. "Maybe I could eat in town. You know, let the family sort this out."

"We should live so long." She laughed. "C'mon Maud, just go in. Please. I'll bring Penny in when I'm sure her food is on the table."

Once in the dining room, I quietly took my seat and watched Beau lavish attention on the young woman whose large glassy eyes and bright orange hair, reminded me of Trinket, a childhood troll doll. Mrs. Barrington, fingering her placemat, seemed to be either praying for patience or plotting a kidnapping. I fidgeted with my napkin ring, anxious for Jamie's natural enthusiasm to warm the air.

Finally, Mrs. Barrington thawed enough to introduce me to her son. He flashed a smile that could have launched my ship, were I unaware of the rough seas ahead.

"A pleasure to meet you, Maud," he said. And with an easy reach across the table shook my hand, holding it until *Trinket* cleared her throat. Dropping back into his chair he wrapped an arm around her shoulder and explained that I was there to paint a portrait of his mother. Turning to me, he added, "Maud, this is Cecilia Fox."

"Nice to meet you both," I said, though 'forced to meet you both' would have been more accurate. I offered my hand to Cecilia and when she reached for it, I noticed ink on her upper arm—a tattoo of a small red fox.

"Did you know," began Mrs. Barrington, "the name Cecilia means blind?"

Her guest responded with a haughty negative and Beau quickly chimed in, insisting she preferred the name 'Ceal.'

"Like the semi-aquatic marine mammal?" asked his mother.

"No, it's C- e - a - l," said Beau.

Mrs. Barrington arched her eyebrows. "And that improves it?"

When Dinah bustled in from the kitchen carrying a large tray, the scowl Beau had turned on his mother dissolved into a grin. He leapt up to help place a platter of roast chicken and two steaming bowls of vegetables on the table.

"Thanks, Sonny. I'm so happy ya got here early," Dinah cooed. She set a glass of milk at the place setting next to Ceal. "But if I'd known your plans, I'da made all your favourites."

"No worries, Nan." He slid back onto his chair and gazed at her, his long brown lashes framing unusually green eyes. "Everything you make is delicious."

"That's my boy," she said, patting his curls. "You be sure to pop into the kitchen later, like always. Now, did I hear somethin' about a fiancée?"

"Oh yeah." It seemed he'd momentarily forgotten. "Nan, I'd like you to meet Cecilia."

"It's Ceal." She made a sidewise glance at Beau, then batted her artificially long lashes at the family's cook. "So nice to meet you, Nan."

"It's Dinah." The family cook smiled at Beau. "Only my Sonny gets to call me Nan." A little squeeze of his cheek and she waddled from the room.

We were taking turns adding food to our plates when Jamie and Penny arrived. With their usual spots taken by Beau and Ceal, Jamie hesitated until she spied Penny's glass of milk. Like synchronized swimmers, Mrs. Barrington put food on her daughter's plate, (good to know she eats more than peanut butter sandwiches) and Jamie folded Penny onto her chair, putting the glass of milk in her hand.

Penelope drank the beverage in one long swallow, then carefully returned the glass to the table. She picked up her fork, held the shining silver utensil aloft, turned slightly and in one swift movement, propelled it into Ceal's exposed arm. The embedded tines pierced the neck of the little fox. Ceal jumped up, toppling her chair, and the fork clattered to the floor.

In a flash, Jamie seized Penny and rushed her from the room.

"Jesus Christ!" Beau grabbed a linen napkin and wrapped it around his fiancée's arm. "Are you okay, Ceal?" Turning on his mother, eyes flashing anger he yelled, "Why in hell does that demon child live here? She belongs in a ... a nuthouse!"

Anxious to see the damage, Ceal lifted the napkin. "That little bitch stabbed me!" We watched as the blood drained from her face and flowed down her arm. In a faint, she collapsed against Beau's chest.

With a force that could have ripped her arm from its socket, Mrs. Barrington pointed in the direction of the stairs. "Take her to the green guest room! I'll send Dinah up with a bandage."

Beau swept up Ceal and cradling her in his arms, teetered at the archway. "Damn it, Mother, she'll need more than a bandage. Call Galen. And I'm taking her to my room."

Chapter 9

With a sigh of exasperation, Mrs. Barrington grabbed the cordless phone from the sideboard. Finger poised to key in the number, she told me to find Dinah, have her fetch the first aid kit, and take it to Beau.

Swinging through the panelled door, I found myself in a small hall with a second door. Assuming it led to the kitchen, I pushed it open slowly and called for Dinah. "Sorry to bother you. We have a problem."

She didn't bother to come to the door. "Nothin' wrong with the food, I hope," she called out.

"No, I'm sure it's fine, but we haven't eaten any of it."

The door jerked open. "Why not? What's going on?"

"Penelope stabbed Ceal with her fork."

"What?"

"In the arm. She just picked up her fork and ..."

"Well, I guess she speaks for all of us." Dinah rubbed her hands on her apron. "So, what do ya want me to do about it?"

I relayed Mrs. Barrington's instructions.

"Land sakes! I might as well deliver their suppers too."

Dinah followed me back to the dining room. On a small tray, she loaded the two dinner plates and carried them from the room.

"Maud," Mrs. Barrington tapped the table, "sit. Perhaps you and I can enjoy our meal. Penelope needs time to ponder her behaviour."

I wasn't sure how much pondering Penny was likely to do, but I was reasonably certain I'd enjoy the meal. I was savouring a second (they were rather small) perfectly baked potato with sour cream and fresh chives when Holbein's Desiderius Erasmus, or at least one of his descendants, entered through the French doors.

"So, Ronnie, where's my patient?"

Did he say Ronnie?

"Galen, thank you for coming. Beau insisted on taking her to his room. I'll show you up." She rose from her chair but he waved her back.

"Don't trouble yourself. I know where it is." Spotting me he said, "Oh, hello."

"This is Miss Maud—no 'e'—Gibbons. She's the portrait artist I told you about. Maud, this is Dr. Patmore. He's also our neighbour."

He bowed and took my hand in both of his. "A pleasure, Maud no 'e' and please call me Galen." The warmth and confidence in his brown eyes was a welcome harbour. Releasing my hand he said, "Set me a place Ronnie, after I see to your guest, I'll join you for dessert."

He left and Mrs. Barrington reached for the phone, jabbed at the keypad, and waited a moment. "Bring Penelope to the dining room." Returning the phone to the sideboard, she pulled on a thick cord, partially hidden by the ornately carved hutch.

Within seconds Dinah reappeared. "You rang Madame," she said with mock seriousness.

"Set a place for Dr. Patmore. He'll be joining us, as will Jamie and Penelope."

Dinah bustled about getting cutlery and dishes from the buffet and added a complete place setting before Mrs. Barrington told her the doctor was only staying for dessert. Tongue clicking, the cook removed all but a dessert plate and fork, then puffed like a steam engine back to the kitchen.

Jamie and Penny returned as Mrs. Barrington and I were quietly enjoying the entrée and all of us were ready for dessert by the time Dr. Patmore joined us. He tipped, an imaginary hat. "Good evening, Jamie, Penelope. Ronnie, where do you want me?"

"Dinah's put you next to Maud."

"Did Ronnie tell you she has the honour of being the first baby I delivered?" he asked me, edging closer to the table.

I shook my head; certain I now knew why he could use her nickname with impunity.

"Now Galen, Maud's not interested in our ancient history," chided Mrs. Barrington. "How's the patient?"

"Miss Fox is upset and will have a visible contusion, along with those puncture wounds, but I've assured her she'll make a full recovery. Better a clean fork than a rusty nail, eh? I guess your eldest will be arriving tomorrow. How go the party plans?"

"Gabriel and Beau were supposed to arrive together tomorrow before lunch. My youngest son, however, took it upon himself to get here a day early and surprise us with Cecilia the Blind. You saw how that turned out."

Dinah swung through the door and Galen stood to greet her. "Dinah!" he said with a broad smile. "Unfortunate circumstances brought me here, but I'm grateful to be offered one of your fine desserts."

With a coquettish smile, Dinah placed a large pie on the table.

"Ah," said Galen taking in a deep breath. "Mmm, cinnamon. Do tell me that's your famous apple pie."

"That's what it is Doctor. I'm so glad you like it." Dinah lingered at the table until her employer dismissed her with a curt 'thank you.'

As she served the pie, Mrs. Barrington said, perhaps noticing my look of confusion. "Years ago, Dinah would have lost a finger were it not for the expertise of our neighbourly doctor. She thinks he's a miracle worker."

Galen chuckled. "I've tried repeatedly to disavow her of the notion, but I consistently meet with failure." He scooped up a forkful of apple pie. "Delicious, as always. You know Ronnie, I'm surprised no one has tried to lure away your amazing cook."

"Oh, they have, Galen, but Dinah stays with us for more than the financial reward."

He nodded knowingly. "Ah, of course. But what will happen when 'her boy' sets up his own household?"

Mrs. Barrington's eyes narrowed. "I think we will cross that bridge when we come to it."

After Jamie escorted Penny from the room, Galen turned the conversation to art and portraiture, showing an extensive knowledge of the process. I was sorry to see him leave, but he did so with the promise to seek me out at Beau's birthday party and as soon as we were alone, Mrs. Barrington affirmed a party invitation. "Best wishes only and casual dress. It will involve a barbecue, not my favourite but then it's not my birthday. There will be music and dancing and the pool is open, of course. Do you like to swim?"

"Yes, very much."

"Then you must make free use of it. The water is kept at a constant eighty degrees Fahrenheit, perfect for an early morning swim." She folded her napkin, laying it across her plate.

I thanked her and before she could leave, quickly retrieved the prints from my bag. Placing the envelope on the table, I promised to get started on her portrait as soon as we decided on a pose.

I expected, if not instant enthusiasm, at least a willingness to move forward. Instead, she sighed as if I'd just asked her to spend the next few hours looking at my holiday snaps. Although her hand moved toward the envelope, it did so with glacial speed. I'd hoped we would be looking at the images together, defining our preferences but instead, my client picked up the envelope and agreed to 'peruse them at her leisure.' Finally, she dismissed me with a stony stare.

Chapter 10

Alone in my room, I felt like Jonathan Harker on a business trip to a Transylvanian castle. Fortunately, my exit, unlike his, wasn't locked and I soon trudged up the narrow staircase to the loft. The sound of my footfall brought Jamie running to the landing. "Am I getting fired?" she asked, in a hoarse and hurried whisper. Her eyes darted toward the puzzle table and Penelope.

"Why would you think that?" I whispered back.

She made a stabbing action toward my arm.

"Right. But that wasn't your fault."

"So you might expect, however, Mrs. Barrington will insist it was my responsibility to prevent her daughter from wielding a weapon."

"Jamie, it was a fork, not a switchblade. How could you or anyone else anticipate what she did?" I saw an untold story in her eyes. "Unless …"

Jamie waved me toward her bedroom, indicated a wicker chair and found a spot on the edge of her bed with a good view of Penny. "As far as I know this was the first time anyone was stabbed with a fork, but …"

"Yes?"

"When I first arrived here, Dinah took me aside and told me to watch my back around Penelope. She referred to her as 'the girl.' I'd already been working with Penny in the classroom and like many children with her degree of autism, she could lash out in fear or frustration. Dinah explained she was referring to unprovoked aggression or as she put it, 'acting psycho.' I asked for details and was told that one of 'the girl's' previous minders fell down the stairs.

Accident? Dinah wouldn't say but she made it obvious that she didn't think so."

"Crikey, what happened to the poor woman? I'm assuming it was a woman."

"It was and by the way, Penny is not that fond of men. Well, she is not fond of anyone but she gets more anxious around men she doesn't know than women. Anyway, that particular woman suffered a concussion and a broken leg. According to Dinah, the Barringtons took care of her." Jamie rubbed her thumb and fingers together. "She left without making a fuss."

"Do you think Penny …?"

Jamie shook her head. "I try not to think about it."

I watched the emaciated girl assemble her puzzle. She was like a spider—her thin arms moving so quickly they seemed to multiply. It was hard to imagine her pushing someone down a flight of stairs but then I wouldn't have expected her to stab someone with a fork either. "Do you think she ever feels remorse?"

Jamie shrugged. "Hard to say. She doesn't display many subtle emotions. Most of the time she's just … tense, locked in her own world, unless something triggers an outburst of anger or frustration. For example, one hot day in early July, she was puzzling, I was on the other side of the room putting her laundry away and her mother called my cell. It was, she insisted, a perfect day to begin her daughter's swimming lessons. Penelope doesn't like the water and 'swimming instructor' is not on my resumé but I agreed and closed the call. The moment I did, Penny scrambled from the table, dashed to her dresser, found her swimsuit and tossed it out the window."

"How did she know?"

Jamie shrugged. "ESP?"

"Probably not."

"Though her senses do seem unusually acute."

"Or, at some point earlier in the day, her mother mentioned swimming lessons."

"That would suggest a level of communication Mrs. Barrington seldom has with her daughter."

"If Penny tends to react strongly to triggers and if her senses are usually on high alert, maybe she didn't attack Ceal."

"Meaning?"

"She put a fork into Ceal's arm, but on that arm is the tattoo of a red fox. The tines of the fork went right through the fox's neck."

"Eww. I missed that." Jamie involuntarily grabbed her upper arm. "I think you might be onto something. Kids on the spectrum often have trouble separating people and objects. Maybe Penny saw the tattoo as a threat."

"In which case, she was simply defending herself."

"Good point, Maud. Maybe you could defend me in a case of wrongful dismissal?"

"Mrs. Barrington won't fire you. She needs you and so does her daughter."

"Ha. These are the Barringtons. Any of us could be replaced before we finished packing." Jamie eyed the Tiffany lamp on her bedside table.

"You'd need a really big suitcase."

"What?"

"Nothing. You've just reminded me that I haven't even finished unpacking. Better get to that. Before I do, I want to see how Penny is progressing with the puzzle."

Crossing the room, I noted she'd assembled almost a third of van Gogh's *Starry Night*. As she continued to pick up and place each piece in rhythmic succession, I wondered if Penny was keying into colour or shape. Whatever technique she was using it was phenomenal to witness. "Wow, Penelope. You're good at this," I told her. "I can't stay but I would like to come back soon, okay?" She didn't look at me, but she did pause for a moment. I took that as a yes.

Back in my room, I picked up my paintbox and carryall and stepped into the hall. Angry voices bellowed from Beau's room. Inching a little closer to his door, I heard Ceal say, "Why the hell didn't you tell me your sister was crazy?"

"She's autistic, not crazy," Beau countered. "And she doesn't usually go around stabbing people."

"Somehow, I don't find that a comfort."

"Okay, I'll say it again. Cecilia, I'm really sorry. I feel terrible." Beau's words were slow and over-enunciated.

"God damn it, Barrington. No matter how bad you feel, I can assure you I feel worse." I imagined Ceal cradling her arm.

"But this was your idea, remember?" Beau was whining.

"I'm the one who got stabbed and now you're blaming me."

There was a smack against the wall. "Enough! I get it. You're angry and hurt and I told you, more than once, I'm sorry. There is good news though. Doc Patmore said you'll be fine for the party."

"You are one selfish bastard, Barrington. I knew this was going to be stressful but I sure as hell didn't expect to get attacked. I want to go home."

"Christ! Now who's being selfish?"

When the door suddenly swung open, I jumped backwards. Beau back from the room, slamming the door as he left. He turned toward me, and two long wooden stretcher bars and a roll of tracing paper fell from my carryall. "Maud, what are you doing?"

"Taking my supplies to the library," I smiled heroically. "I've tried to carry too much." I raised my arms, exaggerating the weight of the box and the awkwardness of the bag.

"Let me help you," he offered. Like a gallant knight, Beau lifted the carryall from my shoulder and bent down to rescue my wayward supplies. "Where do you want these?" His blond curls fell teasingly toward his face.

"Pardon?"

I felt the warmth of his hand when it gently brushed against mine as he took the paint box. "Lead the way."

Beau pulled open the library doors, stepped aside and followed me in. "Ever had a client demand you bring your studio to them?"

"No," I admitted. "But I'm not complaining. Your mother has created a great space for me."

He placed my supplies on the larger of the two work tables. "She's very excited about this commission."

"She is?" She certainly had me fooled. "What makes you say that?"

"It's a birthday gift for my father. Something he's wanted for a while. You knew that, right?" He accepted my casual shrug and kept on talking. "Anyway, it's something he's wanted ever since my mother started investing in fine art. Too bad you won't be here when she presents it to him." He smiled and revealed his perfect teeth. "Maud, I thought I'd get some air. Would you like to join me?"

He leaned so close I could smell his skin. Though his words seemed guileless, my gut told me a different story. "Thank you, Beau. I'm very tempted but," I waved at my carryall and paintbox, "I hope to start work on your mother's portrait tomorrow. I have supplies to unpack, oils to organize, and I need to sharpen my—" I intended to say pencils but it could just as easily have been skills, had he not interrupted me with "some other time, then" and a smile that didn't reach his eyes.

Chapter 11

It was dusk by the time I organized my new studio. I walked the dimly lit hallway, listening to the silence. Perhaps Beau hadn't returned, or they'd resolved their differences, or Ceal made good on her threat and left. And what did Beau mean when he reminded Ceal this had been her idea? At least I now understood why Mrs. Barrington had seriously considered wearing that polka-dot dress. And why not tell me the painting was to be a gift for her husband? Every artist knows it's hard enough to please the client you know, never mind the client you never met.

By six a.m., I awoke tired but determined, first to enjoy a morning swim and then, to get my client to make some decisions about her portrait. The pool water felt like liquid silk and though I may not have frolicked like a dolphin, I did manage ten of the twenty laps I promised myself.

At eight-thirty, I trailed Jamie and Penny into the dining room. Beau's disarming smile came with the news that Ceal was having a lie-in. When he pulled out Jamie's chair she floated, like a leaf on water, to the seat beside him, only to jump to her feet the moment she remembered to assist Penelope.

During breakfast, I kept a close eye on my client. I was intent on catching her before party preparations stole her away. When she placed her cutlery across her plate, I was ready. "Mrs. Barrington I was hoping we could—"

The scraping of her chair as she pushed back from the table drowned my words. "Come with me, Maud." She stepped briskly toward the door. "I've reviewed the photographs."

At the large work table, my client spread out the pictures, pointing at three she felt had merit. Through discussion, compromise and persuasion, we finally agreed, me with enthusiasm, she with uncertainty on the best photo.

The next decision was one of size. As I unpacked two rolls of canvas and set out a selection of wooden stretcher bars, Mrs. Barrington asked, "How did Beau seem to you this morning?"

I told her I thought he seemed fine.

She fingered the linen canvas. "I like this one. Too fine?"

"A fine weave in a canvas is best for a portrait."

"I'm referring to Beau. His cheerfulness was insincere."

"You know him better than most." I laid the linen over the rectangle formed by the stretcher bars, tucking it in around the edges. "My agent said you wanted a half-figure, life-size including hands. This is thirty inches by twenty inches, approximately the size of the Mona Lisa."

"My son has always been too accepting, too quick to form relationships. Charm and agreeableness are often features of the youngest in the family and he does like to help."

I was sure his help came at a cost, but did she just refer to Beau as her youngest child? Perhaps she meant the youngest son.

She glanced briefly at the proposed size. "Maud, I've been to the Louvre and da Vinci's masterpiece is larger."

"Many feel that way, Mrs. Barrington. I think it's because of the painting's larger than life presence."

She flicked her wrist as if to say, whatever, and insisted that her Toronto home could accommodate a much larger painting. Visions of Michelangelo, his profit rapidly disappearing as he laboured for years on the Sistine Ceiling ran through my mind. I grabbed my wooden mallet, and was banging together my largest set of stretcher bars when Dinah appeared in the doorway.

She shuffled across the room, stopped in front of the collage of photographs and hovered over them like a nosy neighbour. When she finally got around to saying the caterers had arrived, Mrs. Barrington told her to tell them she'd be right there and waved her on her way. Before my client could follow her cook, I drew her attention to the larger canvas.

"It's better, Maud, but I don't know. Perhaps we can revisit this after the party."

Unwilling to lose the rest of the day, I offered to use our chosen photograph as a reference and render a full-sized drawing. "And when you approve of the image, I'll transfer it to the canvas and we can begin working from life tomorrow." I braced for an argument but she looked relieved, pausing only to remind me lunch was at noon.

Removing my watch and placing it at the top of my drawing board, I calculated the required ratio to enlarge the photograph and applied the appropriate grids. I was adding greater detail to my drawing when, in my peripheral vision, I caught sight of that pale blue sweater. As one would expect, she said nothing and as I was reasonably sure I wouldn't get a fork in my back, I let her be.

By the time my muscles begged for mercy, I snuck a peek for my audience of one and found myself alone. I was doing a few stretches when Jamie burst into the room. "Did I miss lunch?" I asked.

"What? No. Listen, Maud, I need to find Penny." Her words came out like bullets. "We were in the loft. She was puzzling. I was writing lessons. I looked up. She was gone. Have you seen her?"

I told Jamie about my recent visitor.

"When did she get here? How long did she stay? Where did she go?"

"I don't know. I don't know. I don't know."

"Crap."

"Sorry, Jamie. Isn't Penny allowed to be on her own?"

"No!"

"Okay, well, how can I help?"

"Maybe she returned to the loft while I was talking to Caleb. I'm on my way to the swing. Would you check the loft?"

Jamie rushed toward the door, then stopped. "And Maud, when you get there, don't call out, you'll startle her. She likes enclosed spaces, so check under her bed and in the closet. Do not try to force her out. She scratches. Just tell her you'll take her to the swing. Ditto if she's puzzling. I'll wait there and hope to see you in ten minutes."

Chapter 12

Iapproached what looked like an empty loft, half expecting Penny to leap, ninja-like, from a dark corner. Reaching her bed unscathed, I held my breath as I knelt and pulled back the bed skirt, exhaling when no wild eyes stared at me from the shadows. Getting to my feet, I noticed the closet door was partially open and gave it a gentle push.

Like the incubus squatting on the sleeping figure of Fuseli's *Nightmare*, Penny was on her haunches next to a large wooden toy box. Seeing me, she bolted from the closet, grabbed my arm, and pulled me toward the staircase. When we reached the library, Penny jogged awkwardly to my work table, snapped up a pencil and a small pad of drawing paper, and pressed them to her chest.

"You want to draw," I said, stating the obvious. I rolled the office chair to the smaller work table, and Penny leapt onto it. "Wait." I raised my palm. "I'll get you something to draw." On the étagère, I found two, equally amazing reproductions of Bernini sculptures and chose the one I thought would be the easiest for my new student to draw. Grabbing a couple of thick books to provide a stand, I set them on the small work table.

"This is a statue of David. He used his secret weapon to protect his people from a giant named Goliath." I pointed to the device in the figure's hand.

Stacking the books, I placed the statue on top, then bent down until I was at her eye level. "I think this is a good view of your subject. Can you see it okay?"

Penny looked steadily at the statue and nodded.

"I'll help get you started." On a separate piece of paper, I demonstrated how to build a drawing using a faint grid and explained how ratios help to reproduce a three-dimensional model on a two-dimensional surface.

Penny grasped the process quickly and as she drew, her state of perpetual anxiety was made all the more apparent by its sudden disappearance. Within a few minutes, she seemed almost content, at least until Jamie burst into the room.

"Maud, didn't we say we'd meet at the swing?" Before I could respond she noticed my drawing companion and sprinted across the room. "Oh, thank God. Where did you find her?"

"She was—"

"Wow, what a great outline." Jamie looked from the statue to Penny's drawing. "It's so accurate." Then suspiciously at me. "Wait a minute, Maud. Did you do this?"

I shook my head. "I gave a short demonstration. Her drawing is entirely her own. Do the students at your school receive art instruction?"

"Not really. There are basic art supplies but no qualified art teacher. The kids are expected to create purely from their imaginations—a difficult concept for children with autism. Good idea giving her a model. But, how can she be so accurate?"

"I don't know. Eye-hand coordination is important, and a recognition of shapes and values, so all those hours assembling jigsaw puzzles have helped, but I've never seen anything like this. Most of us draw what we think we see, not what's actually in front of us and this takes training. Penelope is like a human camera."

We watched, like proud parents, until Jamie whispered her need to get something and left the room. Within minutes she was back with a plastic kitchen timer. "A bell rings for recess, lunchtime and home-time—all good things, so the students, as challenged as many of them are, routinely stop whatever they're doing when they hear a bell ring. Living here, I've found further applications." She rotated the dial and set the timer on my work table. "Okay, if I pop back upstairs—get our clothes ready for the party? I'll be back before the timer goes off."

Jamie left, and I returned to my drawing, almost forgetting my new student. When I did look up, I knew she'd forgotten me.

True to her word, Jamie returned a few seconds before the timer rang. When it did, Penny, as if responding to a siren's call, laid down her pencil, slid from the chair, and stood next to the table. I did the same, worried any other response might disrupt the routine.

In the dining room, we once again found Cecilia occupying Penelope's place, and in the spot next to her, Dinah had placed the young girl's peanut butter sandwich and her apple. I waited while Jamie quickly moved the food one place over, coaxed the youngest Barrington into the chair and placed herself, like a buffer, between them.

As I crossed the room to my chair, I felt magnetically drawn to a pair of warm brown eyes. I then noticed the gentle wave of his hair and his classically straight nose, and when his generous mouth curved in a smile, I was sure those dimples were just for me.

"Maud, I'd like you to meet my eldest son, Gabriel."

He stood, quickly pulling out the chair on his left and we grinned stupidly at one another. We'd barely manage a few words of introduction when Jamie interrupted. "Maud, tell Mrs. Barrington about Penelope's art lesson."

"Art lesson?" My client leaned eagerly toward me. Good news being a rare commodity when it came to Penelope, I gave a generous description of the morning's events. By the time I finished, Mrs. Barrington's sigh of rapture told me she was already planning an opening gala at the National Gallery.

"Hey ya know what?" chirped Cecilia. "Maybe Penelope is like one of those savoir idiots."

"Are you referring to a savant?" asked Mrs. Barrington, glaring at her youngest son's intended.

"Yeah, that's it. Idiot savants are stupid about most things but way smarter than most people about one thing."

Her lips taut, Mrs. Barrington said, "Which would certainly be an advantage over those who are stupid in all things. Wouldn't you agree?"

Beau opened his mouth captured a moment of common sense, and closed it. For the next few minutes, we silently concentrated on lunch. Gabriel helped himself to a second scoop of potato salad and offered to add more to my plate, bless him, before asking his mother about the party preparations.

"We've had a ninety percent reply rate and most of them intend to be here so all should proceed as planned."

"I think I can persuade Penelope to wear the pink sundress to the party." Jamie proclaimed, rather proudly, to her employer.

"Penelope will not be attending the birthday party."

Jamie's jaw dropped like a ventriloquist's dummy. "But Mrs. Barrington ... I don't understand."

The Queen B leaned back, crossing her arms. "Come now Jamie, you don't expect an explanation, do you?"

"This means I can't ..." With a quivering bottom lip, Jamie gulped air and blinked back tears. Jumping to her feet, Jamie lifted Penny from her chair. The young girl scrambled to grab her apple before being carried from the room.

Beau turned on his mother. "I know why you're doing this but it means excluding Jamie and I want her at my party." His nostrils flared like an agitated horse and his mother smoothed non-existent wrinkles from the tablecloth.

"I must say, Beau, I'm surprised by the strength of your attachment."

"What the hell is that supposed to mean?"

Ceal glared at her fiancé. "Yes, what does it mean?"

Beau shoved back his chair, stood up, and pitched his crumpled napkin onto his plate. "I take back what I said before, Mother. Penelope is already living in a madhouse."

"I think your word was *nuthouse*, dear."

He stomped from the room and as Ceal ran after him, the door to the kitchen opened. Dinah hesitated. "Another stabbing?"

Chapter 13

"Everything is fine, Dinah. Just pour the tea." From the tray, Dinah deposited a tea service and a plate of cookies onto the table. Placing a cup next to Gabriel, she said, "Nice you could be here to celebrate your dear brother's birthday."

"Good to see you too, Dinah," he teased, and she offered him a cookie.

Adding a cookie to a side plate, Gabriel raised his teacup and invited his mother and me to join him on the patio. I was keen but Mrs. Barrington declined. "Too many party preparations, dear. And Maud," she looked at me, "aren't you going to work on our drawing?"

"Mother, let the artist have her tea." Gabriel extended a hand. "Come into the garden, Maud, I am here at the gate alone."

"Tennyson, I presume?" I accepted his hand.

Exiting through the French doors, he guided me to a glass-top table and a cushioned garden chair. "Thank you, Gabriel."

"To be honest, Maud, I prefer Gabe." He noted my look of surprise and admitted it wasn't a name his mother would ever use.

I confessed to referring to his sister as Penny.

"She's not a copper coin, right?" He winked. "And what about you—an artist named for an Empress. Did you study in Toronto?"

His question led to a discussion of his fondness for visiting art galleries and museums. "Something I'm sure we share," he said. "I think there's a show of Renaissance art coming to the—"

He was interrupted by frantic footsteps across the patio stones and then Jamie, halted in front of him, her arms akimbo. "This is so unfair! Gabe, can you reason with your mother? Penelope is a member of the family." She indicated his sister, safely oscillating on her swing.

"I'm sorry Jamie. Not after what happened to Ceal."

Jamie clicked her tongue and rolled her eyes. "You're right. There's nothing anyone can do."

"I didn't say that. Just because my mother banished Penelope doesn't mean you can't go. If I stayed with my sister, you could spend a few hours at the party."

"Nice idea but it won't fly with your mother."

"What about me?" I offered. "I won't be missed and we can both work on our drawings."

Jamie wiggled like a lottery winner. "Maud, what a perfect solution. And if you needed me, which you won't, I'd be right here."

"But," said Gabe, "I was hoping we could sit together for dinner." He smiled and touched my hand. I smiled back and Jamie pouted.

"I accept your invitation Gabe, and since I also have work to do, I'll come back in about seven. Would that work for you, Jamie?"

She nodded and grinned. "Thanks, Maud. Now we just need the okay from Mrs. B and since the fork incident, she'll be in no mood to favour me."

"I'll talk to her." Gabe grabbed his cookie, promised to be right back and slipped through the French doors.

"Well, well, well," said Jamie, with an exaggerated wink.

"It's just dinner with a bunch of other guests."

"Hey, it's gotta start somewhere, right?" She laughed and jogged back to Penny and the swing.

I finished my tea and my cookie, almost slipped into a trance watching Penny on her swing, and eventually conceded that Gabe was not coming right back. Retreating to the library, I sharpened my pencil to a fine point and completed a basic outline of my subject.

"Maud?" Jamie and Penny hovered in the doorway. "She practically dragged me here. Call me selfish, but I sure hope our girl is as obsessed with drawing as she is with puzzling."

Penny slipped onto the office chair and, like a seasoned conductor, raised her pencil.

"And look at the way she hopped onto that adult-sized chair." Jamie set the timer and promised to be back in twenty minutes.

She wasn't. When the timer rang, Penny laid down her pencil and stood up ready to go, which would be fine if we'd had somewhere to go. I considered taking her upstairs to her puzzles, but on impulse, offered to show her more drawing techniques. She was back on her chair before I could pick up my pencil case.

Using a selection of graphite pencils, and a value strip, a scale of nine gradually darkening values from white to black, I demonstrated how to transfer the various values from model to drawing and the best way to apply an even tone. She accepted a 2B pencil with a kind of reverence. Using it exactly as I'd instructed, she achieved an even and accurate application. I stifled the urge to gush over her brilliance sensing that for Penelope, as in art, *less is more.* "Well done," I told her.

"Sorry, I'm late." Jamie ran into the room, grabbed and reset the timer before breathlessly exclaiming that the Queen B had agreed to our job sharing. "Pen and I will have dinner, then she can puzzle away until you join us."

When the timer rang, Penny slipped off the chair. Before they left, Jamie paused at the door. "You've got thirty minutes. Are you going to the party dressed like that?"

I looked down at my outfit. Mrs. Barrington had said causal dress but perhaps not this casual. I may not have expensive jewellery or designer clothes, but I had packed a favourite and somewhat fancy sundress. When I pulled it from my suitcase, I found a book purchased for my working holiday. The party was "best wishes only," but I couldn't arrive empty-handed. As I wrote Happy Birthday on the inside front cover, I hoped Beau would be interested, if not in the life of Caravaggio, at least in the curious way he died.

Hanging my dress in the bathroom while I showered, smoothed out the wrinkles. I hoped for something similar using the blow dryer on my hair, but within minutes of slipping my feet into my best sandals, the heat and humidity of the late afternoon sprung my frustrated curls into action.

Many of life's great inventions and improvements are the result of perpetual dissatisfaction, but some things just can't be changed. Had genetics given me straight hair, I'd have yearned for curly. And then there are my ears. A knock on the door took me from the face in the mirror to the face of Gabriel Barrington.

He offered his arm. "Your escort has arrived. Love the curls."

Chapter 14

Voices, like rustling leaves, teased my ears as we approached the open French doors. From the patio, I saw strands of fairy lights shining among the trees, and drama masks hanging from their branches. Above two long tables on the upper lawn glowed the birthday boy's name in neon and in the clearing to my left, more white lights extended around the perimeter of a platform built for dancing. I don't like parties but I do like to dance. I couldn't help wondering if the man, literally leading me down a garden path, felt the same.

After I placed my birthday offering on a table overflowing with gifts, Gabe introduced me to many of the guests who made up a sea of strangers. I marvelled at his ability to recall everyone's name, knowing, that despite his careful introductions, I would not.

When a voice from the loudspeakers called us to the west side of the house, we found Dr. Galen Patmore standing on a wooden stage, microphone in hand. Following a warm welcome and a few entertaining anecdotes about the man of the hour, he held up an envelope. Tearing it open, Galen proclaimed, "And the winner of the twenty-fifth birthday award is," he extended his arm toward the house, "Beau Barrington!"

Heralds, in brocade tabards, flanked either side of the door. It swung open and to the crowd's applause, Beau walked the red carpet to the stage. Met by his mother, she presented him with a small golden statuette and an awkward hug. Taking the microphone, Beau revealed his comedic talents with a hammed-up acceptance speech. I anticipated the announcement of his engagement, but at the end of his monologue, he simply waved his prize, thanked everyone, and walked off the stage.

There was too much food to choose from, but decisions were made, and carrying our plates on cafeteria-type trays, Gabe and I found two lawn chairs cooled by the shade of the cabana. I enjoyed people-watching almost as much as Dinah's amazing pasta salad. With hunger sated, I asked Gabe if anyone was going to announce the engagement between Beau and Ceal.

He stared at me as if I'd just suggested they double their employees' salary. "Not a chance. According to my mother, you don't make serious decisions when distracted and you always consider unintended consequences."

Gabe gestured toward an older woman sitting on a nearby bench. "Speaking of distracted behaviour, that's my Aunt Margaret. While vacationing in the Muskoka's, a handsome Hollywood celebrity came into the local ice cream parlour while she was buying a cone. That distraction caused her to leave her change on the counter and put the ice cream in her purse."

"Oh my God. I hope they both saw the humour in that."

He shook his head. "She was too busy running from the scene."

Our laughter was interrupted by a voice over the loudspeaker inviting everyone to gather for the cutting of the cake. At the table, we found an enormous two-tiered birthday cake—decorated with gold stars, an authentic-looking statue of the Oscar and twenty-five burning candles. Following a rousing rendition of Happy Birthday, Beau blew them out and soon, servers, dressed like theatre ushers, carried dessert to the crowd.

"This is Dinah's famous double chocolate caramel cake," Gabe told me as we perched on the garden wall. Using his fork as a pointer, he tapped the filling between each layer. "This is dark chocolate, followed by caramel, then milk chocolate and finally ..."

"Let me guess, more caramel." I felt my hips expanding with each mouthful.

"Gabe." We both looked up to Beau's panicked face. "Have you finished dinner?"

Gabe slipped a forkful of cake into his mouth, chewed and swallowed. "No."

"Aw come on Bro. Mother needs you."

"Did she say why?" He scooped up another forkful.

"It's one of the guests."

Gabe's face changed from bored impatience to wide-eyed concern. "Has there been an accident?"

Beau nodded, rather unconvincingly I thought, but Gabe set down his plate. "Sorry Maud, I'll be right back."

Too curious not to, I followed just close enough to hear Beau tell his brother two of their esteemed guests had arrived at the party preloaded.

"Let me guess, the Drunkin Duncans?"

"Yeah, and Mother wants you to drive them home."

"Aw for Christ's sake." When Gabe came to a halt, Beau grabbed his arm and led him to a temporary car park. By the time they reached a man and woman slumped against a car, I'd seen enough.

Taking a shortcut around the back of the house, I noticed a flash of bright orange hair among a small grove of trees. Assuming no one else at the party had a penchant for hair dye the colour of a plastic pumpkin, I figured it had to be Ceal and that she might be looking for Beau. I moved toward her but soon realized she wasn't alone.

Someone, whose long dark hair was tied in a low ponytail, wrapped his or her arms around Beau's fiancée and she instantly returned the hug—the hussy. Then, as if she knew I was watching her, Ceal wriggled from the embrace and created a barrier by extending both of her arms.

Her companion took a step back, Ceal dropped her arms, he or she moved forward, and the pattern repeated. Finally, a man in a faded green hat rushed in to stand between them. Ceal, like a spooked cat, dashed to the house.

I ran around to the patio and went in through the French doors. She was in the front foyer, collapsed on a wooden bench, ignoring the tears pulling traces of mascara down her cheeks. Twisting the ring on her finger, Ceal was so lost in thought I had to touch her shoulder before she raised her head.

"Are you okay?" I asked.

"Not really." She dragged her hands across her cheeks, erasing the tears. "But thank you, Maud. I appreciate your kindness. There's not a lot of it in this house." She took a deep breath and pushed herself up from the bench. "I can't sit here feeling sorry for myself. As they always say, the show must go on."

"I saw you arguing with someone and you looked frightened. Are you sure everything's okay?"

"I don't know what you're talking about. I just came in here to get out of the sun and fix my makeup." She took a small compact from her bag and added blush to her cheeks and lipstick to her lips. "All right Mr. DeMille, I'm ready for my close-up." She laughed and scooted out the door. By the time I descended the front steps, she was lost in the crowd.

"Hello, Maud." I turned to see Dr. Patmore. "Enjoying the party?"

"Not really," I said, without thinking.

"Oh dear. I'm sorry to hear that." He searched my eyes. "Anything I can do?"

I told him I was missing my dinner partner and he scanned the crowd. "I don't see Gabriel but I think Ronnie's by the pool. Shall we ...? He offered his arm. I thanked him, then quickly explained my arrangement with Jamie before ducking back into the house and up to the loft.

"Wow, you're early." Jamie's pleasure was obvious. It wasn't until she hustled Penny downstairs to the library she asked me why. As my student slipped onto the chair and tucked into her drawing, I described my short dinner date.

"That sucks." Jamie placed the timer on my table and strolled over to the window. "I don't see Gabe, but Beau's right there," she tapped the glass, "standing by the pool and talking to his mother." She wiggled her fingers at me. "Come have a look. Gabe's sure to be somewhere in the crowd."

"Jamie, I've got work to do." I indicated my drawing. "Go ahead and join the party. Penelope and I will be fine."

"I hope so. There's a full moon tonight."

"We're worrying about werewolves now?"

"Of course not, but isn't it supposed to make everyone a little bit crazy?"

I sent her away with a confident wave, tucked the werewolves into the shadows, and dove into my drawing. When I needed a break, I strolled over to check on my student. She was making excellent progress. "Good work, Penelope. You've done an accurate rendering of a difficult subject. Do you want to take a break?" She ignored me and continued to draw. "Maybe exercise your muscles, walk around the library?" No response. Returning to my drawing, I carried on, despite being unable to summon similar praise for an equally difficult subject. One's inner critic can be such a bitch.

"Hey, Maud. Looks like everything went okay."

I looked up to see Jamie. "You're back already?"

"I'm actually a little late." On my work table, she set two cocktail glasses and a large shaker. "I brought us a treat." After a vigorous shake, she poured red liquid into each glass.

I eyed them suspiciously, "I'm not much of a drinker."

"You'll like this. It's mostly cranberry juice." She touched the edge of her glass to mine and I took a sip, then another.

"Mmm, you're right. What is this called?"

"A Cosmo." Jamie swallowed and glanced at the young girl bent over her drawing. "Looks like she didn't miss me."

"What time is it, anyway? My watch must be around here somewhere." I devoted a couple of seconds to a futile scan of my work area. "So, how was it?"

"It was great." Jamie grabbed the timer and gave it a practiced turn. "I had a great time. And Beau," she did a mock swoon. "He was, he is ..."

"Great?" I offered.

She rolled her eyes. "Yes, but I was going to say that he's a great dancer." From the look on her face, she was still in his arms. "Ceal might kill me though."

"Couldn't she turn a blind eye?" I tipped my glass, surprised to find it empty.

"Ha. We didn't see her for ages and when she did show up, she strutted around like an ice queen. Beau, the poor guy, was trying to thaw her out when I left." Jamie refilled my glass and topped up her own.

"What else is in this, besides cranberry juice?"

"Lime juice, vodka and something else I can't remember." The timer rang, Jamie emptied her glass and Penny stood next to her chair. Each time she did this, I anticipated the moment she wouldn't.

"See you tomorrow, Penelope," I said and for just a second, she raised her eyes to meet mine.

"Gabe's waiting on the patio," Jamie called as she left the library.

And wait he would. I emptied the remains of the shaker into my glass and though I turned back to my drawing, it wasn't long before I felt too sleepy to continue. Back in my room, I slipped into bed. I barely remembered my head hitting the pillow when a gentle knock on my door woke me up. I forgot to pack a robe, so I slipped a hoodie over my nightgown and cracked open the door. Gabe was standing a humble distance from the threshold.

"Sorry, Maud. There's still time for dancing."

I pulled open the door.

"Oh jeez, you went to bed. Did I wake you up? Again, sorry. But now that you're awake," he raised his hand to reveal a bottle of wine and two glasses. "I brought a peace offering." His mouth curved, his dimples deepened, and I waved him into the room.

He closed the door, pulled up the blinds and the room filled with moonlight. We drank wine and talked and laughed and shared stories until our individual pasts met our collective present. At some point, I either fell asleep or passed out. Unknown hours later, I slowly crept into consciousness. My head ached as I squinted into the morning light. I was drifting back into a twilight zone when Jamie burst into the room.

"Maud, there's a body in the pool."

Chapter 15

Barely awake, I peeked under the covers wondering if I'd dreamt Gabe's evening visit.

"Maud, what are you looking for? Did you hear what I said?"

"What?"

"Someone's in the pool."

"What pool?"

"*The* pool, the Barrington's swimming pool." She gestured toward its general direction and her gaze fell on the empty wine bottle and glasses. "Are you drunk?"

I gaped at her. Given my aching head and the foggy state of my memory, it was almost certain, but I wasn't going to admit it. Instead, I tried to prove my sobriety by quickly swinging my legs to the side of the bed and standing up. I failed and fell back on the bed. "What were you saying about the pool?"

Jamie threw her head back. "Good God, woman. I said, there's someone in it. Someone who looks very dead."

Those were sobering words. I stood up, a little slower this time, and remained standing. "All right. All right. Let's get down there." I grabbed a pair of joggers from the closet and my hoodie off the back of the chair.

"I can't go." She pointed upwards. "Penny. But you have to promise me that whatever happens, you won't tell anyone I was involved, okay?"

"Why not?"

"Because Mrs. Barrington will pelt me with questions and make it seem like I was somewhere I shouldn't have been. Just come to the loft and tell me what you find out."

Trying to convince myself Jamie saw nothing more than a floating pool toy; I stepped into my shoes and ran out the door. From the path, I couldn't see anyone swimming, floating or flailing but when I got poolside and stared into the deep end, the underwater lights illuminated a head of bright orange hair.

All the energy I'd mustered vanished. I felt small and weak, but still desperate to pull the body from the water. Hoping for a burst of super-human strength, I started taking off my sneakers.

"Is there a problem, Miss?"

It was Caleb, standing behind me with a garbage bag in one hand and a trash picker in the other.

"Yes, can you help? I think it's Ceal. But I don't, I mean I can't ..." Words that initially fired from my mouth suddenly collapsed in my throat.

"Put your shoes back on Miss and get the boss." He pulled off his work boots.

"Don't you need my help?" I asked.

"It be all right. You get the Missus."

I heard the splash of water as I dashed across the deck. By the time I returned with Mrs. Barrington, Caleb was standing guard over a now shrouded body, his wet clothes dripping puddles. Leaving me at a poolside bench, she went directly to him. I watched, shivering in the morning heat, as the handyman bent down to pull back the corner of what looked like a large beach towel. Ceal's face was turned away, but that shock of orange hair was clearly visible. They exchanged a few words before Mrs. Barrington joined me on the bench.

"A completely preventable accident." She might have been referring to a damaged car.

"It's definitely Cecilia?" I asked.

"Oh yes, a life gone too soon thanks to an all too familiar accomplice."

"Accomplice?"

"Alcohol, of course. The source of so many bad decisions." She checked her watch. "Caleb will stay with her. I need you to go to

Dinah. Tell her to wake Beau and Gabriel, and leave our guests in the north wing undisturbed."

I sprinted to the house, and when I reached the kitchen door, pushed it open to declare my news before Dinah could throw me out. Anxious for her 'poor boy,' she hustled off to the back of the house. I went to the living room to wait. I was wondering if she'd remember to wake Gabe when I saw him descending the staircase.

"Maud, good morning." He wrapped me in an embrace. When I didn't return his hug he stepped back, searching my eyes. "I'm sorry about last night. You fell into such a deep sleep I couldn't wake you."

I appreciated the euphemism for passed out. "It's not that," I told him. "There's been a terrible accident."

Gripping my upper arms, he readied himself for the worst. "What happened?"

"It's Cecilia."

His hands relaxed. "Is she badly hurt?"

"She drowned. I just left your mother and Caleb at the pool."

"She's dead?" I nodded, and he released my arms to run toward the front door. By the time I caught up to him, he'd reached his mother. She was asking about Beau and Gabe looked to me for an answer. "Dinah's getting him," I told them.

"Mother, when did you call the police?" Gabe asked.

"I haven't."

"What! Why not?"

"Because Beau is my priority. I need to talk to him first." With an open palm, she gestured toward the body. "No one can help her now. I, however, can help your brother."

"All right. Ten minutes. We can't risk more complications."

"Yes, yes," his mother said, wearily.

When Dinah came plodding along the path, Gabe ran to meet her, quickly returning with the news that Beau wasn't in his room.

Each of us walked to the edge of the pool. We all knew he wouldn't be there but sought confirmation anyway. "Gabriel, your brother must be in the house. Take Maud with you and find him."

Gabe turned to me. "Maud, you don't need to ..."

"It's okay, I want to come with you."

As Gabe bolted up the stairs, I checked the first floor and the patio, though I didn't expect to see Beau lounging on a lawn chair. Returning to the living room, I waited, thinking about Ceal and the finality of death. Did she call for help? Did she reach that point of stillness just before slipping away? Where was Beau? Where is Beau?

A touch on my shoulder brought me back to the man at my side. "Sorry, Gabe. Lost in thought. No luck?"

He shook his head. "Unless he's under a bed or in a closet—Penelope's port of comfort—Beau is not in the house."

Exiting through the side door, I gestured toward a large garden shed. "There seems to be a lot of outbuildings on this property."

Gabe stopped abruptly and smacked his forehead. "Of course!"

Chapter 16

As Gabe jogged toward the cabana, I waited on a deck chair. Caleb continued to stand guard over the body of a woman he'd probably never met and Mrs. Barrington perched on the sandstone bench watching for her son's return.

In the time it takes one brother to deliver bad news to another, they emerged—Gabe, his cell phone against his ear was likely calling 911, and Beau, looking rumpled in yesterday's short-sleeved shirt and chino shorts, walked like a man in shackles. Why wasn't he rushing to the body of his beloved in reckless refusal to believe she was gone?

Mrs. Barrington rose to meet her youngest son, and with what seemed a rare display of maternal comfort, she embraced him. "Has your brother told you about Cecilia's accident?"

Beau's vacant stare suggested he was having difficulty processing the present moment. Finally, he said, "Yes, he said she was … But Mommy it can't be true."

"It is, dear. What do you remember about last night?"

"Nothing. Nothing that would explain this." He looked toward Caleb on the other side of the pool, then quickly turned away. "This can't be happening. It doesn't make sense. A few hours ago, we were—" He raised his eyes to meet his mother's. "It was a great party, everybody said so. And Cecilia was happy, why would she …?"

I waited for the end of his sentence. Why would she what? Leave the cabana, go for a swim, drown herself in the pool?

"Beau, I know this is upsetting."

"Upsetting? Really Mother, getting a bad haircut is upsetting. This is … it's … agonizing."

"Yes, dear. Now, what did you and Cecilia do after the party?"

Beau gaped at his mother and she repeated the question. Raising his hands in defeat he murmured something about hanging with their Toronto friends in the cabana.

"And at any time did you go for a swim in the pool?" she asked.

"Four of us did but not Cissy."

"Cissy?" said his mother.

"Oh yeah, well, it's her nickname."

"I thought Ceal was her nickname."

There was a moment of confused hesitation before Beau insisted a person could have more than one nickname. I expected his mother to comment about their senselessness, but she just tightened her lips and said, "So why didn't Miss Fox join you for a swim?"

He rolled his eyes and tapped his upper arm. "Doc Patmore didn't recommend getting the dressing wet."

"That was sensible. And what did everyone do after the swim?"

"We sat around and talked. C - eal," he stuttered, "made us laugh, lampooning scenes from a terrifically bad play. She can be so funny." He cleared his throat. "Could be so funny."

Mrs. Barrington's eyes narrowed. "She was an actress?"

Beau nodded but offered no details. Pacing two steps forward and then back, she asked, "What can you tell me about your time in the cabana?"

Beau chewed a fingernail. "Sam went to bed early. Liam played his guitar. We had a singalong. It got late. I was tired. I guess I dozed off because the next thing I know, Gabriel's waking me up."

"Where were you sleeping?"

Beau ignored the question, dropping his head and rubbing his temples. His brother answered for him. "He was on the couch in the lounge. I assume his guests were in the bedrooms."

Extending her hand, Mrs. Barrington raised her son's head, forcing him to make eye contact. "Now Beau, this is important. When did Cecilia leave the cabana?"

Turning from her grip, Beau threw up his hands. "I don't know, Mommy. But it's all my fault and I can't talk about it right now." His bottom lip quivered and I saw the child he once was.

"Beau, listen to me." She added emphasis to each word. "It was an accident and certainly not your fault."

Gabe stepped a little closer to Beau, wrapping an arm around his shoulder. "We know it's hard, bro, but the police will be here soon. They'll have questions and Mother just wants you to be prepared."

Beau ducked away. "Prepared! Jesus Christ! Cissy's dead. How does anyone prepare for that?"

"Beau." His mother said sharply. "Not only can you do better than this, you must do better than this. Remember, it was an accident, and the kind of thing people are prone to when they've consumed too much alcohol."

"Cissy wasn't drunk."

"Dear, you fell asleep, so how would you know?" Mrs. Barrington glanced at the cabana. "Perhaps we could speak with your friends."

"You're right, Mother. I wouldn't know and they won't either." Beau shivered. In the distance, we heard a siren. "I'm cold."

"It's the shock, dear."

"I'm getting my jacket." Beau jogged to the cabana, leaving his mother in a state of indecision until she chose to wait on the deck chair next to me.

As we watched for Beau's return, I noticed the lights on either side of the cabana door. "Mrs. Barrington, would those lights have been on last night?"

"Possibly. The light switch is in the cabana. If set, they turn on when detecting motion."

When Beau finally reappeared, it was without the sought-after jacket. "I talked to Liam, Sam and Mike. They didn't hear anything and they don't know anything."

"They must know something, dear. What exactly did they say?"

"I didn't cross-examine them, Mother. Surely you can imagine what they're feeling."

She looked toward the house. "The police are here. They will not be quite so sensitive to our feelings."

Chapter 17

Mrs. Barrington stepped away from our group to introduce herself to the officers of the Ontario Provincial Police. After giving a succinct description of events, she offered to provide a complete guest list and the use of her study.

Following an okay from one of the officers, I was dispatched with more instructions for Dinah. She responded to my message with a lot of sighing and "tsking" but eventually gave in and waddled off to deliver bad news to the guests in the north wing. I headed, first to my room to get properly dressed and then to the loft.

At the sound of my footfall, Jamie rushed to the landing, an index finger pressed against her lips. I slipped off my sandals and tiptoed into her room. As I settled on the wicker chair, Jamie enclosed us behind the heavy curtains. "It's Ceal, isn't it?" she asked, perched on the edge of her bed. "I watched from the window."

I nodded. "Thank God, Caleb was there. I couldn't have done it, you know. I wanted to but there was no way. No way I could have pulled her out of that water." I lowered my head and rubbed my temples with my fingers.

"It's all right, Maud. You were amazing. And you didn't say anything about me, right?" I shook my head. "Not even to Caleb?" I assured her I hadn't even spoken her name. "That's great, Maud. Thank you. So, I guess it was pretty bad down there. What did Beau have to say?"

"Not much really. Four of them went for a swim. Not Ceal though, because of her arm. Then they hung out in the cabana, sang, played guitar, and eventually everybody went to sleep."

"Did anyone see Ceal leave?"

I shook my head.

"While you were being terribly brave, I've been sitting here trying to figure out what might have happened. I told you there's no a/c in the cabana. Now if everyone but Ceal went for a swim, they at least got cooled off. She didn't so maybe she wakes up and it's really hot. She might have left just to get some air and somehow ended up in the pool."

"And that could have been by choice or by accident. And if by choice she's unlikely to be in her clothes."

"I don't know, Maud, she was wearing shorts and a halter top. An outfit pretty much interchangeable with a swimsuit. What did you see when you got to the pool?"

"I was too shocked to notice anything except her orange hair. Did you see Caleb pull her from the water?"

"Yeah. He used the steps at the shallow end. I knew he was carrying her, but all I could see were her legs. He laid her down, and covered her with a beach towel he pulled off the bench."

"I wonder if it was her towel. I mean if she brought a towel out with her then we could assume she intended to go for a swim."

"And I guess you didn't see any clothes carefully folded, or even randomly tossed, by the side of the pool?" Jamie asked.

"No, nothing like that. Even the towel may have been left by another guest. The thing is, if she accidentally fell into the pool, why didn't she just climb out?"

"Good question. Maybe she couldn't swim."

"Seems unlikely. I had the impression she would have jumped in with the rest of them if her arm hadn't been compromised."

Jamie snickered. "Might have been one too many drinks."

"That's Mrs. Barrington's theory. Beau insists Ceal wasn't drunk." I leaned back in my chair and the wicker creaked.

"Beau wasn't qualified to judge. He had a pretty good buzz on by the time I left. Besides, alcohol's a wild card, wouldn't you say? Sometimes you have a couple of drinks, feel perfectly sober, lie down, and the room spins. Nothing for it but to get up or throw up, right? So, she gets up, steps out, and whoops-a-daisy, into the water she goes."

"When you saw Ceal at the party, she was in a foul mood, right?"

"Yep."

"But Beau told us she was happy and enjoying herself."

"Ha." Jamie shook her head. "I'm not buying that. You couldn't miss the dark cloud she was dragging around. Maybe after I left, booze and her fiancé improved her mood. Either way, I'd be bad-tempered too if my future mother-in-law treated me like crap and her kid stabbed me in the arm." Jamie checked the bedside clock. "Shit, it's almost seven-thirty." She jumped to her feet.

I stood up too. "What happens at seven-thirty?"

"Penny wakes up."

"Wait a minute. Are you saying she's going to open her eyes as the clock strikes the half hour?"

"Yes, but I guess you'll have to see it to believe it." Jamie slowly pulled back the curtain and turned the bedside clock toward me. As the minute hand moved to the six, Penny sat up and rubbed the sleep from her eyes.

"Okay. That's eerily Draculian."

"I know. Sometimes her actions are very predictable—a seven-thirty wake-up, her puzzles, the swing, peanut butter sandwiches, then bam—someone gets a fork in the arm."

I followed Jamie into Penny's room and while she tended to her student, I pulled back the curtains from the radius window.

"What's going on out there?" Jamie called from the bathroom.

"An officer is talking to Mrs. Barrington and the paramedics have arrived. They're wheeling a stretcher toward the pool. I guess the on-scene assessment is finished."

Anxious to work on her puzzle, Penny, still in her pyjamas, slid onto one of her little chairs. Jamie joined me at the window and it was like watching a movie. The attendants transferred the stark white body bag onto the trolley stretcher and maneuvered it toward the waiting ambulance.

"What do you think happens after death?" Jamie asked.

"They'll do an autopsy and release the body to the family. If she left a will, which seems unlikely given her age, they'll follow her instructions. Otherwise, they'll make the decisions about things like burial or cremation."

"Okay, but what do you think happens after anyone dies?"

"Years ago, my family had a budgie."

"Wait a minute, Maud, you're talking about a bird now?"

"Yes. He was quite a chatterbox and had a vocabulary of over two hundred words. As soon as I got home, he'd fly to my shoulder, push his little beak against my cheek, and say 'give us a kiss,' in his strange little birdie voice."

"Ah, that's adorable. What was his name?"

"Jack. One day he fell off his perch—a stroke, probably. I cradled him in my hand, thanked him for being such a good little bird, and said goodbye. His final breath came out like a sigh and his tiny eyes dropped closed. The thing is, before he died, I felt his energy or what you might call his soul, leave his body."

She looked misty. "Oh, that's so sad. But do birds have souls?" she asked, her moment of grief quickly forgotten.

"There's no proof any living thing has a soul. It was just my attempt to answer your question and illustrate that we could be more than our physical bodies."

"Oh." Jamie gave it a moment's thought before turning back to the window. "I wonder what the cops are asking the Barringtons."

"You know, they'll also want to talk to us," I told her.

"Really? I hope I get the one talking to Gabe." She tapped the glass. "Though that other guy's pretty buff, too." I rolled my eyes and she shrugged. "I know, I know. I'm ogling the boys in blue while poor Beau loses a second fiancée."

Jamie's words were clear but confusing. "What are you talking about?"

"I don't think they were officially engaged but I had the impression everyone expected them to get married."

"Who was she?"

"I don't know. Beau mentioned her when I told him a good friend of mine lost control of her car and was killed."

"Oh, I'm sorry." I patted her hand.

"Yeah, it was wretched. Anyway, Beau found me crying and told me the woman he hoped to marry had died in a car accident."

"Jeez, what happened?"

"She drove off a bridge." Jamie sucked in a breath. "Holy crap, Maud, maybe she drowned just like Ceal."

"We don't know Ceal drowned."

"Of course she did. What else could it be?"

"A heart attack, a stroke, or an aneurysm, and she was dead before she hit the water. Or she could have been shot or stabbed, although one would expect to see blood. Perhaps the pool filter would take care of that."

"What about suicide?"

"Yeah, that crossed my mind but it's a lot harder to drown yourself in a pool than you might think. You'd have to tie up your arms and legs or somehow knock yourself out. Either way, if the autopsy reveals water in her lungs, she drowned. Although ..."

"Yes?" said Jamie.

"I've heard of something called dry drowning. It's when a small amount of inhaled water causes a spasm that forces the airway to close."

"Hot damn, Maud, how do you know this stuff?"

"My uncle was a cop."

"Crikey, you two must have some morbid conversations." She pushed away from the window. "Oh well, life goes on and Pen can't stay in her pj's all day."

Chapter 18

Jamie began holding up clothes from Penny's closet and I realized she was waiting for the young girl's approval. The first three blouses elicited an exaggerated head shake, for the fourth she simply raised her arms and allowed them to slip into each sleeve before methodically buttoning the blouse from bottom to top. A similar routine followed for shorts. As soon as she was dressed, Penny grabbed her baggy blue sweater from the small clothes tree, pushed her feet into sandals and returned to the puzzle table. Re-hanging the rejected blouses, Jamie said, "Too bad our Pen won't just throw on a tee shirt. She used to be okay with them. Now I can't pull anything over her head."

"Did something happen?"

"Not that I know of. Many on the spectrum have heightened sensitivities. One bad experience, even a minor one, can put them right off. Last year one of Penny's classmates shut her eyes and has remained steadfast in her refusal to open them. Argh, did I just say steadfast? I've spent too long in this house."

I pulled out one of the Lilliputian chairs to watch Penny work on *Starry Night,* but before I sat down, she moved to the far end of the table and opened the box containing the second puzzle her mother recently bought.

"Jamie, does Penny usually begin a new puzzle before finishing the one she's been working on?"

"What?" Shoving the dresser drawer closed, Jamie joined me to watch her student dump out the puzzle pieces for *The Birth of Venus.* "I've never seen her do this. She's usually so methodical, always finishing one puzzle before beginning another."

"Is it because her mother gave her two puzzles at the same time?"

Jamie shook her head. "This is not the first time she received two puzzles."

"Maybe it has something to do with the subject matter."

"What do you mean?"

"You know, *The Birth of Venus*—a woman floating on water. If Penelope saw—"

Jamie raised her palm to silence me before pulling her phone from her pocket. She agreed to whatever her caller requested and re-pocketed her phone. "That was the Queen B and you're right. The police want to talk to us."

Distracted, she grabbed Penny's hand. Like a freshly hooked fish, the girl writhed and twisted until she pulled herself free and calmly returned to her puzzle.

Jamie choked the timer, her frustration threatening to pull off the dial. "That was stupid. I should know better. Sorry Maud, you'll have to go on your own. Tell Mrs. B we'll be downstairs in," she checked the demarcations, "ten minutes."

I made a mental note never to lose the timer—in fact, I thought we should have a spare. When I reached the main floor, an officer in the downstairs hall directed me to Mrs. Barrington's office.

The man sitting behind her oversized mahogany desk introduced himself as Inspector Murray. He wasted no time getting the usual data, including the date of my arrival, my relationship with the Barringtons, and the reason for my visit. He didn't hide his surprise at finding a portrait artist in residence but seemed to accept my explanation.

"What was your impression of Miss Cecilia Fox?"

I found it difficult to provide him with a coherent description. A little more reflection and I realized why. "I found her confusing."

"In what way, Miss ..." he checked his notes, "Gibbons?"

"She had natural beauty but she hid it under crazy orange hair, heavy makeup, and lots of jewellery. And the way she dressed was, well, provocative."

"Meaning?"

"Deliberately revealing." I unconsciously pulled up the neckline of my T-shirt. "She seemed like an intelligent person who said stupid things and tried to draw attention to herself."

He wanted my version of the fork-stabbing incident and asked when I'd next spoken to either Beau or Ceal. I recounted the conversation overheard while carrying my art supplies and Beau's subsequent help. I did not mention what I might have wrongly interpreted as a minor flirtation.

"Thank you, Miss Gibbons. We would appreciate a full statement at our local detachment, ASAP." He handed me a card and as I turned to leave asked, "You mentioned you also have an office job, who do you work for?"

"My uncle, at Gibbons Investigative Services."

"Ah, Sid Gibbons. Great cop, your uncle. Give him my best."

Outside the office, I found Jamie with Penny standing next to her like a child sentinel.

"Maud, can Penelope go with you to the library? This will be too upsetting and she won't talk anyway. I'll come up as soon as they finish with me."

With the image of flailing rebellion fresh in my mind, I mouthed the words *bring the timer* before inviting Penny to join me. My protégée rushed ahead and by the time I reached the library, she was sitting with pencil poised.

Checking on her drawing, I noted that not only was her rendering of David complete, but she'd also started to outline the books I'd placed under the statue. "Penelope, this looks great. Would you like to begin another?"

She answered by tossing her finished drawing to the floor.

"No!" I said, immediately regretting my tone and volume. I anticipated a violent reaction but Penny simply froze—her pencil quivering like a hummingbird. "It's important to respect your work," I insisted, keeping my voice quiet and steady. After picking up her drawing, I placed it, with exaggerated care, on my table.

At the étagère, I exchanged the statue of David for the second Bernini statue and set it on top of the pedestal of books. "This is a statue of Apollo and Daphne. The sculptor chose to illustrate the point in the story when Daphne transforms into a laurel tree. Do you remember how we begin?"

Penny nodded. On a fresh piece of drawing paper, she added the faint preparation lines to set the parameters for the drawing, then confidently began the outline. I was smiling with pride when Jamie returned.

"Maud, I'm sorry. I told that cop about Pen's condition but he insists on talking to her." Jamie dragged the wooden stool closer to Penny. She lowered her voice and said, "Penelope, Beau's friend Ceal had an accident. She died. Your mother called the police because we don't know what happened." Oblivious to Jamie's words, Penny continued to draw. "The police are talking to all of us and they want to talk to you." Jamie took a small lollipop from her pocket, and looking at me whispered, "Don't tell her mother." In one motion she pulled off the wrapper and offered it to Penny in exchange for the pencil.

At the door, my young student looked back and this time it was directly into my eyes. "You'll be fine. We'll draw again soon," I promised.

Chapter 19

Iwas tidying my work area when Gabe crossed the room and wrapped me in affection. "Sorry, Maud. I thought we'd have time for a swim, a leisurely breakfast, maybe even a walk along the lake."

"And then death came to Altica," I murmured.

"That's one way of putting it. I really am sorry."

"It wasn't your fault. And now, I'm sure you want to spend some time with your brother."

"I will. Did you talk to Inspector Murray?"

I nodded.

"Then you know they want an official statement. The best time for me to do that is this morning. If you have time, we could go to the local OPP detachment together."

"I can't do much with this drawing until your mother gives the okay, so it's the perfect time."

"Great." He craned his neck toward my drawing. "Mind if I have a look?" I stepped back and he gave it more than just a cursory glance. "Mother will be thrilled." I raised my eyebrows. "Correction. I would be thrilled; my mother will be mildly accepting." Catching sight of the smaller drawing on my table he said, "Hey, what's this?"

"Something Penelope just finished."

"My sister did this?" I assured him she did. "By herself?"

"Yes."

"Wow, she should never be underestimated."

"I agree and it's amazing to watch. When she's working, she becomes the drawing."

"I'd like to see that," he said. "But it won't be on this trip." He turned toward the door, and I grabbed my purse.

I was buckling my seatbelt when Gabe told me he really would be thrilled to have a portrait.

"Anyone in particular?" I asked, and he framed his face with his hands.

"It's for the boardroom. We usually opt for a photograph but now that I've found you, well, I like the idea of an oil portrait."

I reached into my purse for a business card and set it on the console. "This is my agent's number, but you might want to wait until I've finished the portrait of your mother."

"Why? If my demanding mother hired you, you're good. Besides, how could you resist this?" He crossed his eyes and sucked in his lips. I raised my hands to click an imaginary camera.

At the end of the driveway, Gabe offered the scenic route and made a left turn that quickly led to postcard views. As we passed an alpaca farm, he slowed the car, and each furry face turned to watch us go by. I giggled at what looked like the offspring of a sheep and a camel.

"Nice to hear you laugh," he said, giving my hand a gentle squeeze. "I really am sorry about all this, Maud. Certainly not what you bargained for when you agreed to paint my mother."

"Don't worry about me. Compared to what your brother's going through, I'm only slightly inconvenienced. Jamie told me about his girlfriend dying in a car accident, so I know this is not the first tragedy he's had to deal with."

"Yeah, that was tragic."

"Were the two women anything alike?"

"Hell, no," Gabe said, with a disdainful snort. "We know nothing about Ceal. Her relationship with my brother was a complete surprise and a shock, if I'm being honest. On the other hand, Rebecca was from a well-respected Toronto family, one we'd known for years. She was lovely and certainly someone who was…"

He turned into the parking lot of the OPP detachment, switched off the car and slipped out of his seatbelt. "Well, you know what I mean."

I suspected 'more appropriate,' 'suitable,' or 'wealthier' might have filled in the blank.

At the single-story brick building, a heavy steel door was opened by a uniformed officer. He had the self-confident good looks I was going to enjoy describing to Jamie. Following brief introductions, we were led into a waiting area. Cheerful yellow paint on cinder block walls implied things were never as bad as they seemed. The few cold, grey, metal chairs by the windows told a different story.

We were about to sit when Constable Clark invited Gabe to follow him. A few seconds later my name was called and I turned to face a warrior queen. No introductions were made. Perhaps it was a form of intimidation, like the handcuffs on her duty belt. Not that she needed them. If provoked, Constable Boudica would have no problem squishing me like a bug. When she led the way, I was quick to follow. In the interview room, I got the chair in the corner.

In a space only slightly larger than Penny's closet, I answered questions and despite a bright overhead light, a video camera in one corner and a menacing microphone in the other, I reiterated my initial statement. I described the argument I witnessed between Cecilia Fox and a dark-haired stranger. Before it was over, I struggled to suppress my urge to confess to the illegal U-turn I'd made on my first day through the village.

Released back to the waiting room, it was only a couple of minutes before Gabe joined me and another fifteen before we were in a quaint cafe with a fondness for blue and white gingham. My rumbling stomach entertained us while we perused the menu.

When a waitress finally reached our table, carafe in hand, we wasted no time placing our orders—Eggs Florentine for me, the Farmer's Breakfast for Gabe. "Coming right up," she promised and I believed her.

We sipped our coffee. Gabe asked about my favourite artists and we discussed possible galleries to visit when I returned to the city, authors we loved to read and eventually, foods we liked to eat. Gabe checked his watch. I looked desperately toward the kitchen.

"Do you think those farm-fresh eggs have to be pried from under a sitting hen?" I asked.

"If they do, what does that say about the sausages?"

I was just about to munch on one of those little packets of sugar when breakfast arrived and our food became all-consuming. While enjoying a second cup of coffee, I noticed a bridge spanning distant railway tracks. "Was Beau's girlfriend, Rebecca, alone when she died?"

"No, Beau was with her. They were coming home from their grad party."

"Oh, I hadn't realized they were so young. Jamie seemed to think they were engaged."

"Had she lived, that might have happened. They were both boarders at King's College School. Rex and I went there too, but we'd graduated by then. Do you know it?"

"I know of it." I was reminded that having a few things in common is not the same as having common ground.

"Becca was driving. Beau swore they'd only had a couple of drinks and she was sober by the time they got in the car. His memory was foggy but he thought she swerved to avoid a dog. That's when the car hit a tree. At impact, my brother was thrown clear—the one time not wearing a seat belt was a good thing. His injuries were minor but after hitting the tree, the car careened off a small bridge."

"Wow. Pain, guilt and grief. That's a lot to deal with."

Gabe nodded. "He got through it, without much help from me. And now, it's happening again."

I emptied my coffee cup. "We should get back."

As we walked to the car, Gabe called his mother and learned the sedative Dr. Patmore had given Beau had finally taken effect. "So, Maud, how about that walk by the lake?"

It was a short drive to a headland with an unobstructed view of a sparkling expanse of blue. We scrambled over the rocky beach to the shoreline, and I bent down, stretched out my hand, and caught an incoming wave. "Mercy, that's cold! I can't imagine swimming in this."

"I can," said Gabe, crouching next to me. "When we were kids, Lake Ontario was our playground and I can tell you, there were lots of fun times pushing each other off the boat. Something you might say was an experiment in cryogenics but it didn't take long to get used to the cold." He picked up a flat stone and skipped it across the water.

"Did it make you lightheaded? Jumping into very cold water can be hard on the heart, sometimes causing arrhythmias that make you dizzy." I handed him another stone.

"Could that have happened to Ceal?"

I shook my head. "Your pool has a heater."

"Oh yeah." He sliced the stone through the waves. "Maybe she got a cramp."

"Possible. Alcohol, some medications and even diabetes could have been factors. Was Ceal diabetic?"

"Haven't a clue. We'll have to ask Beau." Gabe offered me his hand and we walked along the shore. "Maybe something spooked her and she fell into the pool. Could have been a perceived danger, or even an actual one."

"A danger? You mean like a bear?"

"Very unlikely. You've got a better chance of spotting a fox or a coyote. But whatever it was, everything's scarier in the dark, right? Maybe she just heard something and panicked."

"It wasn't pitch dark, thanks to the full moon and the lights on the cabana, but tell me more about those coyotes."

"They're smaller than you might expect, about the size of a border collie, but with a stronger bite. Generally active from dusk to dawn, they avoid people and rarely come close to the house. Although …"

"Yes?"

"Food scraps from the party might have lured them in."

He must have seen the fear in my eyes. "Maud, don't worry. Caleb cleaned up and Doc Patmore says more people are killed by stray golf balls or flying champagne corks than even get bitten by coyotes. Having said that, if you do see one, don't run. It'll think you're prey. What you need to do is jump up and down, wave your arms—do anything to make yourself look bigger. Oh, and make a lot of noise."

"I'm sure screaming would come easily enough. Standing still— maybe not."

He squeezed my hand. "Look at it this way, what are the chances you'll be roaming the property after dark, besides, it's more likely Ceal was spooked by a raccoon."

I had no intention of roaming the property day or night. I also thought it unlikely that Ceal, or any Torontonian would get freaked out over a trash bandit. But a coyote—crouching in the shadows, saliva dripping from its teeth, ready to defend a scavenged piece of hamburger—that would be terrifying.

"We may never know what happened to Ceal. An accident is the most likely explanation, homicide is second and health issues, a distant third."

"Homicide is second? Wow. I don't want to say it can't happen here—no wait, I *do* want to say it can't happen here." Gabe gestured toward a large piece of driftwood and we sat, facing the lake.

"Even if it was a homicide, it would be difficult to prove. Ever heard of those celebrities who drowned under suspicious circumstances? People like Natalie Wood and Nerine Shatner had both been drinking and their autopsies revealed unexplained injuries, though Nerine's broken neck was consistent with a dive into shallow water."

"Now that sounds like something Ceal could have done," Gabe said and I agreed.

"By the way, was the Shatner woman related to the Star Trek guy?" he asked.

"His wife. He was a suspect until he produced a receipt proving he was dining out at the time."

After a pause, Gabe asked, "My brother's a suspect, isn't he?"

"At the moment, we all are."

Chapter 20

"Maud," Gabe's voice pulled me from the view outside the passenger's window, "last night you mentioned working with your uncle."

"I did?"

"I think we were halfway through a third glass of wine at that point."

"Sorry about that."

"Don't apologize. I brought the wine. It's good to know you're not much of a drinker."

I didn't tell him about the three Cosmos.

"I was wondering if you know the timeline for Ceal's autopsy?"

"It depends on the availability of a pathologist, but if judged a suspicious death it will have a sense of urgency."

"Suspicious death," Gabe echoed my words. "Not what one wants to hear in conjunction with the owners of a pharmaceutical company. If the press gets a hold of this …"

"I think it's a question of when not if."

"You're right. God damn it!" He smacked the steering wheel. "How am I going to deal with this? I can't be here and I can't trust my mother or my brother." He turned the car off the main highway and onto a back road. "Maud, I realize you'll be busy, but could you —"

"Yes."

He exhaled and dropped his shoulders. "Bet you never thought your detective skills would be needed during a portrait commission."

"A good part of what you call my detective skills is simply insatiable curiosity. I'm already looking for answers."

"That's great. Anything you can find out about Cecilia Fox might be important. If you could get Beau talking, without his usual glibness, he might offer something worthwhile. And what about your uncle? Would he be a resource?"

"I can ask."

"That's great." Gabe flashed a smile. "I said that already, didn't I? But I mean it."

Exiting the car, we saw Dinah waving at us from the side porch. "The cops just hightailed it," she said. "They've been in the cabana, all over the pool, might have even been in the pool for all I know."

"Is the pool area cordoned off?" I asked.

"Course not. The woman had an accident and those cops aren't comin' back. But if you're thinkin' of swimmin,' I'd wait till tomorrow. Caleb's been down there fillin' the damn thing with chlorine. Now, Gabriel, I know you'll want to see your dear brother, but he's restin' and I got some lunch for you and Maud." She glanced at me. "Just go round to the picnic table."

We found the table covered with a white cotton cloth, and decorated with a cheerful red vase holding three white roses. Gabe straddled the bench to sit opposite me. "This is pleasantly unexpected."

I breathed in the scent of the flowers, and Dinah came out the back door. "This is so nice of you," I told her as she put a charcuterie board, a jug of iced tea, and a small plate of brownies on the table.

"Had this set for a couple of the Madame's special guests. They left. Figured you two might as well use it."

The screen door closed behind her. "Had you feeling a little special for a minute there, didn't she?" Gabe whispered.

I laughed. "At least the food won't disappoint." To a slice of Dinah's homemade sourdough bread, I added cheese, pastrami, homemade mayo, and mustard.

"That's why we keep her," said Gabe, making a similar sandwich on rye. "Do you think she's right?"

"About what?"

"The police concluding that Ceal had an accident and they've finished their investigation."

"No." I chewed and swallowed. "But I can see why she might believe it."

"Yeah. It's what we all want to believe."

"And as my uncle would say, hope for the best and plan for the worst."

Gabe nodded. "And I'll plan to get back here as soon as possible. Until then let's exchange phone numbers."

I handed him my cell phone. "You input the numbers. It'll be faster."

He tapped away, then wiggled my phone at me. "You know how to make a call, right?"

"Very funny." I snatched it from his hand just as Dinah appeared at the screen door. "Sonny's asking for you."

Grabbing a brownie and taking the steps two at a time, Gabe paused at the back door to ask if I'd take the photos for his portrait before he left for the city. We agreed to meet in the library and by the time he joined me there, I'd secured a backdrop, put a chair in front of it, and set up the lighting.

"Hey, you don't waste time." He fingered the drapery hanging over the bookcase. "Is this the sheet from your bed?"

My cheeks warmed. "I chose it for the colour—blue is the complementary colour to orange and this particular blue will enhance the colour of your flesh."

"I'm orange?"

"We're all orange. Some of us are dark, some light, some more yellow, some more red, but all orange." I held up my tubes of yellow ochre and earth red. "I use these earth colours. You can lighten them with titanium white, darken them with burnt umber and reduce their chroma with grey or cerulean blue."

"I'm sure I couldn't, but I'm happy you can." He dropped into the chair. "I've said my goodbyes to the family, so we've got about forty minutes."

Knowing he wanted head and shoulders only, I suggested either full face or three-quarter view.

"There aren't many portraits in profile, are there?" he asked.

"There's the Duke of Urbino. The artist painted his left side because the duke lost his right eye and part of his nose in a sword fight."

"Ouch." Gabe stroked the bridge of his nose. "Okay, let's go with a more traditional look."

I explained how his thoughts would affect his expression and added it was best not to have teeth.

"Hey, I'm very attached to my teeth." He grinned. His smile relaxed, and there it was, the perfect pose. I took a few extra shots, shifting slightly to capture the changing light. When he raised his hands in front of his face, I lowered the camera. "Sorry Maud, gotta go."

A hug, a kiss, a promise to call and he was gone. Cradling the camera, I flipped through the pictures. As pleased as I was with the images, I needed prints. A glance at my watch told me only that I wasn't wearing it. Typically, I put it on at the start of the day but this was not a typical day. I checked every surface, including the easel, the floor, my pockets, the bedroom and its adjoining bathroom. Damn. Uncle Sid gave me that watch.

Chapter 21

On the way to my car, I felt a crunch under my left shoe. A quick inspection revealed a broken cookie, likely a remnant from the party and just the kind of thing to attract those ravenous coyotes. A rustle in the hedges, a play of light in the shadows, and I could easily imagine those huge menacing canines. And what if it were midnight, moonlight, and real canines, what then? Would I fight—feet planted firmly, arms raised in a threatening display while screaming insults? Or would I take flight—a reckless race down the path and a probable tumble into the pool? Probably the latter. Would Ceal have done the same?

Tracker-like, I scrutinized the area. A Cinderella shoe would be helpful or the deep toe prints of a desperate runner. Unfortunately, the path to the pool yielded nothing more than a broken plastic spoon.

If not the frantic flight from a wild animal, maybe the heat in the cabana prompted Ceal to seek cool water. If so, did she dangle her feet over the side, wade in, jump in, or make a fatal dive into the shallows?

From a spot on the poolside bench, I envisioned her sneaking from the cabana, wearing what—her clothes, a bathing suit, wrapped in a beach towel? Intent on my vision, I was struck catatonic when it became a reality. In the time it took for Ceal's ghost to reach me, I held my breath.

Her perky "Hi there" sounded worldly enough. I stuttered a few phrases. "Are you …? How is this …? How can you …?"

The ghost tugged at her orange hair. "Ah, you thought I was Cissy." She offered her hand. "I'm Samantha Hansen."

I took it, relieved to feel warm flesh. "You're Sam. You were with the group of friends who stayed in the cabana last night."

"That's right."

"You've probably heard this before, but you could be Ceal's twin."

"I know. It may seem strange but we didn't realize the resemblance until one of my co-workers at Randolph's referred to her as my sister." Sam ran a hand through her hair. "I don't usually look like this. I only did it for Cissy." Her bottom lip quivered and tears filled her eyes.

"For Cissy?" I said, knowing there was a story and hoping she'd tell it.

"Yeah, she heard about a great new play featuring twins," Sam's voice cracked.

"You're both actors?"

"That's right. The waitressing job helps pay the bills. Anyway, Cissy convinced me if I made," she raised her fingers for air quotes, "just a few changes, we could get the parts. So, I cut my beautiful long blond hair and dyed it this crazy colour. Even added a couple more piercings." She tapped an ear before running a hand over her arm. "But no freakin' way was I getting a tattoo. Nobody's putting ink under this beautiful skin."

"Did you get the parts?"

She grinned. "We did." Her smile faded. "Cissy got the lead, of course." Catching my eye, she told me with added emphasis, how very happy she was for her. "But now," her bottom lip quivered, "I don't know what'll happen." Sam covered her face with her hands and wept.

"I'm so sorry. It's such a tragedy." I patted her shoulder and my consoling touch was instantly repelled with anger.

"Tragedy? It's more than a tragedy. It's a crime. My mother is a lawyer and I know pool owners are legally required to keep their guests safe."

The thought of the Barringtons getting sued for negligence hadn't occurred to me though I was sure Mrs. Barrington would have considered it.

Sam pulled a tissue from her pocket. "Sorry, I know none of this is your fault. What did you say your name was?"

Hearing my name she cooed, "Oh, you're the artist. Beau told me his mother was sitting for her portrait. Very retro. I was hoping we'd meet but you'd left the party by the time we arrived."

"Yes, I had work to do. I don't suppose you saw Cissy leave the cabana last night?"

She shook her head. "Unlike my best friend, I'm no night owl. I didn't see or hear anything."

"Beau's mother thinks alcohol may have affected Cissy's judgment."

"Of course she does. The negligent pool owner blames the victim. The thing is, Cissy didn't have the stomach for booze. A couple of drinks, sure, but she *never* got drunk."

I made a casual inquiry about recreational drugs and Sam shook her head and wrinkled her nose. "No way. We're not into that kind of stuff. A little weed sure, but it doesn't count. It's practically legal."

I know it isn't as benign as she would like to think, but kept my opinion to myself. Instead, I asked about the possibility of Cissy going for a late-night swim.

Sam shook her head. "We all went in earlier, but not her. She had this, like, big gauze dressing over her gash." Sam wrapped her hand around her upper arm to demonstrate. "Stay away from that crazy sister, eh?"

I winced. "She's autistic."

"Yeah well, Cissy expected the mother to treat her like crap but she didn't deserve to be attacked by the wacko kid sister with a fork. And if that wasn't bad enough, Bobby showed up and ruined everything."

"Bobby?"

Sam pulled a knitted cloche from her bag and covered her head. "Never mind. It doesn't matter anymore." She looked toward the main house. "They're waiting for me. Gotta go." I called after her but she didn't look back.

While driving into town, I tried to remember if I'd met anyone at the party named Bobby. It's not common for men named Robert to use the diminutive, except maybe hockey players and pop singers. Could I have met him as Bob, Rob, Robert or Robbie? No one came to mind. On my return trip, it occurred to me Bobby could be a she, though I didn't recall meeting a potential Roberta either.

When I entered the dining room, it was with the hope of learning something from Beau. Only Mrs. Barrington, Jamie and Penny were seated at the table. The man about the house had sequestered himself in his room, and Mrs. Barrington's icy silence discouraged even casual conversation. Fortunately, Dinah's chicken and broccoli casserole provided enough entertainment. When we left the dining room twenty minutes later, Jamie invited me to the swing and, though I was anxious to talk to her, there was something else I needed to do first.

Chapter 22

In my room, I leafed through the many images of Gabriel Barrington. Anticipating the perfect pose—a timeless image revealing the subject in just the right light—I was ten pictures in when I found it. Confident my newest client would agree with me, I secured the photos in the drawer of the bedside table and made the call I should have made hours ago.

It was a difficult story, so I told it quickly. He, in turn, wanted to know when I was coming home.

"I don't know Uncle Sid. I've only just started the portrait."

"Wait a minute Maudie, the woman lost her future daughter-in-law. Not only that, whether she admits it or not, the circumstances are suspicious. Doesn't she want to reschedule?"

I described the lack of relationship between Mrs. Barrington and her son's surprise fiancée.

"But her son must be grieving. Doesn't he need his mother?"

"She's more Mommy Dearest than Princess Diana."

"But what about Joe? He must be devastated?"

"Beau."

"What?"

"His name is Beau."

"As in Beauregard?"

"No, Mrs. Barrington hates nicknames. It's just Beau. Jamie, she's Penelope's teacher, thinks Beau's proposal was based on his inner philanthropist and the desire to help someone needy."

"Maud, honey, young men from wealthy families tend to express their altruism by giving to charity not by taking on unsuitable brides.

From what you've just told me, Miss Cecilia Fox would be difficult for any mother to accept."

"Only because Ceal worked so hard at making herself unacceptable."

"Hold on a second—Ceal?"

"Beau introduced her as Cecilia but she asked to be called Ceal. And her best friend Samantha, known as Sam, referred to her as Cissy. In Sam's opinion, Cissy was extremely clever. She believes the pool wasn't safe and blames the Barringtons for her friend's death."

"Anything in that?"

"I don't know. The pool is well maintained. And Ceal, after all, is, or rather, was an adult. Mrs. Barrington blames alcohol."

"Common enough," he said. "Though the majority of those deaths involve a lake, a boat and an intoxicated male between the ages of nineteen and twenty-five."

"She fit the age category. Jamie also thinks alcohol was involved but Sam told me Cissy never had more than a couple of drinks. According to her, cannabis was the drug of choice. So, how does being stoned affect one's ability to swim assuming the woman knew how to swim? That hasn't been validated."

"Surely with a nickname like Ceal," Uncle Sid chuckled. "Sorry, I do realize the poor young woman is dead. So, was she born and raised in Canada?"

"I think so, at least there was no detectable foreign accent."

Uncle Sid said, "Chances are, this Ceal could swim. Over ninety-five percent of us can. As to your question about swimming while stoned, that depends on the quantity of the drug and if she was a regular user. THC can cause decreased blood flow to the brain, leading to time and distance distortions. Also, there could be weakness and confusion but fatalities are more likely when swimming in a lake. If the autopsy reveals a high level of THC in her system, it might push for a verdict of death by misadventure."

"That would be a relief for the Barringtons."

"Unless ..." He hesitated.

"Yes?"

"Unless there are other suspicious circumstances. Did you witness any mistreatment? Was Ceal hurt or threatened? Did you see any outbursts, you know, the kind of thing that could escalate to murder?"

I told him about Penelope and the fork, the argument I overheard between Ceal and Beau, and the confrontation I saw during Beau's birthday party.

"How old is this kid?"

"Twelve, I think, but Jamie is always with her."

"Be that as it may, until the police resolve this thing, watch your back. And if it does prove to be a homicide, you know as well as I do, the fiancé will be the prime suspect. I'd say his angry mother would follow at a close second. So, if that happens, my darling niece, I expect you'll be coming home."

"True, but if and until, what I need is for my subject to choose a pose and sit still. I can't lose this commission, Uncle Sid. Especially since I'm almost sure I have another—a portrait of the eldest son."

"Cripes, is he sitting too?"

I stifled a giggle. "No, if it's a go, I'll be working from photographs and at home."

He sighed. "That's good news. Now, let's get this present commission finished—not that I can help you with it."

"Maybe, you can." I told him about meeting Inspector Murray. "It'll be easier to concentrate on this painting if I have a heads up about the case, particularly any findings from the autopsy."

"John Murray, yeah, I know him. Okay, I'll see what I can do. Be sure to keep your cell phone charged and handy. Won't be much good in the drawer of a bedside table. Now, before you go, I've got a good Sherlock story."

"Great, I love a good dog story."

"Yesterday, I brought him to the office to keep me company. He was snoozing in his new bed—a big plush job, honey, you'll love it. Anyway, at about noon I went out to grab a burger and when I got back, he was sitting on your office chair. I'm not kidding, he looked like a canine temp."

I imagined our furry boy with one paw on the keyboard and the other holding the phone. "Did you get a picture?"

"Naw. He jumped down when he saw me. Sherlock knows it's not his place."

"At least not until he learns to answer the phone and use the computer."

Before we ended the call my uncle asked, "For a woman who hates nicknames, why did Mrs. Barrington call her daughter Penelope? I mean the kid could get Penny, Pen, Nell, Nellie, Elle, Ellie, even Pippa. Besides, what's wrong with nicknames? Maudie, this family is very odd."

Chapter 23

The door wasn't latched, so my gentle tap pushed it open. The sun, on that early summer evening, illuminated the area where Beau, like Rembrandt's *Philosopher in Meditation*, sat slouched on a wooden chair, hands clasped tightly in his lap.

"Beau?" I said, twice before he raised his head.

"Maud? What is it?"

"We missed you at dinner. How are you feeling?"

"Angry." His hands curled into fists.

"That's understandable."

"None of this is understandable, Maud." His voice grew a little louder with each word.

"But anger is, especially when an accident is preventable."

"Maud. What the hell are you talking about?"

"Ceal's, um, condition."

"Her what?"

"I know you said Ceal wasn't drunk, but she had a few drinks, right?"

He nodded suspiciously.

"And when you combine alcohol with drugs, it can mess with a person's judgment."

"Did you say drugs?"

"Yes, but—"

"What the hell, Maud? Who said anything about drugs?" Beau shot from the chair and towered over me. "And how is this *any* of your business?" He brushed past me to stand by the door. "You need to go now."

I made a vain attempt to depart with dignity, before dashing to my room. Sitting on the bed, I spent several moments feeling embarrassed, confused, and wondering what had prompted him to have such an extreme reaction. I could think of only one. Beau had provided the drugs.

In need of a friendly face, and hoping to find Jamie and Penny at the swing, I exited the house through the French doors. They weren't there, but Caleb was weeding the bed of petunias around the patio.

"Evening, Miss," he said, prompting Steady to leap over the flowers and greet me with his usual enthusiasm. As I rubbed his velvety ears, he looked up at me with the kind of doggy adoration that makes the world a better place.

"Great companions, aren't they?" I said.

"Yes, Miss." Caleb tossed another weed into a green plastic bucket.

"Caleb, I wanted to thank you again, for doing what I couldn't." He tilted his head. "What I'm trying to say is, thank you for, getting Cecilia out of the pool."

He looked at me briefly, nodded and returned to his weeding.

"Do you mind if I ask you a question?" He shrugged. "Did you notice if she was wearing a bathing suit?"

More weeds hit the bucket. "I don't know what she was wearing, Miss."

So, she must have been wearing something. I thought back to seeing her on the bench in the foyer. "Was her outfit orange? Maybe the colour of a cantaloupe?"

"Beg your pardon, Miss."

"Whatever Ceal was wearing. Was it orange?"

Caleb thought for a moment. "All I can tell you, Miss, is whatever she was wearing, there wasn't much to it." He tossed the weeder into the bucket and stood up. I hadn't meant to embarrass him but it seemed the only reason for his hasty retreat around the corner. Steady, lingering for one more scratch, quickly dashed after his master, and I padded back to my room.

I was closing the door when Gabe called, anxious to know how his brother behaved at dinner. I told him Beau had remained in his room and quickly segued from his angry sibling to describe my meeting Beau's friend, Sam. I asked if he remembered her at the party.

"I only saw one person with bright orange hair. But if they both altered their appearance to get parts in a play, does that mean hooker-chic wasn't Ceal's usual look?"

"I think so, although Sam seems to have made most of the changes. She referred to Ceal as Cissy, by the way, and insisted her friend couldn't tolerate a lot of booze and never got drunk. Weed was her drug of choice, shared with the others in the cabana."

"So, they were using drugs. Jesus! What the hell was Beau thinking?"

"Whoa, Gabe. You make it sound like they were mainlining smack."

"I work in pharmaceuticals. Never underestimate the power of drugs. One might save your life while another destroys it. I wish my little brother would make better choices."

"Do you think Ceal was only after his money?"

"I'm not saying my brother's not a great guy but, yeah. Don't you?"

I admit it crossed my mind.

"On the upside," said Gabe, "drugs, alcohol, and a midnight swim confirms accidental death, wouldn't you think?"

"Best not to get ahead of ourselves. I'll keep looking for answers. And speaking of looking, I've lost my watch. Could you check your car? It has a stainless steel and rose gold band."

"Will do. Until it's found, your new phone has a clock."

"It does? That's great!"

"You do know we've entered a new millennium, yes?" He laughed and I clicked my tongue. "Sorry, Maud. I agree with you about the intrusiveness of a cell phone, but I'm also very glad your uncle convinced you to carry one."

"Me too," I admitted. A sudden rap on my door prompted an image of Beau's fiery eyes and with a quick promise to talk the following day, I closed the call. Inching the door open, I sighed with relief upon seeing Jamie's smiling face.

"Hey Maud, expecting someone else?"

"Not really. What's up?"

"Pen and I are on our way to the loft," she held up an insulated bag, "with homemade raspberry and lemonade popsicles. Care to join us?"

With Penny in the lead, I was happy to follow. The moment we reached the loft, she rushed toward her puzzle table. Ignoring the unfinished *The Birth of Venus,* she stopped in front of the partially assembled *Starry Night* and like a magician waving her cape, swept the puzzle pieces to the floor.

Chapter 24

Jamie's jaw dropped as Penny trampled over the puzzle pieces on her way to the shelves. Once there, the young girl grabbed another plastic box, rushed it back to the table and poured out its contents, oblivious to her teacher's shocked rebuke.

"This isn't typical behaviour?" I whispered.

"She's no stranger to throwing things but never her precious puzzles. Correction. I don't know if she regards anything as precious."

When I took a step toward the table, Jamie grabbed my arm, whispering a warning and telling me it would be best to leave her to it. I couldn't stop myself from craning my neck for a closer look. "Aren't you curious?"

"Sure, but I'll see it soon enough and when this frantic need has abated, I want her to pick up those puzzle pieces."

I pointed at the bag of popsicles. "At least you have an incentive."

"Exactly. Now come and see what I found." Jamie led me toward two rattan clam chairs in the far corner.

"Very nice," I said, sinking into the thick cherry-red seat cushion. "My grandmother had these at her cottage."

"I found them in storage. Figured we deserved an adult corner." She unzipped the thermal bag and from a silicone mold, pried off two popsicles. Laughing, she said, "Pretend they're made from ice wine."

"Good thing I'm only having one."

"Speaking of which, what's the story behind those two glasses and that expensive and empty bottle of Italian wine on your dresser. A little something from Gabe?"

"Yes." I felt my cheeks warm. "I think it was very good wine."

"A few hundred bucks a bottle, I'm sure it was."

"That much? I wish I could remember more about it."

"What do you remember?"

"We did a lot of talking, laughing, and basically got to know each other."

Jamie snickered. "Is that what you call it?"

"I don't drink often but normally I can handle a few glasses of wine. Between you and me, I think I passed out."

Jamie suddenly had as much trouble making eye contact as Penny. "I may have downplayed the alcohol content of those Cosmos. You're not mad at me, are you?"

I shook my head. "It's all booze under the bridge now."

She laughed and her melting popsicle dripped over her hand and onto the floor. "Shit. Hold on. I'll get a cloth from the bathroom."

With my popsicle under control, I strolled over to Penny's table. She seemed to be working at high speed and had a few puzzle islands assembled—a rectangle of bright yellow and two smaller areas of blue—one light, one dark. Like a divining rod, Penny's hand hovered over a selection of tiles, dipped in for one and popped it into place. Soon splashes of white were added to the darker blue.

"Hey." The voice over my left shoulder caused what was left of my popsicle to fly from my hand.

"Sorry, Maud," said Jamie, bending down with the cloth to sweep up the remains of my frozen treat. "Do you want another?"

"No, I was almost finished. Do you recognize this new puzzle?"

"It looks familiar. Either she's assembled this one before or I'm remembering it from an art book. If it's what I think it is, it was painted by that English artist."

"Could you be a little more specific?"

She laughed. "He did something called pop art if that helps."

"Was it Hockney?"

"Yeah, could be."

"If that's the case, then the yellow is a diving board and the blue is water. Hockney did lots of swimming pool paintings after he moved to California." I sat down next to Penny. "Penelope, did you see something last night? Maybe someone in your swimming pool?"

She closed her hand into a fist and raised her face toward mine. My heart pounded in anticipation.

"Maud, she's not going to talk." Jamie killed the moment and Penny returned to her puzzle.

"I know what you're thinking," Jamie said, waving me back to the clam chairs. "But if Penny had gotten out of her bed last night, I would have heard her."

"Don't you find her insistence to work on this particular puzzle kind of odd?"

"One could argue that there are many things Pen does that are odd. I'm just saying whatever she did, I would know. She's never sneaky."

"I thought you told me she could be sneaky."

Jamie crossed her arms in front of her chest. "I don't think so."

"I think it was when you were talking about Penny's obsessions. You said she needed you to take her to the swing, but with her puzzles, she could be sneaky."

"What I meant was, if Penelope wants to do something, she just does it. She's not quiet or stealthy about it. And in the unlikely event that I didn't hear her get out of bed, I'd certainly wake up if she opened the window curtains. Those metal rings are noisy."

Beads of perspiration appeared on Jamie's upper lip and there seemed little to be gained from reminding her that she forgot to close those curtains.

"I'd better give this cloth a rinse," she said walking toward the washroom.

"I should be going, thanks again for the popsicle." Bending closer to Penny, I told her if she kept at it, I would soon have a name for the puzzle.

Walking into my room, and thinking about the puzzle, I stubbed my toe on the chair I'd awkwardly placed to hide the scratch on the wall. It was a painful reminder.

From the library, I picked up my five tubes of acrylic paint—the primaries plus black and white, my palette, palette knife, and a brush.

Unlike oil paint, acrylic dries darker making it tricky to match an existing colour. Third time lucky, I managed to hide the scratches and returned the chair to its original home.

Later, as I lay awake staring at the shadowy forms of a stranger's bedroom, I wondered if the death of Beau's fiancée would mean an early return for Rex and his father. I fell asleep sure I'd be sent to the distant-sounding north wing, but in my dream, I was tossed outside to scream at the coyotes. Typical of dreams, I managed to crawl back through the window only to hear Rex banging on the door. Eventually, I awoke to the realization that the banging was real and stumbled out of bed expecting to see Jamie. With the words *what now* ready on my lips, I flung open the door. It wasn't Jamie, it was Dinah and she was holding a large mug of hot, aromatic coffee.

Chapter 25

Assuming Dinah was making a thoughtful gesture, I extended my hand to accept the mug. She immediately pulled it out of reach and rubbernecked like a tourist attempting to see around me and into the bedroom. A perverse reflex made me turn and follow her gaze.

"Have you seen Beau?" Despite my denial, Dinah waggled her considerable self past me and into the room.

"Is he missing?" I asked.

"Every day my Sonny goes for a mornin' run." She scanned the room. "But he don't leave until he's had coffee with his ole Nan. I been waitin' so long, I thought he musta slept in. So, I hustled up here with his coffee only to find out he's not in his room."

"Maybe he went for a run first? What time is it anyway? Did I miss breakfast?"

"It's just past seven. Now, like I said," she spoke as if my hearing was compromised. "Sonny always has coffee with me *before* his run." Sidling toward the doorway, Dinah gave me a nudge. "You come with me. I got something to show you."

Suddenly aware of my flimsy summer nightie, I grabbed my hoodie and followed. The door to his room was open, and the first thing I noticed was Beau's obsessive tidiness. "Dinah, what am I supposed to be looking at?"

She set the mug of coffee on the dresser, and I breathed in that freshly brewed aroma. "Maud," she said with the impatience of someone repeating themselves. "Come and look at this." She directed me to the far side of the bed and pointed at the floor.

I was more surprised by the fact that he wore pyjamas than the evidence that he hadn't put them away.

Crossing the room to the closet, Dinah pulled open the door and waved her arm like a hostess on a game show. "And then there's this."

I stepped inside. Aside from it being an ideal spot to manufacture semiconductors, it was otherwise unremarkable.

"Not *in* the closet. Here." She jabbed at an empty hook on the door. "He took his jacket." When I failed to see the significance, she rolled her eyes. "You know the thermometer's been burstin' these last few days. Why would he be runnin' in a jacket?" Point made, she closed the closet door. "And my poor boy is hardly eatin'." Her head swayed like a stressed elephant. "Now he's run off without a word to his Nan."

"Dinah, he just lost his fiancée. Grief messes with the mind, right? Sometimes people don't behave as they normally would."

Her head popped up. "Do you think he would of hurt himself?"

"No, I'm not saying that. However, you know him better than I do. What do you think?"

"He is a sensitive lad and he doesn't like to lose things he cares about."

"I can tell Beau really cares about you. If he did decide on an early run, I think he'd go to your kitchen the moment he returned."

"You could be right. I best get back." Her eyes brightened. Dinah hurried toward the stairs, but I lingered with a plan to secure that mug of coffee. Back in my room, I carried it to the window and savoured every drop. With so much time before breakfast, I would normally have considered an early morning swim but it was too soon for things to return to normal.

My phone clock told me Penny would be awake. I reached the loft and found Jamie in the process of helping her student into the day's outfit. "Hey, early bird. What's up?" Jamie waved me into the room and I told her about Dinah's anxiety over the disappearance of her boy.

"Are you saying Beau didn't show up for his morning coffee? Wow, that's a first. If Dinah thinks Beau might hurt himself, this is serious." Jamie seemed to be visualizing the gun or blade poised for action.

"You know Dinah. Don't you think she might be overreacting?"

"Possible, when it comes to her boy. I'm sure she feels his suffering."

I nodded toward Penny, standing with her arms outstretched. "I think Penelope is waiting for you to help her into her blouse."

"Oh yeah," said Jamie, slipping on one sleeve and then the other. "It's an odd thing for Dinah to say, don't you think?"

"I think it's more of a concern that he's distracted and therefore won't take the necessary care. You know, falling *on* the trail, not *off* the trail. I should have asked her if she checked for Beau's car."

"I bet she didn't."

"I could do that now. Want to come along?" I asked.

With the offer of swing time, Penny slipped into her sandals, donned her baggy blue sweater, and followed us downstairs to the kitchen. A call for Dinah got no response, so Jamie pushed open the door and we crept in for a closer look.

"Now where did she go?" With no sign of food preparation, Jamie told us breakfast was going to be late. She tossed me an apple, pocketed one for herself, and gave one to Penny.

Leaving by the side door and walking to the parking area, we were greeted by my shiny blue baby. However, her sunny Miata companion was missing. Jamie paced the spot as if it was possible to overlook a bright yellow sports car.

"Seems unlikely that his car was stolen, so Beau must have driven somewhere. Wouldn't you agree?" I asked.

"As long as it wasn't off a cliff."

"Don't be silly. That car is beautiful."

"What if he drove to the lake and put rocks in his pockets?" Jamie ignored my sigh of exasperation and suggested we check the pool.

"I thought of going for a swim this morning."

"Eww. Maud. Really?"

"Yes, though I didn't do it. But I was thinking, if Ceal died falling down the stairs we'd still use them, right?"

"I guess." Jamie opened the door of the double-car garage and pointing at the black SUV, told me it belonged to Mrs. Barrington.

"Since Beau left by car and took nothing more unusual than his jacket, I think he'll come back today."

Jamie stared toward the horizon, seeming to will Beau's car to materialize. Indifferent to the search, Penny trotted off toward the swing. "I need to check the pool," said Jamie. "Can you help Pen?"

We reached the swing and Penelope pulled herself onto the seat. "Looks like you're feeling a little more self-confident. That's great, Penelope." I gave her a push to help her get going. I was leaning against the beam of the seesaw when Jamie returned. "I take it the pool was empty?"

She nodded. "I knew he wouldn't be in there but sometimes you get a ridiculous idea and you can't seem to let it go." Jamie hopped on one seat of the seesaw and I took the other. "I'll sit further back on the seat and you move forward a little so we can better equal our weight." As we rose and fell, Jamie speculated on more logical destinations for Beau. "Maybe he had an appointment."

"Sounds possible."

"No, it doesn't."

"Didn't you just say—?"

"Yeah, but Dinah would know about any appointments. She keeps close tabs on her boy. It's the kind of hovering attention that would drive me crazy but Beau seems to like it."

"A symptom of having a somewhat detached mother?"

"Maud, you're being too nice. Try cold and uncaring. Now that you've mentioned the Queen B, Beau could have told her it was an appointment, expecting her to tell Dinah." Jamie levelled the seesaw. "You want to check? The boss will be in her room unless she's disappeared too."

Chapter 26

Mrs. Barrington's open door seemed welcoming, but her impatient 'What?' when she heard my gentle knock was far from it. She didn't even look up, just remained hunched over her desk. Could she be working on the secret project Jamie mentioned?

"I'm sorry to bother you, Mrs. Barrington. Have you seen Beau this morning?"

"I have not." She spun round to face me. "If you're looking for him, and Maud, I can't imagine why you would be, he's likely out for his run. Is there a problem?"

I took a few steps into the room and described Dinah's early morning visit.

"No morning tête à tête with his Nan? How odd. More than most, my youngest son is a creature of habit."

"I suggested to Dinah that yesterday's events might have caused Beau to alter his routine. I checked and his car is gone." I slowly inched closer to her desk.

"When you and Dinah were in his room, did you see his cell phone? He generally keeps it on the left side of his bureau."

I pictured the dresser and recalled only the coffee mug. "There was no phone."

"Good. Wherever he went, he took his phone and will call if he's going to be late." As she turned back to her desk, her elbow collided with a hard-cover book and it fell to the floor.

I moved to pick it up. Intrigued by the cover, I held the book, a little too long. Before I could return it to the desk, Mrs. Barrington picked it out of my hand. "You're looking at Monas Hieroglyphica," she told me. "A book written a long time ago by Dr. John Dee, the man whose portrait hangs in my library. He believed that mathematics held the key to unlocking the universe." She pointed to the centre image. "This glyph is his symbol. He was an alchemist, an astronomer, a mathematician, a navigator, and an advisor and astrologer to Queen Elizabeth I. His code name for their secret correspondence was double-oh-seven."

"Really? That's fascinating," I said and meant it.

"I'm so glad you think so." Mrs. Barrington motioned for me to bring a distant chair closer to the desk. "There's little regard for astrology in today's scientific community, but in Dee's time, it was a respected area of inquiry. I find its complexities intriguing. I use the insights of astrology to complement my study of psychology." Mrs. Barrington opened a folder and slid the top page a little closer to me. "This is Beau's birth chart."

"Amazing. It's a work of art," I said, awed by its complexity and symbolism.

My aloof client practically hugged me with her smile. "It's a pleasure to share this with someone who doesn't assume I'm gullibly trapped in the Middle Ages. But then curiosity is a strong motivator for a Gemini." She winked.

"How did you ...?"

Her laughter was spontaneous and easy. "Nothing supernatural, I assure you. Can you guess my accomplice?"

It had to be someone who knew us both and knew me well enough to have gleaned those kinds of details. I thought of the forms my agent helped me fill out for a grant application and remembered being told his daughter Evie and I shared the same birthday. "Mr. Baer?"

"Correct. As we would be working closely together, I hoped creating your chart would give me insight." She opened another folder. "Here it is. Now remember, you are more than your sun sign. Your ascendant is in Taurus, meaning you can be stubborn and your Scorpio moon suggests you experience more than your share of emotional turbulence. You also have an uncanny ability to ferret out the truth."

I wanted to insist that I wasn't the least bit stubborn but realized that might only prove her point. Besides, I rather liked having at least one uncanny ability.

"Saturn in the twelfth house," she continued, "indicates an interest in secretive work. This is good for you because we all know the language of art can be secretive and though you may resist them, your ordeals increase your artistic language."

"I guess that's one way of looking at it," I said. "Any other good news?"

"Yes, of course," she glanced at her watch, "but it'll have to wait until after breakfast."

"Oh yes, breakfast. I sure hope Dinah's back."

Mrs. Barrington snapped her head toward me. "What?"

"When I went to check for Beau's car, Dinah wasn't in the kitchen."

"Good heavens. Where would she go?"

"Maybe she's running the trail in search of Beau." I imagined Dinah, squeezed into athletic gear, jogging over rough terrain.

"If that's the case, she'll soon need rescuing." Mrs. Barrington pushed herself away from the desk. My offer to look for the family's cook was, thankfully, declined. "If Dinah hasn't returned, I'll need your help in the kitchen and if she's not back by the time we've finished breakfast, I'll send Caleb."

Finding the kitchen empty, it wasn't long before the table was set, the coffee was perking, and the bread was toasting. While Mrs. Barrington fried bacon and prepared scrambled eggs, she sent me to call Penelope and Jamie.

From the side porch, my Dinah holler sounded like a strangled bird but it got Jamie's attention. "So, where was Dinah?" she asked, following me into the dining room.

"I don't know. She's not back yet."

Finding food on the table, and a glass of milk at Penny's place, Jamie seemed surprisingly incredulous. "Who made this?"

"I made the toast and coffee." I was explaining that the lady of the house knew her way around the kitchen when Mrs. Barrington brought in the scrambled eggs. Seeing the look on Jamie's face, she said, "I see I've surprised you."

"No, no. Well, yes. But this is great."

We were enjoying a second cup of coffee when Dinah finally poked her head around the door. She looked dishevelled enough to have struggled out of a bramble bush and seemed more annoyed than apologetic when she realized we'd made our own breakfast. "I went up to that trail near Cranberry Lake. Couldn't find my Sonny but did find an old root cellar. Good place for Caleb to store apples." Dinah dabbed at her forehead with a cotton hankie. Turning to Jamie and me, she said, "Maybe you girls can do a search for Beau? I'm some worried about him."

Mrs. Barrington cleared her throat. "That won't be necessary Dinah. And had you checked for my son's car, as Maud did, you would have realized he was not running around the property."

"Where would he drive to?" she asked.

"I don't know," said her employer, "but he is an adult with, I'm sure, a good reason to vary his usual routine."

"He's got that phone of his with him, right? Maybe you want to give him a call."

"He's perfectly capable of calling," Mrs. Barrington shot back.

Disappointed, Dinah harrumphed her way out of the room, leaving me to wonder why she didn't call him herself. After Jamie took Penny upstairs for her lessons, Mrs. Barrington rested her hand on mine. "Maud, dear, before we go to the library, would you like to spend a few minutes on our earlier discussion?"

Chapter 27

"Thank you for this, Mrs. Barrington," I told her as we resumed our places.

"Please, call me Veronica." She reached across the desk and squeezed my forearm. "Now as you know your sun sign is Gemini. You may not know that it is ruled by the planet Mercury, the sign of communication and therefore, a good sign for an artist. As we look at your other planets, we see Uranus in your fifth house. This means you fall in and out of love quickly and with Mars in Libra in the sixth house, your job demands your inner warrior." Veronica paused to regard me with the same suspicion as Constable Boudica. "It's hard to see how that would apply to a portrait artist."

I would have confessed to working for my uncle's detective agency if I wasn't afraid it made me appear secretive and deceitful, especially as I'm apparently so feckless in matters of the heart.

From a desk drawer, Veronica retrieved a small paperback. "I have this book for you. It's 'Astrology for Beginners,' just the thing for the curious, book-loving Gemini."

I thanked her, and she returned my chart to the file box. "Now," she pushed a photograph toward me, "I want to make some changes to my portrait."

"What?" I must have sounded as impatient as she had been earlier that morning. "Sorry, did I hear you correctly? You want to make changes?"

"Yes. This picture is almost identical to the one we're working from. I agree it has much in its favour and I do like the pose, but it's not me."

"Not you?"

"It's the image of a retired lawyer."

Since she is a retired lawyer, I failed to see the problem.

She tapped the image. "Go to the library and ready your camera. I'll be there shortly."

I did as requested and was attaching my camera to the tripod, when she arrived wearing the evening sky.

"Mrs. Barrington ..." She cleared her throat and I began again. "Veronica, you're right. It's perfect."

She fingered the red silk scarf casually draping her neck. "I seldom wear red, but I think it works better with this heavenly shade of blue."

I agreed and asked her about the addition of the elegant crescent moon brooch.

"A gift from Alton." She caressed its large smooth gems. "These are blue moonstones, and the diamonds, of course, are set in eighteen carat gold."

When Veronica assumed the pose, I adjusted the light to add more drama to the image. It was only after I took a few pictures, that I noticed subtle yet important changes to my subject's expression. She seemed softer, more approachable, and when I showed her the photos, she was pleasingly enthusiastic.

"Maud, if you leave now, you should be back in less than an hour."

"Sorry?"

"The photographs."

"Oh, right." I removed my camera from the tripod and before leaving the room for, what I hoped was, my last trip for prints, I gestured toward the smaller work table. I described the way Penelope had demanded a pencil, her response to my brief instructions, and her obvious enjoyment of the process. "As you'll see, one drawing is finished and the other is in progress."

As Veronica studied her daughter's work, the woman with a love of words was suddenly speechless. And when I returned forty minutes later, I found her in the same place. "The doctors tell me Penelope is unable to empathize and yet, she has succeeded in capturing determination on David's face, terror on Daphne's, and arrogance on Apollo's. Penelope's drawing reveals the strain on their psyches and their muscles as each engages in a timeless struggle. How could she do this without feeling it?"

"I don't know. All I can tell you is she seems to absorb the image and let her hand tell the story. You need to see it for yourself."

"I'm afraid my presence would ..." She left the sentence unfinished as she gently caressed the edge of the paper. Then with a slight shake of her head, she asked me for the latest photographs.

I laid them out on the table and, using the photo I'd been working from as a comparison, we soon found the perfect replacement. Feeling confident that I could incorporate the changes into my completed drawing, I offered, though it pained me to do so, to work through lunch.

"Excellent. We can't, however, have you going hungry. Dinah will come up with a tray." She paused at her daughter's drawing. "Thank you, Maud."

After Veronica left, I assembled the canvas and applied the first layer of acrylic gesso before wrapping my brush in plastic to keep it moist for a second coat. Re-working the cartoon meant erasing, amending, and refining the image through measurement and best guesses. Before long, I was in the zone, my pencil gliding across the paper like a figure skater.

"The police want to see ya in madam's office." It was Dinah shuffling into the room without the promised tray of food. Her words were so unexpected it took me a moment to decipher their meaning, and by then she was gone.

Like Veronica, Inspector Murray also flipped open a file as soon as I took the seat in front of the desk. I imagined him studying my birth chart, zeroing in on that Scorpio moon and accusing me of being a stubborn, overly emotional warrior too fickle to find a mate.

"Ms. Gibbons, on the evening of the birthday party, what did you do after Ms. Conlin took Miss Penelope Barrington upstairs?"

"I finished the preparatory drawing for my portrait of Mrs. Barrington and went to bed."

"And did you leave your room at any time during the night?"

"I did not."

"Can anyone verify that?"

Damn. When you decide to follow an impulse in the privacy of your room, you don't expect to be talking about it to a police officer two days later, but talk I must.

"And by Gabe, you are referring to Mr. Gabriel Barrington, the eldest brother. Correct?"

"Yes."

When he laid down the pen, Inspector Murray placed what looked like my wooden mallet in the centre of the desk. "Do you recognize this?"

Noting my initials roughly carved into the handle (art school is a black hole for one's unlabeled supplies) I admitted ownership. "I don't understand. How did you get it?"

He replied to my question with one of his own. "What can you tell me about it?"

I described how the mallet is used to bang together the corners of four wooden stretcher bars, something I did on Saturday morning. "I left it on my work table in the library and up until now, I thought it was with the rest of my supplies."

"Do you routinely clean the handle of the mallet?"

"No. Are you telling me you found no fingerprints?"

He closed my file. "Thank you, Miss Gibbons. We may need to speak with you again."

I rose slowly and left the room carrying questions I knew he wouldn't answer. What he would do, however, was have someone verify my alibi as soon as I closed the door.

Back in the library, I searched my carryall and work area as if there could be two identical wooden mallets. There weren't. Therefore, a member of the household must have spotted the mallet on my work table and decided it was the perfect tool for the job. I had no idea what that job was, but as I lightly sanded the canvas and applied the second coat of gesso, I considered the possibilities. My mind wandered from the benign to the malignant.

Chapter 28

I was searching for a tin of willow charcoal when Penny did a running walk the width of the room and slid easily onto the office chair. She was tucked into her drawing by the time Jamie came in carrying a lunch tray.

"I need to start working out." She placed the tray on my work table. "Since you're working through lunch, Dinah figured you should have two of everything, plus a heavy pot of iced tea." She rubbed her hands. "You sure missed some excitement."

I suspended my search for the charcoal.

"Pen and I had just joined Mrs. Barrington in the dining room when Dinah shuffled in to tell us that 'The fuzz were in the foyer.' I felt a moment of panic. This had to be bad news about Beau. No reaction from the Queen B. She barely buzzed, just flitted out of the room. I chewed down two fingernails, waiting for her to come back." Jamie gazed at the back of her hand before reaching for half a sandwich.

"And did she?" I grabbed the other half.

"Did she what?"

"Come back."

"Oh yeah, of course. She wasn't gone long. Seems the cops wanted access to the shed containing the pool equipment."

"Did the police talk to you?" I asked.

"No. If they had, I would have mentioned Beau's disappearance. His mother won't file a missing person's report."

"It's too early for that."

"Yeah, that's what she said." Jamie finished the sandwich. "Sorry, I eat when I'm stressed." She paced around the room, picking up a date square on the second lap. "Why hasn't he called?"

"Maybe he has. What time is it now?" I glanced at my wrist. "Damn. I keep forgetting I misplaced my watch. It must be close to two. What did Veronica say over lunch? She seemed so certain he would call."

"Veronica, eh? When did you two get so chummy?"

"I wouldn't say we're chummy." I patted the wooden stool, hoping she'd sit down. She didn't.

"To answer your question, Maud, *Veronica* thinks he's fine, just somewhere without a signal." Jamie balanced on the edge of the stool like an anxious rabbit. "I don't understand how he can be such an insensitive idiot. Taking off, not telling anyone where he's going. What the fu—" she looked toward Penny, "fudge is he thinking?"

I laughed and Jamie rolled her eyes. "The kid's been mute for ages. I'd hate the first word out of her mouth to be the f-bomb." With a sigh, she added, "I wish I could call Beau."

"Why don't you?"

"I don't know." Her body crumpled inward. "I've never called him. It would be weird."

"Are you afraid he might think you're a caring person concerned for his welfare?"

"When you put it that way, I guess ..."

I offered to keep an eye on Penny and Jamie, steepled her fingers, made a quick bow and slipped out the door.

Returning to my drawing, I transferred the tracing to the canvas. Using an India ink pen, I retraced the lines, then with diluted India ink and a brush, created a mass drawing. This was covered with a veil of yellow ochre and earth red. This process causes a moment of panic as the drawing disappears but the magic returns when a lint-free rag is rubbed freely across the canvas to reveal the inked image.

I had captured my subject, but the background was only undecided possibilities. An easy solution would be the darks of Rembrandt, Durer or Vermeer. They understood the power of dark to illuminate light. In the quest for ideas and inspiring colour combinations, I scanned the bookshelves and soon found a resolution I hoped my client would appreciate.

To test my idea for the background I mixed ivory black and titanium white, with cerulean, ultramarine and a little viridian. I was applying it to a small canvas board when Jamie returned.

"So, did you talk to Beau?" I asked. She said nothing. I was about to repeat the question when I realized she was like a shaken bottle of pop. I continued to paint, content to wait.

Grabbing Penny's timer, Jamie wrenched the dial between thumb and forefinger. "I called Beau," she said, her jaw tight. "And it went straight to his message."

"Oh, that's too—"

"Then I ransacked his room."

"What?"

She wagged her finger at me like an angry schoolmistress. "Maud, I see that look. Don't worry. I put everything back. All I wanted was a clue, something to tell me where he went. Instead, I found ... this." She dropped a Tissot watch on the table. "It's yours. I read the engraving."

Cradling it, I checked for my uncle's thoughtful inscription, *To Maud, for whom I'll always have time.* "Wow, thanks so much. Where was it?"

"Don't look so innocent. I guess hopping into the bed of one handsome Barrington wasn't enough for you."

"What? Jamie, what are you talking about?" The timer rang and she pulled Penny out of the room. "Jumping to conclusions leads to a fall, ya know," I said into the empty room.

Strapping on my watch, I followed them, stomping on the stairs to the loft. My righteous anger cooled slightly by the time I reached the landing. "Jamie," I called from the threshold. She kept her back to me. "You've convicted me on flimsy evidence. I haven't spent any time in Beau's bed, nor do I know how my watch ended up in his room. And for the record, not only have I never been in Gabriel's bed, but thanks to you I barely remembered having him in mine."

Jamie pivoted on one heel. "Are you going to tell me you've never been in Beau's room?"

"No. I already told you, Dinah woke me and insisted I go there with her."

"So, your watch just fell off while you were looking at an empty hook on the back of his bedroom door?" She crossed her arms.

"Of course not. Besides, I don't know when I lost my watch. I take it off whenever I draw, and I only noticed it missing yesterday afternoon. Maybe Beau found it, and before he could give it to me, his fiancée died, and gee, it slipped his mind."

She lowered her head. For a few moments, I didn't know in which direction we were headed. Finally, she looked at me, smiled meekly, and pointed to my wrist. "At least I found your watch. It was a gift, right?"

"It was."

"And from someone special who cares for you."

"My uncle." I rubbed my thumb across the crystal, not quite ready to make nice. "I should get back to my painting."

"I understand." I'd turned toward the stairs when she called out, "Maud, see you at dinner." I managed an awkward wave.

Back in the library, I finished a study for the background of the portrait and cleaned my brushes. By the time I reached the dining room, Penelope was quietly munching on a buttered roll, and dinner was expected at any moment.

While I updated Veronica on the progress of her portrait, I could feel Jamie searching my eyes for a sign of forgiveness. I was about to offer a smile when Dinah swung through the door carrying a large tray. At the same time, the French doors opened. Sighs of relief were drowned out by the tray hitting the hardwood and a large wooden bowl careening across the floor spilling its contents.

Chapter 29

Ignoring the tossed salad strewn across her path, Dinah rushed to Beau, alternately hugging and scolding the prodigal son. "I been some worried. Where did you go? What happened?" He didn't seem about to give her an answer nor did she wait for one. "Never mind, dear boy, you're here now. Sit yourself down. You must be famished. I'll get the roast."

Before the door swung shut behind her, Veronica called, "Dinah, bring a broom and a dustpan. And you," she turned on her youngest son before he could take his place at the table, "come with me."

As they exited toward the living room, Jamie and I strained to catch the conversation. Only their fading footsteps were audible. Back with another tray and no broom, Dinah prepared a plate for Penny while Jamie and I admired a dinner of glazed carrots, baked potatoes, and a steaming roast of beef. With two minds and one thought, we agreed to wait no more than five minutes before one of us began carving. We were counting down the last thirty seconds when the mother and, her slightly deflated, son returned.

Attacking the roast with a large carving knife, Veronica sliced enough for the household and most of the neighbours. By the time she sat down, we shared a serving of tension with the meal. And as Beau sulkily pushed more food around his plate than he ate, his mother chewed every mouthful almost as long as his sister.

"When the police were here earlier," Veronica said to no one in particular, "I engaged in a brief chat with one of the officers. He was a young chap, new to the job." She paused for a dramatic sip of water.

"Apparently, something was found on Cecilia's head." She made it sound like a treasure map.

"Did he tell you what the something was?" asked Jamie.

"Not exactly, but piecing his words together, a large bruise is most likely. This suggests the poor woman hit her head as she accidentally fell into the pool. Surely the result of a combination of fatigue and alcohol."

Beau cleared his throat and reminded his mother that Cecilia wasn't drunk.

"She need not have been drunk, dear. Perhaps just a little tipsy—no pun intended."

"Was your fiancée a good swimmer?" Jamie asked.

"She wasn't my fiancée," said Beau.

"What?" The three of us said in unison.

"I said ..."

"Beau," said his mother interrupted, "we need elaboration not repetition."

He poked a potato around his plate, and Jamie asked if they had ended their engagement at the party.

"No, it was, I mean we thought ..." He massaged his temples. "Mother, promise you won't be angry."

Her gaze unwavering, she said, "How can I promise not to be angry when it is your explanation that will directly affect my reaction?"

Beau fidgeted with the linen napkin, set it aside and placed his hands firmly on the table. "A while back, Cecilia and her best friend Sam auditioned for a play called 'Mars Opposing Neptune.'" (Veronica and I shared a look). "The lead character is an unsuitable fiancée. Her life is further complicated by a twin sister. Since Cissy and Sam had been mistaken as sisters, she hoped that with the same wild haircut and makeup, they could pass as twins."

Veronica cleared her throat. "Can we please settle on a name for this woman?"

"Sorry, Mother. Henceforth, I shall refer to her as Cecilia."

"No need to be cheeky, young man." Veronica looked toward me and then Jamie. "Nicknames are a waste of nomenclature."

We nodded more with understanding than agreement.

"So," Jamie began, "Did they get the parts?"

"Yes. Of course, they both wanted the lead but that went to Cissy. Sorry, Mother, Cecilia."

"What's the play about?" Jamie wanted to know.

"It's like *Guess Who's Coming to Dinner* but with more deception."

"Was Cecilia in that one too?"

Veronica regarded Jamie with tired patience. "Of course not. 'Guess Who's Coming to Dinner' was a film from the 1960s. It's about an interracial couple who announce their engagement and then deal with the subsequent reactions."

I asked if Cecilia was pretending to be Beau's fiancée to get material for her part in the play.

"Exactly. And by the way, Mother, Cecilia chose the name Ceal for the character she played while she was here. Cissy was her only nickname."

Veronica laid her cutlery across her plate, "Regardless of the woman's name, both of you blatantly deceived us."

Beau closed his eyes and lowered his head. "That's a bit harsh, Mother."

"Wait a minute," said Jamie. "I'm confused. Are you saying you and Ceal or Cissy or whatever, were never engaged?"

Beau pushed his plate aside and rested his forearms on the table. "That's right. We've only ever been friends. There was someone else in Cecilia's life. One thing I need you all to know, we didn't mean any harm. As Maud suspected, it was research. In the play, the unsuitable fiancée crashes the anniversary party of her future in-laws. My birthday party seemed like the perfect opportunity for her to get a deeper understanding of the character and experience the reactions of a family."

"And we were your unwitting participants."

"Yes, Mother, but it wouldn't have been for long. Our original plan had been to arrive just before lunch on Saturday and we would have explained everything on Sunday morning. But Friday in the city was unbearably hot and I couldn't see any reason not to get out of there. I convinced Cecilia that if we arrived a day early, we could beat the heat and she'd have more time to hone her character." He shook his head. "If I'd stuck to the original plan, she wouldn't have ended up sitting next to Penelope."

"That was my fault," Jamie whispered. "I put your sister there."

"Only because Cecilia took Penelope's spot. She did it because she was in character—think, Eliza Doolittle meets Scarlet O'Hara. I have to say, each of you responded like you'd read the script—except for Penelope. The shock and pain of getting a fork in the arm was bad enough, but Cecilia was furious with me because I hadn't warned her."

Veronica shifted in her chair. "I've certainly never felt the need to warn people about my daughter."

"This was an artificial situation, Mother. Cecilia expected to be disliked, she just wasn't expecting, well, you know, what happened. Aside from the shock and pain, she was worried about having an ugly scar on her arm. It didn't matter what Doc Patmore said, she'd had enough and wanted to go home." He closed his eyes and pressed his fingers against his eyelids, pushing back the tears. "I wish I'd taken her to the train station."

"I hope you told the police this charade was Cecilia's idea and that you hardly knew each other."

"Mother, I didn't say we hardly knew each other. We were never a couple but I knew her."

Veronica clicked her tongue. "Fine, you knew her, but more importantly, what did you tell the police?"

"Well, I ... didn't."

Her eyes popped in disbelief. "What? Are you telling me that you lied to us, and then you lied to the police?"

"I knew you'd be like that."

"Like what?" Her words smacked the air.

"Looking at everything in black and white. It wasn't lying. It was research. Nobody was supposed to get hurt." His voice trailed off.

"You introduced Miss Cecilia Fox as your fiancée. That was a lie. There was no reason not to correct that lie when speaking to the police. Really, Beau, how could you be so, so ..." She looked up as if pleading for a divine explanation.

Hustling in with a large blueberry pie, Dinah addressed her employer. "That Mrs. Whatsit is waiting at the east door. Sure as shootin' she's wantin' your help with the hospital fundraiser again this year. You want me to send her away?"

Veronica pushed back from the table. "No, I'll talk to her."

As soon as we were alone, I asked Beau to describe the real Cecilia Fox. I wanted him to convince me that the woman was doing her best to be unlikeable so I could feel less guilty for obliging.

"I think you and Jamie would have liked her," he said. "She was a good actor—ambitious and confident. She was also generous, clever, and funny. The hair, hot clothes, and that haughty, rude, dumb-ass attitude—that was acting."

"Sensitive, eh," said Jamie, offering Penny a cookie. "She had me fooled. How about you Maud?"

"I saw another side of her, though only for a few minutes." I told them about watching the argument between Cecilia and a stranger and then finding her crying in the foyer at the front door. "She was vulnerable and appreciated my concern, at least until I asked too many questions. Then she blew me off."

"It must have been shortly afterwards that I caught up with her," said Beau. "After Mother sent me to get Gabe, I lost track of Cissy for a while. When I found her, she was wound up, but she wouldn't talk about it." Beau rubbed the back of his neck. "Then Sam told me Bobby showed up and it didn't go well."

At the sound of footfall, Beau straightened in his chair. "That'll be Mother. If she asks, tell her we've been discussing her portrait."

"Ha. She won't believe that," said Jamie.

Chapter 30

"And what have the three of you been talking about?" asked Veronica when she resumed her place at the table.

Jamie smiled broadly and said, a little too quickly, "Beau's been telling us what a great actor Cecilia was and that she was very nice."

Mrs. Barrington's eyes narrowed.

"Maybe not *that* nice." Beau countered. "But, Mother, she definitely was a good actor."

"That I can believe."

Jamie shifted in her chair, getting ready to say something when Veronica told her to take Penelope to the loft. Turning to me she added, "Maud, you should go along as well."

Dismissed like naughty school girls, we rose from our chairs. Jamie paused to catch Beau's eye and jerked her head toward the archway.

"Is there something you wanted to say, Jamie?"

"No, Mrs. Barrington." Jamie quickened her step, only pausing when we reached the stairs. "I hope Beau realizes I want him to join us as soon as he's released from the hive," she whispered.

"Is that what you were doing? I thought you had a spasm."

"Har har. Seriously, Maud, we need to know more about this Bobby person. He sounds like a stalker."

When we reached the loft, Penny rushed past us to get to her puzzle table.

Jamie waved me to our corner. "So, what do you know about Sam?"

I described our brief meeting, including her suggestion that the Barringtons could be sued for her best friend's drowning.

"That's what she was worried about? What a bitch. I guess she and Ceal were alike in more ways than just appearance."

"Sam seemed genuinely distressed at the loss of her best friend. And I'm sure she was, but she's also an actor."

"Exactly, and besides, how are the Barringtons responsible? Ceal wasn't a kid. You'd expect her to take care of herself," Jamie hesitated. "Which, as it turns out, she couldn't, but I don't think that makes the family responsible."

"Are you sure you didn't meet Sam at the party?"

Jamie shook her head. "I would have remembered meeting someone who looked like Ceal."

I thought back to the distinctive hat Sam pulled over her head before she ran up the house. "How about someone wearing a blue hat, a knitted cotton cloche?"

"Yes. That I do remember. It was unique and not a sunhat. She seemed nice. She was also quiet, pretty, and not flashing cleavage."

"I guess two people with the same crazy hair would raise unwanted questions."

"True enough," said Jamie. "By the way, I knew Beau and Ceal weren't engaged."

"You did?"

"Oh yeah. If Beau had danced with you like he danced with me, I think you would have had your suspicions too. At least now I can stop feeling guilty."

"Speaking of guilty feelings, I think Beau went to Toronto today."

Jamie thought for a moment. "To hang out with Sam, Mike and Liam, and mourn their friend together."

"Yes. And, to get their stories straight."

"That explains why he left without saying anything to anyone. Maud, I've got a kettle in my room. I think we need that cup of tea we were denied after dinner."

Curious to take a peek at Penny's progress, I strolled over to the table. The patch of blue had expanded and now included a splash of white. And the yellow tiles now formed what I knew to be a diving board. "Jamie," I called toward her bedroom, "you're right, this is a Hockney. It's a painting called *A Bigger Splash.*"

The instant I identified the puzzle, Penny was out of her chair and back to the shelves. Finding what she was looking for, Penny grabbed a box with such determination that it jettisoned off the shelf and crashed to the floor. Jamie was at that moment strolling back into the room and immediately scooped up the box.

"Phew," she said, finding the lid firmly shut.

"Is she usually this anxious to get started on another puzzle?" I asked.

"No." Jamie turned the box over, searching for a label. "I don't know what is so special about—Penelope, manners!" Penny had interrupted her teacher by reaching for the box. Her eyes darted anxiously but she stepped back and dropped her hands. Jamie inhaled. "That's better." She placed the box in the space next to the Hockney.

Jamie left to make the tea, and I sat down next to Penelope. "May I help you right the tiles? I promise not to assemble any of the pieces."

She hesitated then using her forearm, slid about a third of the tiles toward me. A few moments before I flipped over the last tile, Jamie brought in the tea and set it on the table between our new chairs. With a whispered "thank you" to Penelope, I left the table and joined Jamie.

"I hope you know how special that was, Maud."

"I do. I wonder if she felt the same sense of connection."

"I doubt it." Jamie tipped the teapot to fill our cups.

"Have you noticed that every time we put a name to a puzzle she's working on, Penelope leaves it to begin another one?"

"Yes, and I think I know why."

"Really?" I couldn't hide my surprise.

She spoke with the slow enunciation of a teacher to a failing student. "It's because Penny is joining in our conversation." Jamie watched me and rolled her eyes. "I can see you think there's more to it but how could there be? You've witnessed her consistent behaviour patterns: the puzzles, the swing, the timer, and the 7:30 wakeup. And in all the time I've been here, she never gets out of bed at night. End of story."

With a shrug, I agreed to end our discussion, though I knew it was just the beginning of the story. Sipping my tea, I watched Penny proceed at her feverish pace. "I wish she'd talk to me," I said, thinking out loud.

Jamie told me that Penny occasionally responded to questions with subtle body language. "It's common for children on the autism spectrum to exhibit extreme anxiety. They keep their shoulders raised and heads low—like a turtle ready to retreat at the first sign of trouble. And it's not unusual for Penny to keep her hands in a loose fist. If she agrees with something, like a blouse I've chosen, she might squeeze her right hand. It's subtle, so you might not notice. Less subtle is the two-fisted clench. If you see that, things are not going to end well."

I finished my tea and was ready to say goodnight when Jamie asked about Gabe. She wanted a tale of romance, plans for the future, and long breathy phone calls. The best I had was his request for a portrait. I expected oohs and aahs with all that togetherness, but all she had were warnings.

"Maud, are you sure you want to do that? I assume he's paying you, and money is always good, but think of the potential for arguments. Suppose you want to paint him looking sensitive while he wants to look cool and aloof? Or you want him in a sweater and he wants a shirt. And then when you think you've finished the painting, what if he's not happy with it or doesn't like the way you painted his hair or, I don't know, his chin?"

"His chin?"

"Okay, maybe not his chin but you know what I mean."

I did know what she meant and she wasn't saying anything that hadn't already caused me a few anxious what-ifs. I told her the same thing I told myself—our agreement on the reference photo would resolve most of those issues. "If he doesn't like the way I've painted his hair or his chin, then I'll fix it."

"I'm sure you can do that Maud, but hurt feelings are harder to fix. You should wait until your relationship is on firmer ground, don't you think?"

I agreed to think about it, thanked her for the tea, and on my way out the door, paused at the puzzle. I wasn't expecting to see a lot of progress, however, Penny had devoted all her effort to one small area. Surrounded by a murky brown, was the partial face of a young woman. Its one blue eye was open but unseeing and a tiny pink rosebud was caught in a curl of hair.

"Jamie, where's that art history book?"

She pointed at the small bookcase across from Penny's bed. I lifted the book onto the table and went first to the index. Finding the sought-after reproduction, I opened the page and set the book close to the puzzle. "Come and see this. It's a partial image from John Everett Millais's painting of the drowning of Ophelia."

Jamie dragged herself to the table for a cursory glance. "How can you see a face in that? Geez Maud, I think you have pareidolia."

"Pair of what?"

"Par-ei-do-lia." Laughter eased her irritation. "Seeing things that aren't there, like faces in wallpaper patterns, or tree trunks, mud puddles or fried eggs. It's the kind of stuff you learn when you work for a wordsmith."

"I'm definitely afflicted. But," I pointed at the puzzle, "this is an actual face. So far, I can't be one hundred percent certain it's Ophelia's."

Jamie sighed. "Whatever." Glancing toward the landing she said, "I wish Beau would get here."

"If I see him, I'll tell him you're waiting." She didn't try to stop me from leaving.

Chapter 31

I entered the library, stopped, closed my eyes, and inhaled. It smelled like home. A place where the scent of oil paint, turpentine, and artist medium meant exciting possibilities wrapped in cosy slippers.

But I wasn't at home and those cosy slippers were feeling a little tight. I touched the corner of the canvas. The earth-orange veil would be dry enough by morning to begin one of my favourite stages in a painting—adding drama with the lights and darks.

It was something to look forward to and I carried those positive feelings to bed. I lulled my brain to sleep playing with shapes, brushstrokes and values. In a dream, I swam in the silky water of the Barrington's swimming pool. And when I awoke to the morning sun filling my room, I decided it was a good omen.

With a cover-up over my bathing suit, I grabbed a towel and jogged down the now familiar path. For a few minutes, I sat on the edge of the pool thinking about Cecilia. It all seemed so obvious. The artificial hair, theatrical makeup, and over-the-top comments. Of course, it had all been an act.

I recalled Beau's description of the real Cecilia—confident, clever and ambitious. He extolled her acting ability. He was right about that. But the woman I met in the foyer had been hiding something and it wasn't her participation in their elaborate charade. Whatever she was hiding, I hoped to uncover. I felt sure Penelope was doing her best to help me.

Slipping into the silky water, my nervous energy was expended swimming five lengths. I then lay on my back and let myself float. It was time to ponder Shakespeare's play. The Queen of Denmark insisted Ophelia had climbed a tree. The branch broke and she fell into the water, her heavy dress pulling her below the surface. But in the scene at the cemetery, a sexton was certain her death was a suicide. Did Penelope know the play? Jamie told me her puzzles were the basis for many lessons and if they covered the great works of art, Shakespeare was bound to make an entrance. I was also becoming convinced that whatever Penelope Barrington was exposed to, no matter how tangentially, it found a home in her amazing brain. So, did she see Ophelia's death as accidental death or deliberate? And could she tell me?

I spent a little too long swimming with my thoughts and by the time I reached the dining room, everyone was seated. "Sorry, I'm late."

"Maud, you're not late until Mother has started eating," Beau said with a wink.

Veronica patted my chair. "Don't worry my dear, you are on time. It is we who got an early start."

I selected a fried egg, bacon and home fries from the warming tray. "Veronica, the portrait is ready for your first sitting. Could we meet in the library after breakfast?"

"Of course. I'm very keen to get started."

Beau leaned toward Jamie. "While those two meet in the library, how about a game of tennis? Dinah told me she's cleaning the loft this morning, so I'm sure you can leave Penelope to work on her puzzles." He smiled at his mother and as soon as she agreed, Jamie was able to accept the invitation with minimal swooning.

Dinah breezed in carrying a carafe and four coffee mugs. "Sonny, I brewed up that special coffee you brought for me from the city. It's so good I have to share it will ya all." She filled each cup and Beau helped distribute them.

Buoyed by all this bonhomie, I announced the news that Penelope might to be talking to us through her choice of jigsaw puzzles. Veronica's eyes lit up like a Grand Canyon sunrise, but Jamie gaped at me as if I'd just taken a stick to the Queen B's hive.

"Oh yes," said Veronica, smiling at her daughter. "And what's so special about these puzzles?"

Beau and Dinah, who had been discussing further merits of the coffee, stopped to hear my answer.

"Since Cecilia's accident, each puzzle she assembles seems to be—" The doorbell chimed before I could finish the sentence.

"I'll get that," said Dinah.

While Penelope enjoyed a piece of toast and peanut butter, the rest of us had barely enough time to share questioning looks before Dinah returned. "It's the police again." She rested her hand on Beau's shoulder. "And they're askin' for you, Sonny."

Rocketing to his feet, Beau insisted he had this handled. Unconvinced, his mother and Dinah followed him.

Watching them go, Jamie muttered, "Jesus, Mary, and Joseph, what now?"

"The police are just doing their job."

She spun round to face me. "And speaking of jobs. I'd like to keep mine. Why did you have to mention those damn puzzles?"

"What's the problem? Didn't you say Penelope was simply joining in our conversation?"

"Yes, but ..."

"Then it's good news. Why not tell the family?"

"Because one of them, specifically the Queen B might come to the same conclusion you keep harping about."

"So, you think it's a possibility?"

"No. But I don't need my boss to even entertain the thought. My job is twenty-four hours a day, every day."

"She knows you sleep, right? What's the problem?"

Jamie left her chair and joined me on the other side of the table. Keeping an eye on her student she cupped her hand around her mouth and whispered, "The problem is she could burn us in our beds."

I stared at Jamie in semi-comprehension.

"It happened last summer during a cold spell. She got up in the middle of the night and went downstairs to the fireplace. She created a tower of newspapers beside, not inside, the fireplace before getting the matches from the mantel and lighting one. Luckily, Dinah couldn't sleep and was in the kitchen heating a cup of milk. She smelled smoke, grabbed the fire extinguisher and doused the blaze before it did more than ruin an expensive carpet."

"Holy sh—" I raised my eyes toward Penny, "—ucks."

"Holy shucks?" Jamie snickered.

"I admit it's not as imaginative as what the fudge."

Our nervous giggles erupted into laughter as Veronica returned. Tense and distracted, she glowered at us. "I hope the two of you are not enjoying a joke at my son's expense."

"Absolutely not." I said.

Veronica slipped back onto her chair and tapped an index finger on the table.

"Where's Beau?" asked Jamie.

"The police have requested his assistance." Veronica pressed at the creases in her linen napkin as if to smooth out the day's events.

"Did he go with them?" Jamie asked, a quiver in her voice.

"Of course."

"When is he coming back?"

Veronica rose from her chair. "Excuse me, I'm expecting a call." At the door she paused to tell me we would meet in the library at ten o'clock.

When Penny finished breakfast, the only one of us to do so, she was ready for her swing. Jamie and I followed as she led us through the French doors.

At the swing, Penny's reed-thin arms had barely wrapped around the chains when Jamie pulled back the swing and pushed like she was throwing a caber.

"Whoa!" I yelled as the youngest Barrington scrambled to remain upright. "Let's keep her on the swing."

Distracted, Jamie dropped onto the picnic bench. "Goddamn it! We had a date. Maud, what's really going on?"

"I don't know." I stayed close to Penny until I was sure she had a good grip on the chains. "Maybe the cops really do have more questions for Beau. At the end of the day, sometimes a cigar is just a cigar."

"That's stupid, Maud. What else could a cigar be? If the cops show up and take you away, doesn't that mean you were arrested?"

"Not necessarily. The police need reasonable grounds before they can make an arrest."

"And that means?"

"Reliable evidence—like the suspect's prints on a murder weapon, incriminating photographs, a video, eyewitness accounts, and of course a confession is always helpful."

"Well, I don't think we have to worry about any of that." She waved me over to the seesaw, holding the plank level until I climbed onboard. With more power than necessary, she sent me slamming into the ground. "Maud, you need to move your weight forward."

I shifted closer to the handrail. Squatting frog-like, I thrust upward propelling Jamie to a gentle descent. "Bear in mind that Beau lied to the police and they don't take kindly to that sort of thing."

"He wasn't actually lying." She left me dangling in the air. "He was acting. It wasn't done to hurt anyone or to do anything illegal. And we can't ignore Ceal's role in it."

"Jamie, I'm starting to get vertigo. Let's sit at the picnic table."

She sent me back to the ground, then leveled the plank allowing me to slide off.

Sitting across from me she asked, "If Beau hasn't been arrested, he can leave whenever he wants. Yes?"

"Arrest at this point is unlikely but the police might detain him."

"Detain? What does that mean?" she asked.

"It's what the police do while they gather enough evidence for an arrest. Worst-case scenario for Beau, foul play is suspected and they're running some tests or waiting for the results of the autopsy, or someone has come forward with incriminating testimony."

"Incriminating testimony? That'll be one of those Toronto friends. Maybe that one who accused him of not having a twenty-four-hour lifeguard."

"It's not Beau's pool, so if Sam is accusing anyone, it'll be Veronica." I glanced at my watch. "I have a few things to do before Veronica meets me at ten. You know, it's possible Beau is, as his mother said, assisting the police. Maybe he'll get back for an afternoon tennis game. If that happens, Penny is welcome to join me and work on her drawing."

A good morning turned bad, Jamie rose from the picnic table and started to pace. I was sorry to leave her in such a state, but I had paint to mix.

Veronica arrived on schedule, immediately joining me at the easel. Although only in the early stage of the underpainting, the image visible through the veil was the foundation for all to follow, and it needed my client's approval. I hoped to hear a few words of praise. As silent seconds ticked by, I longed for a murmur of appreciation. A few more seconds and I prepared for the worst.

Finally, she said, "It will do, Maud. Shall we proceed?"

I nodded and directed her toward the chair. Using my painting and the photograph for reference, I made a few adjustments to the pose and taped strips of masking tape as an outline for the position of her hands and feet. "This will make it easier to find the pose after each break," I explained. Since my client wanted to participate in the process, I explained the use of oily egg tempera mixed with titanium white pigment to establish the lights.

When she slipped comfortably into the pose, I dipped a sable brush into the tempera mixture and prepared to lay-in the lightest areas of the face. I stopped the instant I saw the creases of tension. This was not a look she wanted immortalized in paint. Her anxiety told me Beau's departure to aid the police had not been as willing as she wanted me to believe. I focussed on the costume and hair until her face relaxed enough to accurately establish the lights.

After thirty minutes, I suggested a break. I'd hope we might talk about what was really going on with Beau but Veronica preferred to pace the room. Stopping at the small table to look at her daughter's latest drawing, she caressed the edge of the drawing paper. "Penelope does not welcome my touch," she said, more to herself than to me.

"I invited Jamie to bring Penelope for a drawing session later. Would you like to be here?"

"I think not. I would be a distraction."

"I don't think so. Once Penelope tucks into a drawing, she won't notice you." I quickly added, "Your daughter has an amazing ability to focus."

"Yes, she does," her mother said, slipping into the pose.

After mixing more pigment into the tempera, I turned my attention to a tricky bit of drawing—the hands. Even accomplished artists can turn fingers into sausages. My subject's long elegant fingers deserved every ounce of concentration and thanks to her absolute stillness, I was reasonably pleased with the result.

"Okay," I grabbed a rag to clean my brush, "the lights are established. I appreciate your ability to hold the pose. Have you modelled before?"

"No. However, many years ago I learned to meditate. It helps keep me in the present."

Laying down the brush, I invited her to the worktable where I propped the small canvas board against my carryall. "This is a possible background for your painting. My intent is to evoke the night sky. And into it, I thought I could add your constellation."

"Maud, that's an excellent idea. My sun sign is Virgo—the second-largest constellation." Veronica went to one of the bookshelves, and removed a volume.

"I think you'll find this useful." Her phone rang and she carried her conversation from the room.

She was right, there were a few very good pictures of the constellation of Virgo. I chose what I thought would be the best image for my painting. Returning to my easel, I remixed the night sky.

Chapter 32

Beau's absence from the dining room ensured another sombre meal. While a grey cloud of disappointment hung over Jamie, Veronica appeared dampened by tension and fatigue. Throughout most of lunch, they remained focused on the soup, which, in my opinion, deserved our attention. Cream of asparagus was never one of my favourites, but I intended to beg or bribe Dinah for her recipe. I was ladling another helping from the tureen when Veronica asked, "Maud, this morning you mentioned something about Penelope communicating through her choice in jigsaw puzzles. To which puzzles do you refer?"

I looked at Penny and tried to convey a silent apology before answering Veronica's question. "There are three so far: *The Birth of Venus*, David Hockney's *The Bigger Splash,* and Millais's *Ophelia*. I should add that *Ophelia* isn't completely verified."

"Penelope may have assembled *The Birth of Venus* because it was a new puzzle. By following it with Hockney's *Bigger Splash,* she has shown us someone on water, in water, and with *Ophelia,* a name that means 'help,' underwater. May I assume my daughter has been with you both during your discussions of Cecilia's accident?"

We nodded warily.

"Because Penelope does not speak, you may think she does not listen. I assure you, she hears every word. My question is," Veronica looked directly at Jamie, "has Penelope used the subject matter of a puzzle as a form of communication before Cecilia's accident?"

"I... I'm sorry Mrs. Barrington, I don't understand the question."

"In July, Dr. Patmore's daughter was visiting. She and her friend rode here on horseback. Do you remember?"

Jamie's eyes sparkled with the memory. "Oh, yes they were each on a Canadian horse." Jamie turned to me. "It's a wonderful breed, Maud. So gentle."

"Yes, they and Penelope were smitten, in the same way she is with Steady. After that event, did she assemble one of her horse puzzles?"

"I'm sorry, Mrs. Barrington. I can't recall. I'll give it more thought and let you know."

"I would appreciate that. I fear you may have missed Penelope's attempts to converse. It is something to be cognizant of in the future."

"Yes, Mrs. Barrington."

Dinah brought us a plate of oatmeal cookies. As I reached for one, Veronica rose from her chair. "Come along Maud. It's time for the darks." I grabbed a cookie and followed her to the library.

Settling into the pose after only a couple of minor adjustments, Veronica assumed her meditative state. For the addition of the darks, I used burnt umber oil paint directly from the tube and a little medium. The large areas were painted first, with particular care around the graduated darks in the folds of material and the hair. From broad brush strokes to the more detailed, I eventually concentrated on the face.

I'd originally drawn the mouth using the reference photo but when compared with the model who sat before me, whether through mood or fatigue, Veronica's lips had drooped into a frown. Cleaning my brush, I suggested we take a break.

Veronica rose from the chair and walked over to the easel. After only a moment of examination, she said, "I realize it's early days, Maud, but do you think the mouth is quite right?"

And there it was, the reason I preferred to work from a photograph. Had she looked at me, my client would have noted my insincere smile. She did, however, hear my words. "Veronica, there is still much work to be done. I suggest re-evaluating when I begin working with the local colour."

"As you wish. I simply don't want you to throw good paint after bad."

I let my silence speak for me. Veronica lingered like a queen inspecting her troops, then slowly returned to the pose. I unclenched my teeth and Dinah ambled through the door.

"That Ms. Arnott's here."

Veronica jumped up as if bitten by the chair and raced from the room. Dinah, like a factory foreman, paused near the work table, examined the floor and pointed to a few pencil shavings, scrapes of canvas, and loose threads. "I haven't been in to clean 'cause I didn't want to be disturbin' your stuff."

She walked to the far end of the room, opened a door I hadn't realized was there, and returned with a broom and dustpan. Pausing at my easel she said, "This is comin' along."

Not exactly a compliment, but better than telling me there was something wrong with the mouth. Walking past the small table, her gaze fell on Penny's drawings. "Hey, these are good. Somethin' you do when you're not paintin'?"

I tried to describe Penelope's amazing talent, but Dinah cut me off. "How can that be? Kid can't even dress herself."

"I can't explain it, Dinah. Drawing could be like her jigsaw puzzles. Perhaps she sees the world in unique shapes and, once she zones in, she simply puts them together."

"Zones out is more like it. Well, I gotta be gettin' back downstairs."

Thrusting the broom and dustpan into my hands, she left me to clean up the bits of debris. At my easel, I taped the reference photo next to the portrait. My plan was to use it as a guide in redrawing my subject's mouth. I soon realized it was a battle I was too tired to fight. I abandoned it to continue painting the background.

Penny was the first one through the door, making a bee-line to her drawing. Jamie followed, asking questions about Beau before she even sat down. I had little to tell her, except the visit from someone I thought must be the family's lawyer.

"Well, that settles it. He's been arrested." She dropped onto Veronica's chair.

"Jamie, don't disturb the tape."

She leapt up. "What snake?"

"Tape, not snake." I pulled the stool from under the work table. "Sit here. It's not part of my painting."

Ignoring the offer, she paced the room. "Do you think the police have taken Beau's phone? Not that it matters. He probably won't call me, anyway. And forget about the Queen B. What about your uncle? He's a cop. Can he help?"

"He's a retired cop, but I'll talk to him."

She stopped walking. "That would be great. Where's your phone?"

"It's in my room."

"Please, Maud?"

"Okay." I jogged to my room and returned with my phone. Not wanting to disturb him at work, I called the home number and left a message. "He'll call back. Why don't you go for a run or something—activate a few endorphins?"

She didn't need much convincing. After she left, I checked on Penelope. She seemed to have more confidence with her second drawing and was working so quickly, she would soon need another model. I scanned the shelves and spotted a set of antique scales. They wouldn't be easy to draw, but given what she'd already accomplished, I thought she was ready.

By the time Jamie returned, sweaty and distracted, my portrait had a night sky awaiting the constellation of Virgo.

"Feel better?" I asked her.

"Did your uncle call back?"

"Not yet."

"Maybe we'll get some good news from the Queen B. It's time the Gods smiled on us, don't you think?"

Chapter 33

The Gods were not smiling and neither were my dinner companions. Dinah wasn't with us but she revealed her state of mind with a lacklustre meal of creamed salmon on toast and what I call a humdrum salad—tossed greens and little else. Dessert was left-over blueberry pie, fortunately made before the latest calamity.

Veronica had little to say, certainly nothing by the way of good news, and by the time we left the dining room, Jamie's dark mood had grown darker.

"I'll check my phone and if my uncle hasn't called back, I'll call him," I promised her as we climbed the stairs to the second floor.

She brightened slightly, and I agreed to come to the loft with an update.

Uncle Sid answered on the second ring. "Hey Maudie, I was just about to call you back. Everything all right?"

I related Beau's probable detention or possible arrest, which lead to the real story behind the unsuitable bride.

"Sounds like a dangerous way to prepare for a part in a play."

"Dangerous?" I asked.

"Behaviour has consequences and bad behaviour has negative consequences. It's hard enough to gauge the reactions of people you know, never mind those you don't. Mrs. Barrington had good reasons to see this woman as a threat. Even the youngest son might have felt the whole charade had gone too far. And if he's been arrested, you know it's not without due cause."

"Yes, about that. Could you find out what's going on? The tension is showing on his mother's face—not a good thing when I'm trying to paint that face. And the cook is off her food."

"The cook?"

"Let's just say the atmosphere is dark and, as an artist, I need light. Please Unc, find out what's going on? And one other thing, Mrs. Barrington told us a small bruise was found on Cecilia's head. She seems to think it proves the woman was tipsy in more ways than one."

"If it helps you, honey, I'm on it. I'll call you when I have something."

Climbing to the third floor, I found Penny at her puzzles and Jamie putting away her clean laundry. Hearing my news, she clutched a pair of denim shorts to her chest. "Thank God. Maybe now we'll get some answers." She stuffed them into the dresser drawer and offered to put on the kettle. "When do you think he'll call back?"

"As soon as he knows something."

While Jamie tended to the kettle, I checked in with the puzzler and her current project. I also checked the art book for the Millais reproduction, and in comparing it to the assembled bit of puzzle, all doubt was removed. The background with its drooping willow and delicate flowers was unfinished, but Ophelia was complete. Arms back, eyes open, she was resigned to the weight of her heavy Victorian gown and its inevitable pull to the bottom of a murky river. It wasn't hard to imagine Penny, lured to the window by the glow of the moon, witnessing another young woman disappearing under dark water.

"Hey, Jamie," I called in the direction of her room, "it's Ophelia."

"I know Maud," she yelled back. "I saw that sinking dress—damn it."

Turning from the puzzle to the window, my attention was drawn to a ride-on mower traversing the lawn near the pool. I couldn't see the driver's face but I recognized that faded green hat. "Is that Caleb mowing the lawn?" I asked Jamie when she joined me.

"Yup, that's him."

"What can you tell me about him?"

"Not much. He's a bit of a mystery. I know he came to Canada as an itinerant worker from Jamaica, to pick apples. He was probably young—early twenties. After a few seasons, he made extra income working in local gardens, and doing handyman stuff. When Dinah's husband died, he was hired by the Barringtons. Dinah is suspicious about his immigration status."

"Why?"

"She says one day Caleb simply didn't get on the bus to the airport."

I watched the handyman manoeuvre the mower around the large trees. "Speaking of mysteries, I know who intervened between Cecilia and Bobby."

"Caleb? He never makes an appearance at the Barrington's parties. And why would he be looking out for Cecilia?"

"Maybe he wasn't. Maybe he was there for Bobby."

Her eyes lit up like a kid offered candy. "If Caleb knows Bobby, he might know something that could help Beau. You've got to talk to him, Maud. He'll be finished mowing in about an hour."

I yawned. "It's getting late. I'll go tomorrow."

"You can see him at seven."

"In the morning?"

"Why not? You're an early riser. He'll be tending to his bees or his own garden."

"And where exactly is his garden? Do I need a map?" Laughing, Jamie pulled me to the side window and pointed across the lawn.

While we were watching Caleb, Penny had chosen another puzzle. She slipped out of her blue sweater and draped it over the back of her chair. With both hands, she shoved the partially completed Ophelia, its message identified, toward an empty space at the corner of the table. Like a cardboard waterfall, it cascaded over the edge. Before all of the pieces hit the floor, I grabbed its plastic container and caught the deluge.

"Great reflexes, Maud," said Jamie, watching me slide what was left into the box.

Penelope, busy overturning the pieces of her next selection, ignored my valiant rescue. When I sat next to her and asked if I could right the upside-down tiles and organize them by colour, she slid some toward me. I was struck by the disproportionate number that were either dark green, brown or black, and suspected this one would be a challenge, even for our little puzzle champ.

My job complete, I picked up the lid and noticed a label bearing the number four, stuck in the corner. Showing it to Jamie, I asked if the number referred to the puzzle or something else.

She took closer look. "When our girl had only a few puzzles, they were numbered instead of named. So, this must be an old one."

"It promises to be a very unusual image, too. Come have a look. Maybe you'll recognize it."

Jamie did a quick scan and shook her head. "No idea."

"You hardly looked at it. I know Penny only put a few pieces together but look at all the dark tiles. Ever seen anything like this before?"

"Nope, haven't a clue. I don't know why she's doing this either. It's creeping me out."

"She wants to tell us something."

Jamie rolled her eyes.

"At least there's nothing that looks like water," I said.

"Speaking of water, I forgot our tea. I'll be right back."

Returning with the tea tray, Jamie brushed against Penny's sweater. It slipped from the back of her chair and hit the floor with a thud. Leaving the tray on the table, Jamie picked up the sweater and checked a side pocket. "Maud, look at this." Dangling between her thumb and forefinger was a lady's watch.

I looked for an inscription. "How did she get it?" I whispered, watching Penny, her head bent over the puzzle. I sat on one of the clam chairs and clasped it to my wrist. "I've been so careful. And when I'm not wearing it, I keep it in the top draw of my nightstand."

"She probably took it just before we left the room—bit of a magician, our Pen."

"Magician or kleptomaniac?"

"I know you're annoyed, Maud, but she doesn't do it often. And she only takes things from people who seem to mean something to her. She's like a puppy stealing a slipper. I'd been here for a week when I found my cell phone under her pillow, but she hasn't taken stuff in ages." Jamie laughed. "Of course, that could be because there are so few people she likes."

"I wonder whether she took my watch the first time it went missing and put it in Beau's room?"

"Why would she take it from you and give it to her brother?"

"A birthday gift, or to atone for something she did that upset him like, say, stabbing his fiancée."

"Geez, that would be weird. Possible, but weird."

We finished our tea, and, just before leaving, I stopped at Penny's table. Unclipping a barrette from my hair I placed it next to her. "Would you like to have this?" I asked. She dropped a puzzle piece and wrapped her hand around the tortoise shell hair clip. I hoped it would be a substitute for my watch, though I had no guarantees. Checking the puzzle, I saw the islands of dark green and brown, and a section that was primarily yellow ochre. "I'm looking forward to naming this one, Penelope," I told her before saying good night to them both.

Chapter 34

Returning to my room, I was annoyed to find a dab of paint on my navy shorts. Fortunately, I had a solution and made a quick sprint back to the library for my brush cleaner. Hearing my phone and assuming it was Gabe, I ran back to my room and answered it with a breathless hello.

"Hi honey, are you busy?"

"Uncle Sid?"

"Yeah. Were you expecting someone else?"

"Sorry, I'm distracted by some paint I found on a favourite pair of shorts. If you ever get paint on your clothes, I have this brush cleaner that works great."

"That's nice, honey. Do you have time to hear some news about the case."

"I guess we're calling it a case now. Yes, I'm all ears."

"There's evidence that Miss Fox had sexual intercourse shortly before she died."

"What?"

"There's also the possibility that it wasn't consensual."

"That's not good. What did they find—scratches, bruising, broken fingernails?"

"Maudie, I don't know. What I do know is that Mr. Beau Barrington got on his high horse and refused to consent to a DNA sample. Probably thought his Mama was going to swoop in and make it all go away. They left him cooling his heels until he finally consented. It won't lift suspicion, but it could clear him of a possible rape charge and allow him to come home."

I sighed with relief. "Phew, that's excellent news."

"You care about this fellow?" I heard his scowl of suspicion.

"Only as one cares for another human being. His return is less about Beau and more about his mother. I need her to relax and let me create the look I think she wants."

"Maudie, you didn't ask for it, but I did a background check on the Barrington lad. Last summer he was charged with impaired. A first offence. Ultimately, the case was dropped. Before that, there was a caution when driving a boat on Rice Lake—no alcohol involved. Then six years ago, a car accident. His girlfriend was driving, the car went off a bridge, she died and the Barrington lad escaped with minor injuries. One could say he's very lucky, but I suspect there's more to it."

"Money and privilege."

"And the expectation of being above the law."

We said our goodbyes and I returned to scrubbing away unwanted paint. It wasn't until I was propped up in bed with my newly acquired astrology book that I heard from Gabe.

"Hi Maud. I know it's a little late but I have some news from Mother. Beau will soon be returning to the fold. She provided no details, so I'm counting on you."

"Sure. I'll let you know when he arrives."

"I wish I could visit you but with my father and Rex away, I'm swamped. Any chance of you coming here? I'd like to see you and I can promise a long lunch with great company—the day, time and restaurant are up to you. And as further incentive it would mean a day away from my mother. What do you say?"

"I say, yes. The *when* depends on a few factors, but the portrait will soon need a drying day."

"Wonderful. You can give me the details when I call tomorrow."

I wasn't sure I'd have details by the following day but Gabe, like the rest of his family, was accustomed to calling the shots and setting the parameters. Caleb, I felt certain, had a very different life experience, one I hoped would make him more receptive when I showed up in his garden just after sunrise.

Waking just before six, I donned my bathing suit, covered it with a sundress, and went into the library to check on the portrait. The lights and darks were dry enough to receive the local colour and since we're clothed in skin before being covered in clothes, I always preferred to start with the flesh.

Yellow ochre and earth red combine to make a mid-value orange. I mixed enough to separate five puddles. To three of them I added increasing amounts of titanium white. To the other two, I added burnt umber for the shadows.

Finishing my work, and after cleaning my palette knife and covering the palette with plastic wrap, I grabbed a towel from my room and found the well-trod path that would take me to Caleb and his coach house. The delightful fragrance of roses told me I was close to my destination.

Through a break in the trees, I spotted Caleb, one arm resting on the handle of a rake as he surveyed his vegetable plot. He saw me, and his face registered more surprise than welcome. At least my cheery hello brought Steady from the shadows, his tail wagging enthusiastically. He got some well-deserved attention before I met Caleb at the perimeter of his garden.

"I'm sorry to bother you. If you have the time, I've got a couple of questions I think you can answer."

"Yes, Miss." Caleb directed me to the shade at the side of the house and a pair of recently painted metal lawn chairs. I ran my hand along the arm rest. "I was never sure if the backs of these were supposed to be shells or daisy petals."

"Shells, I think, Miss."

I perched on the edge of the seat. Shells or petals, in a shady spot at seven in the morning, that metal was cold on my skin. Protected in his shirt and overalls, Caleb filled the chair across from me.

"My first question is about something I saw on the night of Beau's party."

Caleb leaned forward slightly, and I described the argument I'd witnessed. "Initially, I thought they were being affectionate, then it turned aggressive. And soon, you came to Cecilia's rescue. Which was very gentlemanly of you." I smiled and he averted his gaze. "Anyway, when talking to Beau afterwards, he told me the person I saw Cecilia arguing with was a man named Bobby. Do you know him?"

"Not really, Miss."

Hmm. It looked like we were going to have a short visit. I asked if there was anything at all he could tell me about this young man named Bobby.

Caleb lowered his head, then raised it. "He's my son."

"You have a son?" I don't know why I was so surprised. There was no reason he couldn't have a son, but to say he didn't know him suggested a few possibilities—none of them happy. "Am I right in assuming he grew up without you?"

"His mama and I want to marry. We talk about having a son. A son we would call Marley." Caleb rubbed the fingers of his leather gardening gloves, pressing and re-pressing each one. "But her Toronto family don't want this Jamaican boy. No one tells me about the baby. I never knew I was a daddy until after his mama died. But I knew she loved me, because she named him Marley. We only just found each other, but we have distance and his life is busy."

"Your son's name is Marley? I thought it was Bobby."

Caleb explained, without bitterness, that the family of his son's mother renamed him Bobby. "When my son called wanting to visit, I'm happy he has time for me. We sit on these chairs and we hear the party. He says he heard his friends talking about it and he wants to go. I tell him no but he go anyway."

"And you followed him?"

Caleb hung his head, fidgeting with his gardening glove. "No way he crashes the party. Not right. I find him and make him come with me."

"Did he tell you why they were arguing?"

"No, too much shame."

"And have you spoken to him since?" I asked.

Caleb's shoulders sagged and he shook his head. "We talk only one way. He calls."

"I'm sure he just needs time. Does he work in Toronto?"

"Yes, Miss. My son is an artist too. At the York Theatre where he design and make sets for the plays."

"Is that where he met Cecilia?"

Caleb nodded.

"Was he in love with her?"

"He didn't say, but …"

His gestures confirmed what I suspected. When he got to his feet, I knew my welcome was wearing thin. I thanked him for his time and enjoyed Steady's companionship to the edge of the garden.

Chapter 35

I arrived to the dining room with one minute to spare, and Veronica greeted me with a broad smile of anticipation. "Beau will be returning before lunch."

"That's wonderful news," I said.

Jamie reminded me of a bubble about to burst. "It is, isn't it? We've been really, really worried. Haven't we, Maud?"

"It has been on my mind."

The improved quality of our breakfast, told me Dinah was thrilled too. I was about to enjoy a second serving of her cheese and mushroom omelette when Veronica laid her napkin across her plate. "Maud, let us see how much progress we can make on my portrait before Beau arrives. I'll meet you in the library in ten minutes."

I rose from the table and Jamie offered me a cranberry muffin. "Take it with you."

I patted my belly. "Pushing a paint brush around a canvas isn't burning off a lot of calories."

"Your hair is still damp. How many laps did you swim?"

I took the muffin and finished it before reaching the library. When Veronica arrived, she was carrying an insulated bag. Without a word, she left it on the large work table, and settled into the pose. Continuing our painting partnership, I described my procedure for adding local colour to the canvas. I was explaining the difference between value, hue, and chroma when I noticed my subject wasn't wearing her costume.

"Oh dear, you're right," she said, looking down. "I was distracted by my detour to the kitchen. Shall I get changed?"

"Since my focus this morning is your skin, you can stay as you are. I'll start with your hands."

I was finishing the lightest areas when Veronica's voice broke through my concentration. "That's forty minutes."

"Good for you, another marathon pose."

She went to the table and unzipped the bag while I cleaned the excess paint from my brush. "Maud, I brought us sparkling pomegranate juice and Dinah's cranberry muffins."

I accepted the juice and a muffin, it would have been rude not to.

Veronica took a sip and lowered her cup to the table, "Do you have an approximate date for the completion of my portrait?"

"Depending on your availability for posing, I expect to complete the addition of local colour over the next few days. The portrait will need a day to dry before I can add the final glazes and another day to refine and perfect the image. Add another day for any areas that need correcting and it could be close to a week." Seeing the look of disappointment on her face, I added, "Sorry, I can't be more precise."

"If I made myself available for four one-hour sessions and you worked using our reference photo could the timeline shorten?"

"Yes, I expect it would."

She finished her drink and got to her feet. "Then let us resume. I know you want to fix the mouth, so I'll try to match that forty-minute pose."

We were halfway there when Dinah lumbered into the room. I was struck by her ear-to-ear grin and realized how seldom she smiled. It delivered her message better than words and Veronica was out of the chair and the room before I could tell her to say welcome home from me too.

With the loss of my model, I was pleased to have permission to use the reference photo and taped it next to the canvas. Casting my eyes from photo to painting, put me on familiar ground.

When painting fabric, it's the accurate rendering of the folds and the play of light that explain texture and tell the viewer whether it's satin or velvet, burlap or cotton. After strengthening the contours of the face, working on the mouth and blocking in the large shapes of her scarf and suit, I stepped back from the easel to evaluate my progress.

My pleasure with the work ended just below the nose. The mouth still wasn't right, reminding me of Sargent's definition of a portrait—'a likeness in which there was something wrong about the mouth.'

Because of its flexibility, it's a facial feature that can alter more than any other and small errors soon compound to affect the likeness. My most obvious error, I decided, was the bottom lip. Using mineral spirits to thin my burnt umber oil paint to the consistency of ink, I chose a fine pointed brush and began a line that suddenly slid off recklessly when my phone rang. I couldn't disguise my irritation when I answered the call.

"Honey, is everything okay?"

"Sorry, Uncle Sid. I'm fighting with Veronica's mouth."

"Many people wouldn't understand that comment." He laughed. "I don't want to keep you from your battle, but I just heard Beau should be on his way home. Any sign of him yet?"

I checked my watch, "I suspect he arrived about an hour ago, because that's when the cook came to collect my model. I'm working from a photograph so I haven't actually seen him. I have, however, learned about another man in our victim's life." I laid my brush across the palette and told my uncle what I knew about Bobby.

"I can see that it would have been awkward to invite one's actual boyfriend to one's pretend fiancée's birthday party. Sounds like she wasn't too happy to see him. Which raises more questions, doesn't it? Got a last name for Bobby?"

"His biological father's last name is Moses but since he's only recently met his son, I'm almost positive Bobby has his mother's family name. I'll try to find out for sure."

"Okay. Now about that bruise on Cecilia's head. Apparently, it displays a unique patterning, which should help in identifying the weapon."

"Could she have been knocked unconscious?" I asked.

"Don't have that info but I can tell you there was water in her lungs, so she definitely drowned."

I wandered over to the wall of windows and looked down at the pool. "If she was hit with a hard object that will eliminate my 'fell while fleeing a coyote' theory."

"Unless he came at her wielding a big stick." Uncle Sid cleared his throat. "A little gallows humour."

"Or she slipped and hit her head while fleeing."

"But Maudie, that kind of fall would most likely impact the knees, hands and possibly the forehead. There's no sign of injury to any of those areas. And falling into the pool full of water provides a pretty soft landing."

"Hmm, I see what you mean. What if she hit her head on the way out of the pool. There are concrete steps at the shallow end."

"I didn't know about the steps. Also not impossible, but honey, a slip when climbing up a set of stairs would more likely result in impact to the front of the head."

"You're right, Unc. I guess we need more info. What about her drug-alcohol level?"

"You'll be surprised to learn her blood alcohol level revealed impairment. As to the full impact of recreational drugs when combined with alcohol, the hound and I have been hitting the sack early so I can spend time on a little research. Some of the literature says THC levels after death are unreliable, but I'll keep reading."

"Thanks, Uncle Sid." He was about to close the call when I interrupted his goodbye. "Wait a minute. Did you just say the dog is sleeping on your bed? Because you told me—"

"Sorry Honey, there's a call coming in on the landline. Gotta go. Stay safe."

Chapter 36

With the image of Sherlock hogging a good portion of mattress real estate, I turned back to the errant line of burnt umber. The tip of a clean brush is a good eraser and erasing a mistake is a lot easier than covering it up. To trick my brain into seeing a mouth as nothing more than a simple shape, I turned the canvas and the photograph upside down. Adding the lines I hoped would fix the issue, I righted both images just as Jamie and Penny breezed into the library—Jamie being the breezier of the two. Penny, with her usual determination, went straight to her drawing.

"Maud," Jamie grabbed my forearm as if to ground her excitement. "Beau wants to take me to the village for ice cream."

"Terrific. Will you bring one back for me? I'm starving."

"You haven't eaten?"

I shook my head.

"That's not good. I thought Dinah would have brought you something."

"No such luck. Her excitement at Beau's return likely erased any thoughts of the poor artist struggling in the garret."

Promising to be right back, Jamie ran from the room. I returned to the easel with fresh eyes and critical judgement. Convinced the right colours were in the right place, I strolled over to the small work table to check on Penny. Her drawing of Apollo and Daphne was complete and before she could draw the books supporting the statue, I promised her a new model. She laid down her pencil. I grabbed the antique scales and set them on her table.

"Scales are used to weigh things but they're also symbols of justice and truth. You know it's important to tell the truth even when you don't want to, right?" She didn't look at me, but she didn't fidget either. "Although scales are complicated to draw. I believe you're ready. Would you like to try?"

She clenched her right fist, and I thanked her for not tossing her finished drawing to the floor. After exchanging the statue for the scales, I put my hand on the table and crouched to see the model from her vantage point.

"That looks good to me. What do you think?" In response, Penny briefly covered my hand with hers. Suddenly, my eyes got misty and I found it hard to swallow.

Rising to my feet, I blinked rapidly and cleared my throat. By the time I tore a clean sheet of drawing paper from the pad, I'd regained my composure. "These weighing platforms are made of circular pieces of white glass but from your viewing angle, they appear to be ovals." I demonstrated how to create an ellipse and soon my student was wiggling her pencil, a sure sign that she was ready to draw. I slipped back to my easel and Jamie returned with a tray of food.

"Leftovers from lunch. It was good. You'll like it." Jamie sat on the wooden stool and asked about my meeting with Caleb. She was equally surprised to learn Caleb had a son. "I wonder if Beau knows Bobby is Caleb's son."

"You should ask him. And if he knows Bobby's last name and anything about his relationship with Cecilia? And confirm where he went on Monday."

"Jeez, Maud, I finally get to spend some time alone with the guy and you want me to turn it into an inquisition. Can't you ask him this stuff?"

I pointed out that he'd be more willing to confide in her if she asked him. She looked vaguely convinced and scurried from the room.

Jamie was right about the avocado halves stuffed with chicken salad. When I finished lunch, I got the number from directory assistance and called the restaurant where Samantha worked.

Back at my easel, and feeling satisfied with the state of the mouth, I tackled my subject's hair. When painting hair, it's always a balance between doing too little and too much. As a student, I was warned that painting every strand would destroy its weightless quality. Not only would the subject appear to be wearing a hair helmet, it would be a mistake not easily corrected. The streaks, or balayage or whatever she called it was going to make colour mixing a challenge. I had created four values of similar hue when Jamie reappeared.

"How was it?" I asked, cleaning my palette knife.

Jamie pulled an elastic from her pocket and, after gathering her hair, wrapped it in a high ponytail. "Hot."

"Are you referring to more than just the weather?" I teased.

"Ha, I wish." She paused to set the timer for Penny. "It started off well. Beau can be very entertaining, and the ice cream was good, but the guy just can't sit still. First, we did the local history walk. Not usually my thing but I was surprised at how many buildings in the village are over two hundred years old. And to finish off our 'date,' we went for a jog along his favourite trail."

"Did Beau say anything about where he was on Monday?"

"It's very hard to chat while jogging. You were right about Monday. When I finally got him to sit in the shade for ten minutes, he told me he'd been hanging with this city friends. And," she did an imaginary drum roll. "I found out Bobby is a set designer at the York Theatre."

"Good sleuthing." Nothing to gain from telling her it was information I already had. "Did Beau know about Bobby or tell you his last name?"

"No. I was going to ask but he got broody after I asked where he went on Monday. I don't think he likes answering questions. He only perked up when he talked about his move to New York but then that made me feel broody. I wish he knew how much I want him to stay."

"He'll know if you tell him."

"I tried, sort of. He just looked at me like he was seeing me for the first time."

"Maybe he was." Before the timer ran out, I checked on Penny's drawing and noted that not only had she rendered an accurate outline of the image, her ellipses—a challenge for even an experienced artist—were expertly done. "I'm beginning to think this child can master any shape."

Jamie laughed. "Are you calling her a shapeshifter?"

"Given the way she assembles the various shapes of her jigsaw puzzles and replicates those of the models I set before her, it's a description that fits."

The timer rang and Penny slipped from her chair. At the door, Jamie turned back. "You've got twenty minutes and Dinah's pizza night is one meal you won't want to miss." She lowered her voice to a whisper. "Though your friend Veronica would disagree. Madame is not partial to pizza. She dines out."

I was surprised to find pizza night was more than just the food. It included a change in décor—the formality of white lined was replaced with casual red and white checks. It was a pleasant change but the meal was made more memorable by the attitude of the diners. In the absence of the Queen B, there was more laughter and chatter.

When Dinah brought us chocolate pudding, she stayed to listen to Beau's funny anecdotes about stumbling actors. Seeing him so caring, relaxed and happy, I was almost convinced he couldn't possibly be a murderer.

Chapter 37

Veronica returned in time to join us for tea, keen to know how the painting was going. "Maud, I know my mouth was giving you problems. Are they resolved?" Before I could respond, she waved an index finger at her son. "Careful Beau, I know you're itching to make a comment."

He smiled with exaggerated innocence. "Only to say that even I have heard mouths can be challenging to draw." He turned his smile on me. "Though I'm sure Maud has it handled."

"I'll soon find out. Maud, it's six-thirty. Let's have one more session. I'll dress in my costume and meet you there."

We arrived at the library at the same time. I expected Veronica to pass judgement on the painting but she surprised me by settling directly into the pose. Grateful for a reprieve, I focussed on the portrait and let the world around me fade like an old photograph. Only the dimming light told us our work was over for the day. I turned from the easel to clean my brush and suddenly, Veronica was standing next to me, her nose inches from the painting.

"Make the bottom lip fuller and you'll have it."

I don't consider myself a violent person, but I instantly thought of one way to make her bottom lip fuller and it wouldn't be with paint.

"It won't take much, Maud. You're almost there."

"I'm happy to hear that," I said, feeling a slight rise in blood pressure.

"Yes, given what you have accomplished thus far, and your obvious talent, this portrait will undoubtedly be complete by Sunday. Do you agree?"

Swept up by her sudden praise, I might have signed an agreement in my own blood had she asked. I nodded and said, "Yes, I'm sure I can do that."

"Excellent. We'll celebrate with a grand unveiling and a small dinner party. The entrée will be eaten in the dining room, then we will relocate here for dessert and drinks." She waved an open palm toward the far corner. "We'll put the easel there. You can provide a short talk about the process and answer any questions."

Completing the painting by Sunday suddenly seemed like a lark compared to this new proposal. "How many guests will there be?" I asked, thinking of a recurring nightmare in which I'm pushed on to a stage naked.

"Just family and a few neighbours. Dr. Patmore of course and his daughter's family."

"Is there a Mrs. Patmore?"

"No, she died in a boating accident eleven years ago."

"How sad. He must have been devastated."

"It was a shattering summer. He lost his wife, and I learned the reason my fourth child never wanted to be held." She walked slowly to Penny's table. "I see she's drawing the scales. How appropriate. I hope her interest in drawing will bring some semblance of balance to a rather circumscribed life." Veronica picked up one of Penelope's pencils, examining it as if it was a foreign object. "Would you consider continuing Penelope's art lessons after we return to the city? I would pay you of course, and the timing could be whatever fits into your schedule. Alternate Saturday mornings from nine to noon would be ideal."

"Well, I ..."

"We'll settle the details before you go home on Monday." Veronica replaced the pencil and walked from the room.

Overwhelmed with what seemed like too many things to do, I took a pen and notebook from the drawer of the tabouret and listed what had to be done for the Sunday deadline. The painting would need a day to dry before I could apply the final touches, and that day would be Friday.

I made a quick call to Gabe to confirm the day and our details for lunch, returned the book to the drawer, and headed to the loft to check on Penny's puzzle progress. At the landing, I found the room dim and silent, its usual occupants nowhere to be seen. Flicking on the nearest light, I tiptoed across the room to steal a peak of the puzzle. Given the similarity of so many of the pieces, I expected even Penelope might take a little longer on this puzzle, but her lack of progress came as a shock.

"Maud, what the hell are you doing here?" Jamie's voice cut through my concentration, and Penny joined me at the puzzle table.

"Sorry, Jamie. I just popped in for a visit. I'll leave."

"Please don't. I just wasn't expecting to see you." She rattled the cookie tin. "Pen and I helped Dinah make gingerbread men. I know Pen wants one but first, she needs to jump into her pjs."

Penny was out of her day clothes and into her night clothes with such co-ordinated precision, that she hardly missed a second of puzzle devotion. Jamie placed a cookie next to her and waved me to our corner.

"Jamie, I couldn't help noticing," (especially since I made a point of looking) "there's not much progress with the latest puzzle."

"No big deal. Now that drawing has been added to her usual activities, Pen hasn't had a lot of time to work on it. And tomorrow, Beau is taking us on a hike." She offered me a cookie. "How's the portrait coming along?"

"The Queen B, as you've aptly named her, has decreed that her portrait will be ready on Sunday."

"Does that work for you?"

I told her about the grand unveiling and dinner party. "With that to look forward to, finishing the painting is the easy part."

"Jeez, Maud, couldn't you, like, drag it out for another week?"

"Not a good career move. Besides, you'll all be returning to the city at the end of the month."

"Not all of us."

"Ah, this is about Beau."

"Not entirely. I like your company too, Maud. It's just that you keep the Queen B busy and without a distraction she might discourage her baby boy from spending time with me."

"I agree, the woman is a snob, but at the end of the day, she wants her children to be happy. And even though it was a ruse, for a little while Veronica thought her son was engaged to a crazy person named Ceal. That alone has to make her more accepting of you." I bit off the leg of my gingerbread man. It seemed kinder to leave the head till last.

"Then there's New York."

"A lot can happen in three weeks." I could add that depending on the results of the investigation, Beau might have an entirely different destination, but that wouldn't cheer her up. When the phone rang, I munched my cookie and waited for Jamie to take her call.

"Aren't you going to answer that?" she asked, indicating the side pocket of her shorts.

By the time I disentangled it, the caller had hung up. "That was my uncle."

"You're going to call him back, aren't you?"

"Of course." I set my phone on the table. "After I finish my cookie and check on the puzzle." The subject matter was still a mystery, but Penny had made good progress in a little time. "Jamie, I think she might soon have enough assembled to reveal its subject."

"It's her bedtime shortly, so she'll have to do it tomorrow."

I checked my watch. "Wow, where did the time go. I'll call my uncle from my room and we can catch up tomorrow." As I approached my room, I decided to take a quick look at the portrait. Doubts always creep in when I'm away from a work-in-progress, especially when I've made what could turn out to be an unachievable promise. A few minutes with the portrait helped to alleviate most of my worries. I headed back to my room ready to return my uncle's call, at least I was until I realized I'd left my phone in the loft.

I climbed to the loft on tiptoe and peered into a space lit only by a light from Jamie's room. A sudden movement at the puzzle table grabbed my attention and I squinted into the darkness expecting to see Penny. As my eyes adjusted, I recognized Jamie. She was disassembling the jigsaw puzzle.

It was not the time to confront her. I turned around, tiptoed halfway down the stairs, and climbed back up with a heavier footfall. Jamie met me at the landing.

"Do you have news from your uncle?" she whispered, the glint in her eyes more creepy than attractive.

"No. I was going to call him and realized I'd forgotten my phone. I think I left it on the table in our corner." It was quickly found and I was soon back in my room, more than ready to talk to Uncle Sid.

Chapter 38

I told my uncle I thought Jamie was disassembling enough of the puzzle to keep its story a secret. I thought she was doing this because she was afraid Penny had gotten out of bed that night.

"And why would that be a problem. You might want to know what she's trying to say."

I told him about the fire and the expectation that Jamie was to be on the job 24/7.

"The kid tried to burn the house down? Cripes Maud, the place is a house of horrors."

"Jamie's always on the job, and if she hadn't had a few drinks Saturday night, she probably would have heard the kid get up."

"So, drinking on the job. That's her secret."

"It certainly explains her determination to keep Penny quiet."

"Jamie will want you to stay quiet too. What do we know about her? Not prone to violence, is she?"

"Jeez, I don't think so."

"All the same, keep you phone handy and your guard up."

"I know you're worried. You'll be happy to hear I'm committed to finishing the portrait by Sunday. And since it needs a day to dry before I add the final glazes, I'm driving into the city on Friday."

"That's great, Honey. The hound and I will be waiting with bells on."

I would have mentioned my lunch date with Gabe but as my uncle had a dim view of the family it was a conversation to avoid. Instead, I told him I hoped to talk to Samantha, a.k.a. Sam and also to Bobby. "They work in the same neighbourhood and between the two of them maybe I can find out why Bobby crashed the party."

"Maybe it was to whack Cecilia on the head and toss her into the pool, though I'm sure he won't tell you that. If you do talk to him, gain his confidence and don't back him into a corner."

"It'll be fine. I'm not meeting him in a dark alley."

When I awoke the following morning, the air held the slight chill of summer's end and the sky glowed with a blue I never took for granted. I had plenty of time for my swim but hurried through breakfast to get some paint mixed by the time Veronica arrived in the library.

By the end of the morning, my model, having managed three sittings of forty minutes, was ready for lunch.

"There's more to do on the hair. I'll join you shortly," I told her.

Within fifteen minutes, Veronica was back. "Maud, dear, I appreciate your efforts to meet the date for the unveiling." She set a tray on the large work table. "I've brought us quiche and a salad. Beau has taken the girls on a hike today, and I don't want to eat alone." Passing me a plate, Veronica casually asked if her daughter had completed another jigsaw puzzle. I could honestly say she had not.

"How unusual." She eyed me suspiciously.

"She has been spending more time on her drawing. Does her birth chart show anything about her artistic ability?"

"An excellent question, Maud. And one I've not investigated. Before Penelope was born, astrology was a curiosity, something to be satisfied by that little book I found in London. Soon after Penelope's birth I recognized she was different from my other babies. Until I received the diagnosis of her autism, I was desperate for answers. An acquaintance suggested I consult a professional astrologer."

"Did it help?"

"I wasn't sure what to expect but yes, it did. It helped me accept that many things are out of our control and we deceive ourselves if we believe otherwise. Now, if you've had enough to eat," Veronica put her plate on the tray, "I'll take the pose for one more session."

Setting a date for the unveiling meant Veronica not only continued to hold the pose well, she also seemed to be enjoying the effort. It was an infectious attitude. Soon the mouth, with its full bottom lip, curved in perfect symmetry, the hair took on the sheen of health, and the subtle nuances of my subject's personality found their place.

When the session ended and Veronica took a step toward the easel, I raised my palm to stop her. "Would you mind waiting until Saturday to talk about my work? It needs a day to dry and I've made plans to go to the city tomorrow. First thing Saturday morning we can ..."

Her initial expression of annoyance faded into acceptance. "Saturday morning then," she said with a nod and left me to clean my brushes. I took them to the bathroom sink for a final wash and was returning to the library when Jamie poked her head from around the canvas. "Hey, Maud."

"Yeezus, you almost gave me a heart attack." I glanced beside me and saw Penny working on her drawing.

"Sorry." Jamie tapped the side of the canvas. "This portrait is amazing. You're really good."

"Thank you, but do you have to sound so surprised?"

"Is it finished? I thought you said ..."

"There's still work to do but it needs to dry for a day."

"That's good. I'm not ready for you to go." She spent the next several minutes telling me about her hike with Beau. "Could I ask for a favour?" she clasped her hands in supplication, "We've got a few hours until dinner, and Beau wants to show me a geographical wonder."

I bet he does.

"It's called the Lake on the Mountain. Penelope hates the car, and she's already tucked into her drawing, so she can stay with you, right?"

Certain of my answer, she handed me the timer, thanked me with a quick hug and practically skipped out of the room. Setting the timer for fifteen minutes and grabbing a pencil and paper, I made a list of questions I intended to ask Sam. Digging through my carryall, I found a piece of linen to drape loosely over the portrait. When the timer rang, Penny and I stood up. "Come on Pen, let's spend some time on your puzzle."

In the loft, we sat side by side. I told Penny I was very good at assembling the outside edges of jigsaw puzzles and asked if I could help. She folded the fingers of her right hand into a loose fist.

"Thank you, Penelope," I whispered and got to work while my co-puzzler returned to rhythmic picking, placing, and forming puzzle islands. By the time I joined one long strip and two corner sections, she had assembled a rectangle of faded green, edged with deep yellow ochre and another section that looked like a note or letter.

Letters in paintings are not unusual. Johannes Vermeer did at least four paintings involving letters, though only one, *Lady with her maid holding a letter,* has the same deep brown background. Holbein's Erasmus is depicted writing a note, and his dark cap and coat take up a large portion of the painting.

Another of Penny's puzzle islands seemed to be white drapery in a Vermeer-like technique, more hints to the Lady and her maid, though how that related to a swimming pool and the drowning Ophelia I had no idea.

With the edge complete, I collected and assembled tiles of the same streaked yellow. Some of these pieces had matching marks that, when joined, formed a distinctive capital letter M. Excited at the possibility of discovering the artist's signature, I eventually pieced together an A and an R but found nothing to join any of these together.

Meanwhile, Penny had assembled what looked like the closed eye of a sleeping figure. It's a rare subject for most of the masters, though Vermeer did paint an exhausted servant. As I looked on, Penny added tiles to form a forehead and what could have been a headband or scarf. My concentration was so intent, I got a shock when I looked up and saw Dinah standing in front of us.

"Don't mind me," she said holding up a large cloth bag. "I'm just here for the laundry. Should be a decent breeze tomorrow morning and her majesty thinks we'll save the planet if I don't use the dryer." Disappearing into the bathroom, she re-emerged dragging a cloth bag toward the stairs. "I already picked up what you had in your hamper," she told me.

"Thank you," I called after her.

"Dinner out of the oven in ten minutes," she called back.

"Ten minutes, Penny. Let's get our hands washed." I was relieved when she followed me into the bathroom. I lathered my hands while waiting for the water to run warm and, on impulse, made a circle by touching my index finger to my thumb and blew gently into the film of soap. A large bubble formed and hung from my hand. Penny's eyes widened like the bubble. When it suddenly burst, her jaw dropped in surprise. "Shall I make another?" I asked. She responded with a vigorous nod. After five big bubbles elicited the same excitement, she put her hands next to mine and we washed together.

We were the first to arrive in the dining room and, as Penny slipped onto her chair, I sat on the one next to her. Dinner sat on the rotating tray and Penny's meal was on her plate. As she picked up her fork, I had a moment of déjà vu and felt tense until she stabbed a piece of chicken.

Jamie and Beau breezed in, enveloped in the pleasure of companionship. Jamie sat next to Beau and gushed about the amazing lake that really does sit on top of a mountain. "I know this is hard to believe but—" I expected her to say the ever-energetic Beau jumped in and swam across it, "—no one knows how deep it is."

Veronica, the last to arrive, removed the lids from the serving dishes to reveal crispy chicken and pasta salad. As talk continued about the mountain lake enough interesting facts followed for me to consider making the drive to see its phenomena for myself.

"You should go and see it, Maud," said Jamie.

"You could go tomorrow," Beau suggested. "The forecast is for good weather."

"Actually, I'm driving to Toronto tomorrow. I'm having lunch with Gabe and a short visit with my uncle."

"What time will you be back?" Jamie asked, the hint of anxiety in her voice made me think she and Beau had made plans.

I couldn't give a time but as Dinah bustled in with lime sherbet I promised to be back in time for dinner. When we finished out tea, Veronica told me she had some interesting research I might like to see.

"Don't go yet," said Beau. "I picked up a bottle of ice wine. Give me a minute to get a tray and the glasses and we can sit on the patio."

"None for me, dear, thank you." Veronica reached over to touch my arm. "You go ahead Maud. I'll be in my room."

On route to the swing, Jamie said, "So, Sweet Pea, I bet you got a lot done on your drawing this afternoon. I can't wait to see it."

Once Penelope was in motion, we walked the short distance back to the patio and I confessed she hadn't spent much time drawing.

"Why not?"

"Because I decided to help her with the latest jigsaw puzzle. I wish you'd seen the way she let me assemble some of pieces. We made good progress."

"I don't get it, Maud. Why can't you just leave the damn puzzle alone?"

I might have asked Jamie the same question had Beau not swept in like a waiter, tray held high. I finished what tasted like a thousand calories in a tiny glass and left to keep my appointment with Veronica.

She waved me into her room, a new chart proudly displayed on her desk. "I have Penelope's, however, I first want to show you Cecilia's. Before you ask, I managed to glean her natal information during Beau's party.

"In her eighth house is Uranus, the planet of the unexpected, and Mars, the planet of violence. It's on the cusp," she tapped a line on the chart, "of Aries. This indicates sudden, possibly violent death involving the head." She next pointed to a red line in the inner circle. "This is a difficult aspect with Neptune, God of the sea, so drowning is not unexpected."

"Gosh. What does my chart have in the eighth house?"

She pulled it from a banker's box. "No planets in your eighth house, but its cusp is in Sagittarius, suggesting travel challenges."

"I don't think I have an inner compass."

"If that's the case, Maud, you should take extra precautions. Know where you're going and don't let uncertainty affect your driving."

She placed her daughter's chart next to mine. "In the twelfth house, Penelope has Saturn rising in Capricorn. This compels her to finish her puzzles, and of particular interest are these quintiles that speak to her drawing ability."

I didn't need an astrology chart to tell me Penelope had drawing ability. Before getting bogged down in too much detail, I mentioned my plan for an early night.

"That's an excellent idea Maud. Navigating North America's busiest highway demands a rested driver."

Chapter 39

Apathy, rather than resolve, is the key to a good night's sleep. I know this, but I still tried too hard. When I finally dozed off, I overslept and left without breakfast. Traffic remained light for the first half hour. Forty minutes later, it was so congested I missed my exit.

Annoyed and flustered, I took a few deep breaths. However, changing lanes to merge into the collectors was like joining a massive herd of stampeding buffalo. Desperate not to miss another exit, I edged my car toward the far-right lane. The loud blast of a car's horn threw me into an alternate reality.

Time slowed. I looked to my left and stared into the face of a terrified fellow driver—his car just inches from my own. Intuitively, I steered back into my lane, eased off the accelerator and waited for the driver, now doing his best to recover from a panic attack, to get past me. He did and there was just enough time to cross into the lane and make the exit.

With trembling hands, I carried on. Only after I turned into the over-priced municipal parking lot next to Randolph's fine dining establishment did my heart rate and breathing return to normal. I made it as far as the restaurant's foyer before a stern middle-aged woman in a classic black dress told me they wouldn't open for another twenty minutes.

"I know I'm early but I was hoping to see Samantha Hansen."

I was told to wait a moment and shortly a young woman with shoulder-length blond hair breezed into the foyer.

"Samantha?" I asked.

"Maud, isn't it? From the Barrington's place? I forget what they call it."

"Altica," I told her and she rolled her eyes. "I'm meeting someone for an early lunch and remembered you said you worked here. It's a long drive so I'm early."

She checked her watch. "You're not that early. How about I show you to a table?" She grabbed a couple of menus and led the way into the dining area and a table by the window. I sat down brushing aside the fronds of a large fern. "Sorry, Maud. The planter seems to be as far into the corner as it'll go."

"It's fine and if my date doesn't show up, I've got this fern for company."

"Felix."

"Pardon?"

"The fern, we call it Felix. Can I bring you something to drink?"

"Ice tea please and a glass of water for my new friend?" I stroked a frond and we both laughed.

Sam returned with a tall glass of ice tea, a pitcher of water, and an extra glass. "I thought the two of you could share the water," she said.

"Sam, I didn't recognize you at first. What's happening with the play?"

She sat down, cupping her hair, "It's the wig. The play's going ahead. I have the lead and they're auditioning for the part of the sister. The director likes the orange hair. For me, every time I look in the mirror I see Cissy." She shook her head. "For now, I have this."

"Have you talked to the others—Mike, Liam and the other guy. I think you said his name was Bobby."

"Bobby Jenkins. I haven't seen him, but Mike has. Apparently, he's creating an amazing art deco set for a new rendition of Hedda Gabler." She straightened the already straight cutlery. "He used to meet Cissy here for lunch, …"

"In happier times."

Sam nodded, clasping and unclasping her hands. "Bobby was crazy about her. Unfortunately, sometimes he was just crazy."

"In what way?"

"Jealous, insecure, temperamental. Though I have to admit, his jealousy was occasionally warranted."

"Like Cissy not telling him about the fake engagement?" I asked.

"Yeah. She told him she was spending the weekend with me, which wasn't a total lie. She had no idea he'd be visiting his new-found father that same weekend."

"How long had Bobby known about his father?"

"Not long. Less than a month, I think. Anyway, I didn't blame him for being angry at Cissy. He embarrassed her by showing up at the party. That must have been awful for him too." Her face revealed a mix of sympathy and longing. I suspected she had stronger feeling for Bobby than she would admit.

"Do you think they would have made up if Cissy hadn't ..."

"Probably. They were always breaking up to make up. Lately, I've been wondering why she left the cabana after we all fell asleep. Maybe she agreed to meet him." Sam's eyes filled with tears and she pulled a tissue from her pocket. "Shit. I can't talk about this." She hurried from the room.

Grabbing my notebook from my purse, I wrote down Sam's comments. I turned my attention to the menu, eventually deciding on the spinach salad. While sipping my iced tea, I remembered Felix and gave him a long drink of water.

"Hey, who's your friend?"

I turned from the plant to the man, pleased to see Gabe's honey-brown eyes searching for mine. "This is Felix." I stretched a frond across my shoulder. "He's been keeping me company."

"Ah, Felix the filix-mas." Gabe leaned over to kiss my cheek before taking a seat. He nodded toward the fern. "Good to know my competition."

"And filix-mas is?"

"Latin for male fern. They were once used to expel internal parasites."

"Really? Sounds nasty yet impressive."

Gabe leaned back, raising his chin. "One picks up this kind of thing in the drug trade."

"You make it sound like a cartel."

"How many drug lords do you know who can tell you about the common fern?"

"Honestly, Gabe? Not one." I tapped the menu. "I've decided on the spinach salad."

"I'm going to have the beer battered fish with fries. Dinah doesn't do fish. She thinks we'll all get mercury poisoning."

"At least she's looking out for you."

"And here's someone else who's looking out for us," Gabe said, as a waiter arrived to take our order. "Tyler, nice to see you."

"Nice to see you too, sir."

Gabe introduced me, greetings were exchanged, and Tyler took my order. He asked Gabe, "And will you be having your usual?"

Gabe laughed. "I'm too predictable. Perhaps one day I'll order your crispy chicken."

Within a minute, Tyler was back with a beer for Gabe and another ice tea for me. As we sipped our drinks, I told him what I'd learned from Sam. "If Sam is right and Cecilia left the cabana to meet Bobby, he was the last person to see her alive."

"Someone should talk to this guy."

I was sure Gabe had never met Bobby and didn't know he was Caleb's son. I decided it wasn't the time to tell him. "I'm hoping to talk to him after lunch."

"Alone? Do you want me to come with you?"

"I'll be fine. He works at the York Theatre. I'm just going to talk to him, get a sense of who he is which wouldn't happen if you came too."

"And you'll be careful, right?"

"Always."

"Mother mentioned someone complaining to the police and I think that was Sam."

I thought back to Sam's anger the day we met. "Is this about the pool being unsupervised at night because, wow, is that even a thing?"

"Everything is a thing if lawyers get involved. Mother also thinks Sam has been making accusations against Beau."

"Really? Such as?"

"That Cecilia begged my brother to take her home and he refused and instead, kept her a virtual prisoner."

"The incident with Penelope was upsetting, I'm sure but Cecilia could have called a cab or asked someone to take her to the train station. And according to Beau, she may have been crying earlier but she resolved to have a good time. I guess Sam had already gone to bed when Cissy, as she calls her, kept everyone laughing."

"Stoned audiences will laugh at anything." Gabe cleared his throat. "Sorry, Maud. That was flippant. It's been a long week and this morning I missed breakfast."

"I hope we don't wait as long for lunch as we did for our café breakfast."

"Hard to believe that was just five days ago." Gabe looked across the room and pointed at an approaching waiter. "Here comes Tyler."

We shared only a little conversation until Gabe finished half of his meal. I asked if his mother had told him about the dinner party and the unveiling of her portrait.

"Ah yes, and not just an unveiling, it's the 'grand' unveiling. I will definitely be there." He studied my face. "Why do I have the impression you would rather I not?"

"I guess I'm just feeling the pressure."

Gabe reached across the table for my hand. "Don't worry, Maud. There will only be a few of us there and we're all close friends. You'll receive lots of support, even from my hypercritical mother. Then you'll be back in the big city and ready to paint me." He offered a broad grin, before pressing his lips together. "Sorry, I forgot no teeth. But the portrait will be easier because, unlike my mother, I'm happy to have you work from photographs. Speaking of which…"

I put down my fork, pulled an envelope from my bag and handed it to him. "There's one image a little more perfect than the rest."

"You read my mind." He took out the photos. "And you want me to find this image."

"I do."

Going through them like a deck of cards, he selected one and set it in front of me. I shook my head.

"Hmm. I know for sure it's not this one." He handed me an image with his head down and his eyes closed.

"At that point you were either falling asleep or dying of boredom."

He squeezed my hand. "Never in your company, my dear." From the remaining photos, he selected three. "In my humble opinion, any of these would make an excellent painting. Can we agree on at least one of them?"

"Yes, we can." I pointed at the picture in the middle.

"Okay. I talked to your agent; the image is chosen and we have an agreement, right?" I nodded, he smiled and shook my hand.

I gathered the pictures and returned them to the envelope. This was all good news—unless it turned out we couldn't agree on how to paint his chin.

"Maud, I'm sorry. The office beckons." He slipped on his suit jacket, broke a frond from the fern and pressed it into my hand. "A memento of Sir Felix."

"Such delicate leaves." I slipped it between the pages of my notebook.

"Don't be deceived by appearances. Ferns are robust survivors."

On the sidewalk outside the restaurant, we parted ways but not before a warm hug and a lingering kiss. Then I walked to the York Theatre.

Chapter 40

A bubbly twenty-something approached me when I entered the theatre. With a little persuasion, she happily told me the location of Bobby Jenkins's workshop, and directed me toward the stairs.

Fortunately, the studio was clearly marked and since the door was open, I called his name with a cheery hello. He stepped out from behind a prop, and I was struck by his height and intense good looks.

"And you are?"

He relaxed after I introduced myself as an artist and let him know I'd been chatting to my friend Sam at Randolph's. "Sam told me you're working on the sets for *Hedda Gabler* using an art deco theme. It's one of my favourite styles, so I hope you don't mind a short visit."

"No problem. I was just about to break for lunch." He led me to the far wall where he'd taped his initial inspiration—a *Hedda Gabler* poster featuring the Russian actress, Alla Nazimova. "This was my starting point."

"She was stunning. And those eyes."

"I know, eh." He waved a hand toward a nearby table strewn with articles, books, and images, many of them I noticed from the Society of Decorative Artists. "One can never have too much research material." While viewing the flourishes he'd added to the theatre's existing props, we shared stories about the joys and frustrations of a life in the arts—both the financial and the emotional rollercoaster.

"Would you like a coffee?" He gestured toward an espresso machine.

I accepted a small cup. "Wow, that packs a punch."

"It's liquid creativity. I can't work without it." He pulled over an old wooden desk chair. "Have a seat."

"I think a big part of that emotional rollercoaster you mentioned is rejection. An artist needs a thick skin, though maybe that's not as true in your position."

"Ha," he snorted, "I've had plenty of rejection, both on the job and off."

"Sam told me you both recently lost someone very dear. Cissy, I think she said her name was."

He collapsed inward, and I wasn't sure if I was seeing guilt or grief.

"And you were all at the same party—that's tragic. And poor Sam. She said she'd fallen asleep and you and Cissy had an argument." I put on my most empathic face. "She really hoped you two had a chance to make up."

"It's the one thing I'm grateful for." His voice was shaky but he held it together.

"Did you meet her by the pool?"

His eyes narrowed. "Wait a minute. Who are you and how do you know Sam?" With each sentence his voice got louder.

I hadn't anticipated that question. "I met her through Beau." It was the best I could do with only a second to prepare and it was the truth, if only tangentially.

"Beau Barrington?" He spat the name at me and I involuntarily pushed against the back of my chair. "Yes, actually but ..."

"All right we're done." Bobby rose. Taller than Beau he loomed over me and I felt the hair-trigger craziness Sam described. I was off the chair and out of the door in a flash.

"Stop!" he yelled from the landing as I sprinted down the stairs. "What did you say your name was?"

I didn't answer and I didn't look back. It felt like a long trip to the front door, but finally I was out and running toward the parking lot. My car never looked so welcoming. The drive to my uncle's office was just long enough for the sweat to dry and my heart rate to return to normal.

"Maudie!" Uncle Sid wrapped me in a hug. "What took you so long? The hound and I have been waiting impatiently." Sherlock's body wagged like an articulated bus and his tail threatened to clear every item from the coffee table. I grabbed the sagging skin around his neck and stared into a face framed by two droopy ears. His mournful eyes confirming my uncle's words. "You have missed me, haven't you Mr. Holmes?" I kissed the top of his furry head.

"Honey, you look a little flushed. How about a cold drink." He brought me a bottle of soda water from the bar fridge behind the desk.

I sat down, took a long sip, and I told my uncle about my visit to Sam and then to Cecilia's boyfriend, Bobby. I left out the part about running to my car.

"I may be reading between the lines here, but it sounds like their makeup included consensual, possibly very energetic, sex? Did you get that sense?"

"I did. Sam said the relationship was volatile. Bobby was jealous, insecure and temperamental. Seems they liked to breakup to makeup which sort of goes with the territory."

"When do you figure this joyous reunion occurred?"

"Caleb took Bobby back to the coach house after I saw them, so sometime after Caleb went to bed and the Toronto gang went to sleep."

"And where? By the pool, do you think?"

"Hmm. There are sensor lights outside the cabana and lights in the pool, so not too close. I'm sure the police won't have too much difficulty getting the details from Bobby." Sherlock left my side to circle in front of the office door. "Someone has to go out."

"Good timing. We have something to show Maudie, don't we Mr. Holmes." From the coat closet he brought out what looked like a double collar. "Sherlock and I were in the pet store the other day and two of the salespeople were enthusiastic about this new, no-pull collar, I decided to give it a try. I think you're gonna love it."

Bloodhounds are the noses of the dog world, and walking Sherlock can be a challenge. The only thing he seems to like better than following a scent is finding one. My uncle slipped the halter-like device over Sherlock's snout, clipped it behind his head, and we were off, my pooch walking steadily beside me, head held high. "You're right, Uncle Sid. I love it."

"What does Mrs. Barrington think of her portrait?"

"She hasn't seen it since I started the local colour."

He glanced at his watch. "She's probably had a good long look at it by now." He chuckled. "Unless you hid it under your bed before you left."

"I draped it with a piece of linen, but if she cancels the unveiling, I'll know why."

"Stop worrying, Maudie. She'll love it."

As expected, the traffic heading back was like an ever-growing swarm. My shoulders only dropped when I reached the outskirts of the city. When I finally ascended the white pebble drive, I felt relaxed and grateful to be back at least until I saw Jamie running toward me. Judging by the way she was flailing her arms she didn't have good news.

Chapter 41

"Maud, thank God you're back. I ... I ..." Panic swallowed her words.

"What's wrong? What happened?"

"I can't find Penny." She grabbed my arms. "This time, I really can't find her. I've searched everywhere and there's nobody here to help me. Beau and the Queen B went to a meeting with their lawyers. After that, they were going ... shit, I don't remember where they were going."

"It doesn't matter. Just breathe and tell me what happened, and how long she's been missing."

Jamie inhaled and exhaled. "It seems like an hour but it can't be that long. Maybe thirty, forty minutes."

"Okay. Did anything special happen today?"

"Beau took Penny and me on another hike. We got back, went for a swim. Actually, Pen just sat on the edge of the pool. Beau and I did the swimming. Then we had a picnic lunch on the patio. She ate her usual. We went upstairs to change out of our suits. Naturally, she wanted to work on that damn puzzle ..." Jamie paused for a moment, blinking back tears. "Look about what I said—"

"Forget it. What happened next?"

"I called my mother—it's important to her." Jamie's bottom lip quivered. "Sorry. That's a lie. The truth is my mother has early onset Alzheimer's. Some days aren't too bad, others are terrible. Today was terrible. I got angry. After I ended the call, Penny was gone."

"What about Dinah? Have you talked to her?"

"No, she went grocery shopping."

"You know Penny better than most people, even her family. Where do you think she would go?"

"Hiking. I know that sounds weird and it's not something she'd normally do, but Beau made it such fun, pointing out birds, butterflies, squirrels." Jamie pointed toward the woods behind the house. "We went that way yesterday. An easy walk with a good path. Earlier today, we went this way." She indicated the other side of the play area. "With two of us, we can search them both."

I pointed at the path behind the house. "I'll check that one. Will I be going west."

Jamie laughed. "No, that's north. Use the position of the sun. Remember it rises in the east."

We wished each other good luck. Starting down the well-trod path put me in mind of search and rescue movies—seekers finding pink hair ribbons or pieces of torn clothing. Penny didn't wear ribbons and finding torn clothing would be more upsetting than encouraging. I was a few minutes into the forest when my phone rang. I answered, expecting Jamie to tell me she'd found our wayward girl.

"You're back?"

"Sorry, Unc." I explained my reason for not calling as promised.

"Has she run away?" he asked.

"I doubt it. Jamie thinks she's repeating an earlier hike to see more wildlife."

"And how wild is the wildlife?"

I told him not to worry. I was on a well-worn path through a small wooded area. I sounded convincing but as soon as we ended the call my mind conjured up foxes, coyotes, and wolves. Wolves?

Refocusing on the deep scent of a healthy forest and appreciating the coolness of the shade, I plodded along the path. If I had kept hungry predators out of my thoughts and if I wasn't anxious and straining to see Penny at every turn, it would have been a pleasant stroll.

When the path veered to the left, I cupped my hands to amplify my voice and called her name. I paused to listen. Nothing. I called again. Same result. I trudged on.

Eventually, I slipped into a pattern; walk five minutes, call for Penny, survey the area, repeat. Thirty minutes into this routine and I began to hear desperation creeping into my voice.

I certainly didn't expect to be trekking through an Ontario woodland when I dressed for my lunch date in an upscale Toronto restaurant. My choice of footwear, ill-suited for a search and rescue operation, was taking its toll, as was my lack of insect repellant. I considered calling Jamie to ask how long it took to reach the end of this trail, but decided ignorance would be more comforting than knowledge.

Stopping for another futile shout-out, I inadvertently startled a flock of birds. Watching them fly from a cluster of branches, I consoled myself with the knowledge that Penelope had not only spent all her summers around these woods, she'd walked this route yesterday. This reassuring thought lasted until the forest grew so dense it felt ominous, and the shadows filled with curious coyotes and hungry wolves. A few minutes later my positive thoughts about Penny faded and I decided that someone with her challenges could never find her way home alone.

I was pining for my comfy old sneakers when I spied a tree trunk decaying beside the path. Satisfied it would hold my weight, I sat, rested my feet and dialed Jamie's number. Nothing happened. Two more failed attempts. I vaguely remembered something my uncle said about signal strength and decided that sitting in the middle of a forest was a problem. I needed to find an open field.

Forcing myself to move one blistered foot in front of the other, I slogged on. As tears of anger and frustration threaten to break through my resolve, I spotted the peaked roof of a weathered outbuilding about 150 metres off the path. the sort of miniature house that Penny might find irresistible.

I couldn't find a direct path and stepped off the trail into the undergrowth. My feet disappeared into decomposing vegetation and my head filled with a new terror—snakes. I told myself it could be worse. It could be raining and I could be walking in the kind of mud that sucked the flimsy, once beautiful, sandals right off my feet.

When I finally reach the outbuilding, scratches were added to my blisters and I'd swatted so many mosquitos, my arms were stained with my own blood. A walk around the shed revealed no windows and there was nothing to see through the slim gap between the frame and a door kept closed with a pioneer-style latch

I lifted the latch bar and pulled the door open. As my eyes adjusted to the shadows, I saw Penelope. She was sitting cross-legged on the wooden floor, with the calmness of a Tibetan monk. I shoved a rock against the door, and stepped inside. Avoiding a collection of old rakes and shovels, I crouched in front of Penny and gently placed my hand over hers. She raised her head, met my eyes, and said, "Maud?"

Oh my God. Did she just say my name? "Yes Penelope, it's Maud. I'm so happy I found you. Are you all right?" I wanted to hear "yes" or "no" or even "mind your own goddamn business."

Without a word she got to her feet and moved toward the open door. I followed, ready with a steadying hand as she adjusted to the sunlight. A quick examination told me she was in better shape than I was—not even a mosquito bite.

"You look okay. Are you okay?" I asked, hoping for a word or a nod but she kept her head bowed. "How did you get trapped in this shed." I shoved the makeshift door stopper out of the way, let the door swing shut and as it hit the frame, the latch bar dropped into its cradle, securing the lock.

"Ah, maybe that's what happened."

Stepping into the clearing next to the shed, I promised Penny we'd be on our way as soon as I made a quick call to Jamie. Sadly, the excitement of bringing good news was short-lived because now the phone battery was dead.

"For crying out loud!" Irrationally, I continued to press the power button while demanding that the stupid thing work. I let my anger and frustration take me in what I hoped was the direction to the path and expected Penny to follow me. She didn't. I should have known better. It was Jamie's angry words on the phone that drove Penelope out here in the first place. Trudging back to her side, I apologized.

"I'm not angry with you. I'm mad at my phone and myself." I held it up and said, "See, I'm putting it back in my purse. Everything's going to be fine." And, like Dorothy and Toto we were off to find, if not the wizard, at least the path back to the house.

My forced optimism lasted until the pain in my feet went from inconvenient to intolerable. At the same time, the labour of lumbering about the forest was making me sweat. The sweat was attracting more blood-sucking bugs, threatening my sanity. If a snake had slithered by, I would have totally lost it.

I forced myself to stop, take a deep breath, and do a slow scan of the area. It was something one of those professional trackers might do. Since I'm no tracker, I had to admit we were getting nowhere fast.

"Penny, I'm so sorry. I can't do this. I don't know how to get us home." I wiped my tears with the back of my hand, too disheartened to even reach for a tissue. "I should have joined the girl guides when I was a kid or gone on one of those outward-bound things. I've never even been camping."

Penny suddenly grabbed my hand, and pulled at me to follow her. Within a few minutes she had us back on the path.

"You clever girl, you've done it!" I hugged her without thinking. A quick look left then right, and I asked. "Which way?"

She confidently turned to her left, and had I been able, I would have skipped along beside her. Instead, I limped with self-pity, at least until we rounded a corner and I saw movement rippling in and out of the tree-cast shadows.

It was a hound of the Baskervilles and it was racing towards us. I stopped breathing and adrenaline prepared me for flight, but I couldn't leave Penny. Like a superhero, she stepped in front of me and extended her arms. I exhaled a nightmare when Steady greeted her with tail-wagging doggie jubilation.

Reaching us, Caleb said, "Miss Jamie told me you took this path. She's going to be laughing and crying when she sees you two. Good for you, Miss, finding the little one."

"I may have found Penelope, but she's the one bringing us home."

He slipped a backpack from his shoulder. "I got 'ere a few things you might be needing." Like a magician reaching into his hat, Caleb pulled out two bottles of water. I opened the first for Penny, then gulped gratefully from the second. Next came a container of insect repellent and I sprayed my exposed skin. I offered it to Penny, but she took cover behind her canine companion. "It's okay. I won't put it on you if you don't want me to."

"Miss Jamie thought you could use these too." Caleb held up my well-worn sneakers.

I thanked him and leaned against the nearest tree, prying the soles of my feet from the leather sandals. "I thought I was going to have to crawl back."

He lifted the flap of the backpack to accommodate my sandals and I dropped them in. "No worries," he said, "we be back at the house in easy time, you'll see."

He was right. Relieved of the stress of the search and ensconced in a comfortable pair of shoes, I almost forgot how bad it was. As we came round the far side of the garage, Jamie ran toward me, arms extended, and we collided in a hug. "Maud, I can't thank you enough." She drew back for a long stare. "I don't want to say you look terrible, but how bad was it?"

"I coped—more or less. Less more than more."

"And your poor feet? Watching you set out, all I could think was—damn those sandals are not gonna hold up. After I walked the hike we took this morning, I thought of Steady. Dogs are natural born trackers." She patted his furry head. "Good boy." And bending close to Penny she whispered, "Sweet Pea, I was so worried. We all were. Promise me you'll never wander off again."

Caleb gave Jamie the backpack. "Miss, I got to finish my chores."

"Yes, of course. Thanks again. And thank you too, Steady Eddie."

"Are Veronica and Beau back yet?" I asked, as we walked toward the house.

"No, thank God. I don't even want to think about her majesty's reaction if she were to find out I lost her daughter. Promise me you won't tell her."

"I can certainly promise not to volunteer any information."

"Maybe we shouldn't say anything to Beau either. He might accidentally let something slip." When we reached the side of the house, Jamie insisted we use the front door to avoid Dinah.

"Are you afraid she might ask questions?"

"Maud, you need to look in a mirror."

Chapter 42

The mirror revealed a frightful sight. I appeared to have been pulled through a hedge by my ankles. My carefully coiffed hair was a tangled mess and there was more mascara under my eyes than on my lashes.

After a fifteen-minute shower, I felt clean, if not invigorated. Donning comfortable clothes, I hobbled to the loft wearing the only footwear that didn't antagonize my blisters. Penny, completely unfazed by her experience, was assembling the puzzle like a pianist playing Rachmaninoff's fifth piano concerto. The face emerging with each added piece was the same one she'd almost completed the previous evening. Jamie's handiwork again? At least she left the perimeter puzzle pieces Penny let me put together and the two rectangles of green and yellow.

"Is that you Maud?" Jamie called from her room. "I'll be right out."

"Okay," I called back before noting that the letter Penny had partially assembled was gone. I bent close to her ear and whispered, "Finish the face, redo the letter, and try to find the artist's signature."

Jamie joined us at the table. "You cleaned up well. Do you feel better?"

I would have felt much better if she'd left the puzzle alone. "My feet are sore but I'll live." I collapsed on one of the clam chairs.

Jamie joined me with the offer of a banana. "Dinner is in half an hour and there'll just be the three of us."

"Great. I am starving."

"Yeah, traipsing around the woods can work up an appetite." She leaned back against the cushion. "Okay, tell me the gory details."

Though I couldn't tell her how long I was walking before I found the shed, I gave her a fairly accurate description of the building.

"What else was in the shed?" asked Jamie.

"A few rakes, shovels, maybe other gardening stuff. I should have asked Caleb about it, but I was too distracted by the pain of the journey and the joy of the rescue."

"I didn't see it on our hike yesterday but Penny might have. I'm just grateful you found it."

I swallowed a mouthful of banana. "It was such a relief to find her." I lowered my voice to a whisper. "And when I did, something amazing happened. I crouched down next to her, Penny looked up at me and said my name."

"Get outta town," Jamie said, a little louder than she intended. "Are you saying she spoke? Out loud?"

"Yes! I'm like eighty percent sure, though under cross-examination I could be convinced I imagined it. She only said it once."

"All the time I've worked with this kid and I've never heard her voice." Jamie looked toward the puzzle table.

"It was thanks to Penny that we got onto the right path and more importantly, walking in the right direction. Left to me, we'd still be roaming around out there."

Jamie raised her arm in a fist pump and called to Penny. "Good for you, Sweet Pea. You saved the day." To me, she whispered, "Too bad we can't tell her mother any of this."

I argued that Veronica would be so proud of her daughter she wouldn't be angry, but I couldn't convince Jamie.

"I'm paid to watch Penelope, not to lose her. It's not worth …Wait a minute Maud, what are you doing? What's wrong with your ankle?"

I stopped my hand in mid-scratch. "It's itchy."

"Ever had poison ivy?" She took a closer look. "Could be just bites. Not everyone who comes in contact with poison ivy gets it, but if you do, scratching will make it spread. I'll be right back."

Jamie dashed to her room and returned with a small jar and a couple of cotton balls. "This is calamine lotion." She dabbed it on my ankle—it was instant relief. And from the pocket of her denim shorts, she handed me two small packets. "I have this too. It's colloidal oatmeal for your bath. Use one tonight and one tomorrow."

"If it gets rid of the itch in time for Veronica's unveiling, the portrait that is, I'll be grateful."

"Her what?"

I described Veronica's plans, and Jamie saw it as another event from which she and Penny would be excluded.

"I don't think so. She wants her family there and that includes Penelope, which means it also includes you. I'm going to suggest we show her daughter's drawings. Penny will be finished three by then. Speaking about finishing things ..." I pushed myself up from the chair and limped toward the table for another check on the puzzle.

Penny had linked the previously assembled islands. The headscarf looked more like a turban resting on what could be a pillow and it put me in mind of a sleeping figure. The face was haunting and familiar, but I couldn't place it.

"Chow time," said Jamie.

After dinner and afraid to fall asleep in the bath, I decided all I needed was a decent night's sleep, the oatmeal packets could wait until morning. Before closing the blind, I moved a small plant from the window sill and in doing so realized it was an aloe vera. I broke off a leaf and managed to get enough gel to cover my ankle.

By morning, the aloe had done such a good job I felt sure I'd had no contact with a poisonous plant. As an extra precaution, I replaced my morning swim with a medicinal oatmeal bath. Putting the astrology book next to the tub, I settle in for a healing soak.

After the required fifteen minutes, I dropped the book to the floor leaned back and let my consciousness drift. A few minutes later, I was startled into full awareness. I suddenly recognized the face from Penny's latest puzzle. It belonged to a man who had also sought relief in a warm bath. When he died, it had not been from drowning. So, Penelope the Weaver, why have you assembled this message?

Chapter 43

The question of Penny's puzzle occupied me during breakfast. Only when I reached the library to confront the portrait did it slip from my thoughts. After rendering more detail, and adding glazes to give more depth, I stepped back for a critical view. Overworking a piece is a road no artist intends to travel, but it's so easy to misread the signs and ignore the belief that constant improvement is possible.

To check the drawing, I once again turned both the painting and the photograph upside down. Seeing no issues, I put both images to rights, and standing with my back to the easel, used my hand mirror to see the image in reverse. My final test, was to remove the photograph, stand before the portrait for a full minute with my eyes closed, and then open them. In that instant I hoped to see, not oil on canvas, but real life. Did the painted Veronica appear to breathe? I thought so. The final judgement would be from the flesh and blood Veronica. I found her in her office.

"Veronica, whenever you have time, your portrait is ready for an evaluation."

Her reaction was swift and her enthusiasm unexpected. I really hoped that attitude continued after she saw the finished portrait. As we approached the easel, I watched for signs, both positive and negative, and quickly decided she must be a good poker player. She examined the painting from a distance and then moved a little closer. She crossed her arms over her chest and said, "Beau often tells me I'm a control freak, which, I assume, means predisposed to finding fault. That may be true but," she paused and I held my breath, "in this case, I need more time." She tilted her head toward the door. "Do you mind, dear. I need a few moments."

With effort, I strode into the hall, not easy in a pair of flip-flops. After popping into my room to sacrifice another aloe leaf, I called Jamie's cell.

"Maud? Where are you?"

"I'm waiting for a verdict on the portrait, and in need of a distraction."

"We could chat on the phone," she said, laughing. "But it would be an even better distraction if you joined Pen and I in the loft. I'm sure her ladyship will find you when she needs to."

I arrived to find Jamie sitting on Penny's bed, towelling the young girl's hair.

"She refused to leave that thing this morning," Jamie said. "I don't recognize this image, so it could be she's never assembled it before, at least not since I've been here. It looks like a guy who fainted while sitting in a box."

"I only realized who he was this morning while taking my bath."

"The dude is napping in a bathtub? That makes more sense—I guess." Jamie dropped the towel on the floor and grabbed a hairbrush.

"It's a painting by Jacques-Louis David, a French artist, working at the time of the Revolution. His subject suffered from a skin condition relieved only by soaking in a tub."

"Really? Well, at least no one's drowning."

"That's true, but he is dead."

Jamie threw her head back and gazed at the ceiling. "Oh, for fudge sake, of course he is." With a glance toward me she added, "Still it might not mean anything, right?"

Penny tried to wiggle off the bed. "Wait, I'm almost finished. You don't want to leave tangles in your hair." Jamie's cell phone rang. When she set down the brush to answer it, her captive escaped. I heard her say 'yes' and 'okay' before pocketing her phone. "I told you she'd find you. Her majesty awaits in the library."

I felt reduced to a moment in time. "How did she sound?"

"I don't know, Maud. How did you want her to sound?"

"Gleefully thrilled to impart the excellent news that her portrait is perfect."

Jamie snickered. "We are talking about the seldom satisfied, often judgemental Lady of the Manor, are we not?"

"I know," I grumbled. "Not gonna happen."

What Veronica did say when I joined her at the easel was, "Maud, I require an important addition to the painting."

I inhaled. "Really?"

"Yes. I have a large emerald and diamond ring of familial significance and I would like you to add it to my portrait."

I exhaled. "I can do that."

She displayed the ring finger on her right hand, and if I were the type of person impressed with expensive items of jewellery, I would have been duly dazzled. Grabbing my camera, I asked her to take the pose. "I need a picture of your hand with the surrounding information and a detail of the ring. Then I won't need a print."

I got a good photo, but since she was also willing to keep the pose, I mixed a little of the white pigment with oily egg tempera, and using a fine pointed sable brush, drew the ring. When dry, the opaque white would ensure my glazes of local colour created sparkling gold and lustrous gems.

As I rubbed the paint from my brush, Veronica said, "There's something else."

Uh oh.

She walked to the easel. "I look ... sombre. Am I always like that?"

"Well—" I paused. There was no good way to end the sentence.

"What I want is to look strong, yet pleasant. It's something I know you can do, right Maud?"

I nodded, she smiled, and when she left the room, I spread all of the portrait reference photos across the work table. Studying the face on each one, I concluded the woman had only three expressions: sombre, stern, and severe—sombre was almost pleasant by comparison. It was a problem, and not one I wanted to tackle on an empty stomach.

I found the remedy in a lunch of deviled eggs and pasta salad. "This looks delicious," I said, pulling in my chair.

"Go ahead," said Veronica. "We won't wait for Beau. He's taken Dinah on an errand." She tapped a metal tin. "And for dessert, we have the world's best cookie."

"How do we know?" I asked.

Jamie laughed. "Because that's what they're called."

"And according to Dinah," added Veronica, "they are made using a recipe handed down from her grandmother."

My client was still wearing her emerald ring and I watched it play with the light as she raised her fork. I had hoped my next brushstroke would be used to sign my name. Though painting this gem was a joy, creating the pleasant expression she asked for was going to be a challenge.

"What puzzle is my daughter working on at the moment?"

"I think it's David's painting of Marat," I told her.

Her brow creased in thought. "That must be an old puzzle. Perhaps one we brought over from the coach house. I realize we have someone dying in water but a revolutionist in a bathtub is an odd choice." She looked from me to Jamie. "Is it in any way related to a recent conversation?"

We sat in silence until Jamie perked up and said, "Maud's itchy skin."

"Itchy skin?" questioned Veronica.

"A mosquito bite, I think. I scratched too much and now the skin around it is red and sore."

Veronica's brow wrinkled and I waited to be caught in a lie. Fortunately, there was something on her mind more important than my rash. "Maud, have you had an opportunity to peruse our photographs for the ideal expression?"

"I set them out just before coming down for lunch and will study them as soon as I return to the library."

Veronica rose from the table. "If you need me, I'll be in my office."

After she left, Jamie said, "It seems your friend Veronica is never going to let up on this communication through puzzles thing. At least we know why Penny chose the one she did. I only thought of it when I was put on the spot."

"Sorry to throw water on your idea, but Penny started the puzzle before we went on the hike."

Crestfallen, she murmured, "Oh yeah."

"One other thing though, Veronica said the puzzle was moved from the coach house."

"That's because it's an old puzzle."

"And she said it was from the *coach house.*"

Jamie's eyes lit up. "It's Bobby. Penny's trying to tell us he's involved with what happened to Cecilia."

"I don't think Penny even knows Bobby. But she does know Caleb."

Chapter 44

"What could Penny be trying to tell us about Caleb with a painting of a dead guy having a bath?"

"It's more than that. It's a man, water, and death."

"Man, water, death," she echoed. "I get it. The man is Caleb, he pulled Cecilia from the water and she was already dead. Pretty clever when you think of it." Jamie wagged a finger at me. "See, our girl didn't get up to anything in the middle of the night, she is simply a very good listener."

"Possibly, but the verdict of accidental death isn't in yet. And they found a suspicious bruise on Cecilia's head. What if Caleb is somehow involved?"

"But he's such a nice guy and he didn't even know Cecilia."

"If the motive is strong enough, even nice people become aggressive. We know he had means—he's a strong man familiar with the property. And opportunity—no one seems to monitor his actions. As to motive, we know his son was involved with Cecilia. Maybe they argued and—"

Jamie looked over my shoulder. "Beau! You're back. I thought you were out with Dinah?"

"It didn't take as long as we thought it would. How about that game of tennis?" He held up two rackets.

Jamie swiveled toward me.

"Fine with me. We should ask—" I turned to check with Penny, and she slipped off her chair ready to go. "That looks like a yes. I'll bring her to the swing in a couple of hours."

My student settled into her drawing without a moment's hesitation, and I perched on the stool in front of my portrait. My goal—to give my subject a pleasant expression. The photographs offered no help. I needed to find another way. I grabbed my hand mirror, looked into it, and smiled. I compared my face with that of the model. After mixing a small quantity of paint, I gently smoothed a few of the worries from her forehead and reduced the creases between her eyebrows. A light touch with a slightly darker value hinted at laugh-lines around the eyes. Finally, I smudged the corners of her mouth so that if you were looking for a smile, you'd see one.

Satisfied enough to think Veronica would approve, I moved on to my client's second request. By the time my painted lady sported her iridescent jewel, Penny had almost completed her drawing of the scales. A quick scan for the timer told me it was in the loft. Given Penny's powers of concentration, I was reasonably certain she'd stay put if I ran upstairs to retrieve it.

With the promise to be right back, I closed the library door behind me, and raced down the hall and up the stairs. The timer was on her puzzle table and as I reached for it, I noticed she'd added a few more pieces around Marat's left arm and completed the letter he held in his hand. Had she assembled this puzzle first, I would never have understood her message.

A quick jaunt back to the library found my student hard at work. I set the timer, cleaned my brushes and carried the wooden stool to Penny's work table. After praising her work, especially the excellent ellipses and accurate values, I made her a promise. "Penelope, I want you to know I understand why you're assembling *The Death of Marat*. I also want you to know I'll take care of it."

The timer rang, Penny slipped from the chair and put her hand in mine. She left it there until we got to the swing. Leaving Penny to benefit from its calming motion, I sat under the shade of a friendly red maple, pressed my back against its trunk, and closed my eyes. The gentle whine of galvanized chains carrying Penny on her endless journey mixed with the chatter from the tennis court—Beau's words of encouragement and Jamie's of frustration—helped me concentrate. I'd made a promise to Penelope and, as the sounds around me faded, I developed a plan to catch a killer.

"Hey Maud, wakey-wakey."

I opened my eyes and got to my feet. "Where's Beau?"

"He's gone to the house for water. How's the painting? Finished?"

"I think so but I could be wrong. How was tennis? Looked like a love-love game."

Beau arrived carrying the same insulated bag his mother brought to the library. "Hey, what are you two talking about?"

"Puns. It seems Maud is a lot more like your mother than I thought."

I left them enjoying their water. Arriving in my room, I closed the door and called my uncle.

"Maud, honey, did Mrs. Barrington like her portrait?"

"She seemed generally pleased—just a couple of changes," I explained how I painted her from sombre to pleasant.

"Ah, if only every sour puss could be changed so easily."

I joined in his laughter and then got to the real reason for my call.

"From what you've told me, Maudie, I see no cause to doubt the young girl's message. I think we both know there's only one way to verify it."

I explained my plan and together we refined it. Uncle Sid promised to call me as soon as the players agreed. "In the meantime, honey, don't talk to anyone about this."

"I won't. Don't worry."

"I mean it, Maud—no one. Put it in the vault. It's the only way to protect yourself."

I agreed before ending the call. When I was an angst-filled teenager, my uncle told me to create an imaginary strong box, a vault. It was a place to keep secrets and things I didn't want to think about, and knowledge that would someday be needed.

A knock on my door was accompanied by Jamie's call. "Hey, Maud."

I called for her to come in, and she poked her head around it. "We're waiting for you on the patio. Didn't anyone tell you we're having a barbecue?"

I checked my watch. It was ten after five. "Gosh, I didn't notice the time." I grabbed my trusty hoodie and walked with Jamie to the patio. "Sorry I'm late," I told Veronica when she patted the chair next to her own.

"Is everything all right?" she asked.

Perhaps I hadn't properly sealed the vault. "Yes. I was talking to my uncle and lost track of time."

"And what does your uncle do?"

"He's retired. While I'm here, he's looking after my dog—well actually, he's more like our dog." I went on to relate the long and, since no one listening had met either my uncle or my dog, perhaps tedious story of finding him at the humane society—the dog not my uncle.

Veronica asked me what kind of dog, though I think she did so more from politeness than actual curiosity, and Beau announced he was planning a visit to New York. "I need to fly down next weekend and make sure everything is ready for September."

His mother straightened in her chair and reminded him that until the police finished their investigation, he wasn't going anywhere. With an exasperated tongue click, he insisted he'd go crazy if he had to stay locked up in the house. His mother said being locked up is exactly what he was trying to avoid.

When Veronica asked about the painting, I told her the ring was finished and her expression was now pleasant yet strong. I hoped my assurance would influence her judgement.

"Let's finish up here and have a look at it, shall we," she said.

Once in the library, she went directly to the easel and in exactly thirty seconds, said, "Very good. Thank you, Maud. You have created a true image."

Her comments, though brief, were so unexpected I hardly knew what to say. She filled the gap with her eagerness to get to her office and make final preparations for the dinner.

"Veronica, before you go, I thought we might buy some frames for Penelope's drawings and have them on display at the unveiling."

"That's a wonderful idea. And with it, you have given me another. Children are often bored by grown-up things. When we gather in the library, could you supply Penelope with paper and pencils? I'll have Caleb move her small table to a suitable spot and we'll provide her with a model. For the frames," she checked her watch, "there's a store in the town mall that will be open for another two hours."

Sent off on an unexpected mission, I was relieved to find a good selection of readymade frames at the mall. I chose a simple dark grey with a white mat and regular glass. I also purchased three stands to prop them on a table or shelf.

Back to the library with my purchases, I pulled out my phone and let my uncle know the unveiling was proceeding as planned. Finally, I had one more addition to make to Veronica's portrait and it was an important one.

Adding one's signature with paint and a small brush to a vertical surface is even harder than it sounds. I'd been painting for a few years before I realized I could lay the painting on a table and support my hand with a book. For my signature on Veronica Barrington's portrait, I decided on a wise bluish-grey and thinned it to an ink-like consistency. When completed I returned the painting to the easel.

"Hey, Maud. Feel like some company?" I turned to see Jamie and Penny.

"Sure, your timing's perfect. I just signed the portrait."

"It's finished. Can I see it?"

"You can if you promise to be suitably surprised tomorrow."

"Oh yeah, it's the big reveal. Maybe I'd better wait. I'm a lousy actress." She sat with her back to the easel and set the timer. "I gotta say I'm impressed with your courage. All those eyes judging your work. And you know how people are, even someone who's never held a paintbrush is going to have something to say."

"Gee, thanks. Up until now, I'd been successfully ignoring those thoughts."

She patted my hand and looked at me as if my ice cream just fell out of its cone. "It'll be okay. Besides if you have to fix something you'll stay longer."

I reminded her she had Beau to keep her company.

"Yeah, but not for long. I do want the cops to close this damn case so the poor guy can get his life back, even if it means he's off to

New York." She shook her head. "Much as I'd like him to stay, stress fractures are beginning to show."

"Stress fractures?"

"Everybody's got a breaking point, right?"

"Have you talked to his mother?"

"Really? C'mon Maud, you must have noticed that she's not the easiest person to talk to."

"Then you should talk to him. In the morning, I'll take Penny to finish her drawing and you and Beau can spend some time alone together."

She laughed. "Maybe we could book a motel room."

"Is someone going to a motel?" We turned to see Veronica in the doorway.

"I was just telling Jamie you're an excellent model." She squinted at me with suspicion, but the timer rang and Penny stood up ready to go.

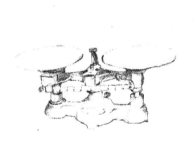

Chapter 45

When my uncle called it was to let me know that everything was set for the following day. We discussed not only Plan A but also Plan B. Uncle Sid always has a Plan B. When we ended the call, I realized I'd missed an earlier one from Gabe. I tried his number but ended up leaving a message. I fell asleep waiting to hear from him.

The woodpecker making a living in the tree outside my window woke me just before seven—the perfect time for my last swim in the Barrington's pool. Clad in my bathing suit and cotton cover-up, a towel draped around my neck, I walked quietly past Beau's room, down the stairs and to the front door. Grabbing the doorknob and pulling it open I stifled a squeal when I found myself face to face with someone it only took a second to recognize.

"Gabe! Holy crap! I just about had a heart attack."

"Sorry, Maud. I misjudged the early morning traffic and got here faster than planned. I intended a pleasant surprise, not a moment of terror."

He stepped back and eyed my outfit. "Ah, you must be on your way to the pool."

"I am but now that you're here we can go inside."

Dropping his overnight bag inside the door, he said, "I don't want you to miss your swim. Much more fun to join you. I have a suit in the cabana."

While Gabe changed, I draped my towel and coverup across one of the deck chairs. Normally, I would leap in from the side of the pool but as he could reappear at any moment, I opted for a more elegant entry using the metal step ladder. I grabbed hold of the rail, but my descent was far from graceful. A sudden spasm in my right hand propelled me awkwardly into the water.

Time and space became strangely muddled. I was vaguely aware of Gabe shouting my name. When I felt a hand reach for me, I tried to help but I was a rag doll with no mental capacity.

It was through his strength that I was saved from the water. Cradling me in his arms, Gabe said words I couldn't understand. He repeated them until I slowly deciphered his intention to call an ambulance. A terrifying image flooded my brain: pool—ambulance—body bag.

"I'm okay. No ambulance. Call Galen. I'm okay." I could only manage two-word sentences.

"Maud, my phone is in the cabana." He gently laid me on the deck with a towel stuffed under my head. "I'm going to get my phone. Don't move." He hovered over me. "Maud, did you hear me? Don't move, okay?" I managed what I hoped was a nod and he promised to be right back.

Weak, numb, and left to stare up at the sky, I felt suspended in blue infinity. When my awareness eventually sharpened to take in the presence of Gabe, I had no idea how long he'd been sitting next to me. "Did you call Galen?" I asked and Gabe pointed toward the path.

"Yes, and he's coming now."

Kneeling next to me, Galen took my hand. "Maud, you've had a nasty shock. Did you, at any time, lose consciousness?"

My short-term memory had short-circuited. Raising my eyes to Gabe, I hoped he could respond for me.

"I came out of the cabana the moment Maud stepped on the ladder. Her whole body went into spasm. Though she's been sort of spacey since—sorry Maud,—I'm pretty sure she hasn't lost consciousness. Why did this happen?"

Galen opened his medical bag. "It sounds like she received an electric shock. If electricity finds its way into your swimming pool, the current is strongest closest to the source. That metal ladder is a good conductor. So when Maud touched it, the current travelled through her extensor muscles causing them to go into spasm." Galen pulled a stethoscope from his medical bag.

"Are you worried about her heart?" Gabe asked.

"I'm listening for an arrhythmia. Wet skin is less resistant to electricity and its flow can affect internal organs."

He pressed the chest-piece over my heart, and I froze. In that instance, I thought if I didn't move, talk, or even breathe, I could improve his diagnosis. And it worked. He lifted the chest piece, wrapped the tubing around the headset and assured me everything seemed fine.

Then, before I could breathe a sigh of relief, he insisted we had to go to the hospital. I searched his eyes, sure the tears forming in mine would convince him to reconsider.

"It's just a precaution. An EKG will give us a snapshot of your heart and they'll attach a monitor to watch your heart's rhythm. The process should only take about an hour. We need to verify nothing unusual is going on. Don't worry, I'll stay with you."

Tears spilled onto my cheeks but I had no energy to argue. I simply wanted to sleep. "I just need to rest for a minute," I bargained.

"I'm sorry dear," Galen shook his head. "You can have a nap when we get back."

While Galen helped me slip on my coverup, Gabe ran back to the cabana and when he returned was wearing his shorts and a short-sleeved shirt. Picking me up, he carried me to his car, tenderly placing me in the back seat next to my attentive physician.

During the drive to the hospital, Galen did his best to distract me with childhood stories about the Barrington boys. "You haven't met the middle son, but I think Gabriel will agree when I say he's the most accident-prone in the family. You'd think with a name like Rex he'd be able to stay on a horse. Fortunately, most of his tumbles resulted in only cuts and bruises, except for the time when he was about sixteen. It was a bad fall. He broke an arm and gave himself a mild concussion. I don't think Ronnie let him go horseback riding after that."

Gabe laughed. "No, but she let him get his driver's license."

"Luckily, he can control a car better than a horse," said Galen. Patting my arm, he asked if Ronnie told me the meaning of her eldest son's name. "I'm sure you've noticed her interest in words and their derivations."

I shook my head. I thought she might have, but at that moment, I felt fortunate to simply remember my own name.

"Gabriel means hero. And Maud, if your hero hadn't pulled you out of that pool as quickly as he did, well, let's just say fatal electrocution in swimming pools is not as rare as you might think."

It was a short drive to the hospital but a long wait before an emergency room doctor checked me over. First, she looked for obvious burns and then for what she called tiny charred craters that indicate internal burns—a much more serious condition. She couldn't find any, but cautioned that the problems after an electric shock could sometimes show up days, even weeks, later. While I pondered that delightful news, a technician attached a series of electrodes, and ordered me to lie perfectly still because any movement, could distort the results. Next, I was hooked up to a heart monitor. Fortunately, I was allowed to sit up, sip a cup of tea, and enjoy the chatter of my male companions.

When we got the news that my heart rhythms were normal, we made a hasty escape. On the drive back, I began to feel the kind of subtle throbbing that warns of a headache. Galen watched me rub my temples and asked if I was in pain. I told him I was just tired.

"There's a remedy for that." He smiled. "We in the medical profession call it bed rest."

I was certain I didn't need a nap, at least until we got to the house, then I could think of nothing else. Gabe offered to carry me to my room and though it made me feel like a Victorian invalid, I accepted. He tucked me under the covers and I had just fallen into a dream, one that had me floating weightless in space when there was a knock on my bedroom door. This was followed by Jamie's sudden appearance on the edge of my bed. "Holy shit, Maud, Gabe told me you were almost electrocuted. What the hell is going on?"

With effort, I pulled myself up and pushed a pillow against my back. I looked from Jamie to the door. "Where's Penny?"

"She's picking flowers with Caleb."

My voice was shaky, my eyes watery and I apologized for my lack of control.

Jamie held my hand. "Hey, Maud, what's this, now? Everything's fine. Tell me what they said at the hospital."

I did my best to relay events in chronological order.

"Yikes, charred craters sounds nasty. Good thing that didn't happen. And with normal heart rhythms, you'll soon be ripe as rain."

"You'll find the expression is *right* as rain."

We looked up to see Gabe standing in the doorway.

"It is?" Jamie moved to the adjacent chair, offering her spot on the bed to Gabe.

He suppressed a smile and rubbed my cheek. "Do you feel any better now that you've had a nap?"

"I had a nap?" I could have sworn Jamie had appeared only a few moments after I'd closed my eyes.

"When I peeked in on you an hour ago you were doing a mighty fine imitation of someone napping."

"An hour? Wow."

"Gabe, I saw you and Dr. Patmore checking around the pool," said Jamie. "What were you looking for?"

"We were trying to find out how electricity was getting into the water. We think one of the underwater lights has been damaged."

She hunched forward, forearms across her knees. "How could that happen?"

"I'm not sure. Maybe general wear and tear. Neither of us knows much about swimming pools."

"What about the chlorine? I hear it's corrosive," Jamie said, and Gabe agreed.

They speculated about the odds of an accident, of something hitting the light during cleaning. "You don't think the damage could have been deliberate, do you?" Jamie asked.

"Deliberate damage," I echoed. They turned toward me as if surprised to find me in the room. "Are you saying electricity was sent into the swimming pool on purpose?"

Jamie's eyes widened. "Shit, that would mean someone was trying to kill you."

Chapter 46

"Let's not get ahead of ourselves," Gabe cautioned. "Like I said, Doc Patmore and I don't know much about swimming pools and even less about underwater lights."

"Okay." Jamie flicked her hand as if to erase the idea. "Besides, why would anyone want to hurt you, Maud?"

I thought I knew, but let a shrug do my talking.

Jamie stood up. "I gotta get Pen. I'm so glad you're okay, Maud." She blew me a kiss on her way out the door.

"And I can't stay either," said Gabe. "Mother wants me to find an electrician who's willing to come out today." He gave me a gentle kiss. "You get some more rest, and I'll be back to take you to lunch."

I felt sure I was almost back to normal but, seconds after he left, my head throbbed and my fingertips tingled. Psychosomatic? Muscle memory? Those lingering problems the ER doctor talked about? I decided it wouldn't hurt to have another nap, a short one, and set the bedside alarm clock, switching it to the softest ringtone.

I awoke with the alarm, my brain still feeling a little foggy. A warm shower may have helped but I was a water-shy. Though if I'd thought about it, it would have made more sense to avoid light switches. Dressed and ready to leave my little sanctuary, I pulled open the door to find Gabe, his fist upraised and ready to knock. I'd forgotten he was coming for me but covered it with a compliment on his perfect timing. He thought it indicated our psychic bond.

"Really? What am I thinking right now?"

His arms closed around me and his mouth warmed mine.

As we entered the dining room, Veronica lifted the lid of a soup tureen. "Welcome, Maud. Dinah made your favourite asparagus soup. She thinks it has recuperative powers." She held up a bowl. "You'll have some, won't you?"

Gabe pulled out my chair for me and I thanked her as I nestled closer to the table.

"Did Gabriel tell you a qualified electrician will soon be checking the pool?"

"He did."

"No need to dwell then. At least this evening can go ahead as planned."

"Mother, you might at least ask Maud if she would like to proceed with events as planned." Gabe echoed her last two words with extra emphasis.

"Maud?" Veronica may not have been drumming her fingers on the table, but her stare was just as effective.

I pushed aside doubts that hung like tiny black bats and fibbed with conviction. "Thank you, Gabriel. I'm fine and looking forward to it."

Veronica looked to her son with raised eyebrows. "You see, she's fine. Now, Caleb will be clearing the extra furniture from the library. Maud, when you pack up your supplies, please set aside whatever you think Penelope will need."

When the cook brought in the tea tray, Veronica said, "Dinah, your soup has had a restorative effect on Maud. We will continue," she glanced at Gabe, "as planned. I trust you have everything you need for serving the desserts."

She dipped her head like an army recruit.

"Anything I can do?" asked Beau.

Dinah beamed at him. "You can pick up a couple of things in town for me."

Veronica clicked her tongue. "Dinah? I thought you just indicated you were completely ready."

"I am ready," she propped one hand on her hip, "With my Sonny's help, I'll be even more ready. Pop into the kitchen when ya finish your lunch."

Beau insisted he didn't mind, and Gabe opted to go with him. "Unless you need me, Maud."

"I'll be fine." The weariness of telling everyone I was fine was making me less fine. I hoped no one noticed or it would only get worse.

When the door closed behind Dinah, I asked Veronica if Caleb would also be joining us for the unveiling, and, though it sounded cryptic, she assured me he had his job to do.

"Speaking of Caleb," said Beau, "Mother, why not ask him to have a look at the pool?"

"It's best to wait for the professional."

"But Caleb knows the pool better than anyone."

Jamie looked at me, and I knew exactly what she was thinking.

"Caleb may have a general knowledge of our swimming pool, but he's not an electrician."

Beau clicked his tongue. "Sometimes Mother, you can be very, um, dismissive."

"Dear, the word dismissive means to consider something as unworthy of consideration. I, however, am merely stating a fact."

Before tempers flared, Beau went to the kitchen to get the list from Dinah. Veronica left to speak to Caleb. Gabe placed a hand on mine. "Maud, when I get back, how about a nice quiet walk in the woods?"

A sharp intake of breath caused me to inhale rather than swallow a tiny piece of apple. I coughed, gagged, and sputtered. While I struggled to regain control, I heard the words Heimlich Manoeuvre.

"No!" I waved them away and managed to clear my airway before becoming a medical experiment.

As soon as I could breathe normally, I took a cautious sip of water. Like an anxious nurse, Gabe patted my hand. "Okay now?"

"Yes, Gabriel, I'm fine."

"Good. So, what about that walk?"

Jamie's eyes met mine and we laughed so hard I almost started choking again.

"What are we missing?" asked Beau.

"Nothing really, it's just nervous tension." By avoiding eye contact with Jamie, I managed to explain that I would be busy framing Penelope's drawings. "She's welcome to stay with me. It will give her time to finish her third drawing. When it's complete, I'll show her how to frame it."

Jamie and Beau were out the door. Gabe lingered until I shooed him out with a wave of my hand. In the library, my student got to work while I cleared out the tabouret, and packed my paint box. All my other supplies, except what Penny would need for this evening's drawing, went into my carryall and I left both the box and the bag at the library door ready to take to my room.

Penny had her third drawing completed in the time it took me to frame her first two. She joined me at the work table to watch as I framed her final piece. We then spent a few minutes selecting the best spot to display her work.

Gabe returned to find us standing in silent admiration. He carefully examined each drawing. "Your drawings are really impressive, Penelope. They look very professional in the new frames. Good work. And you too, Maud."

"Sorry to bother you." Caleb stood in the doorway.

Gabe waved him into the room and offered to help with the furniture removal. This seemed like the perfect time to take Penny to her swing. When she refused to leave her drawings, I dashed to the loft to get the timer. David's Marat was still on the table. Little had been assembled since the last time I saw it.

I raced back to the library. Not only was Penny still guarding her drawings, but she was anxiously alternating her weight from one foot to the other. I felt sure the timer would not provide its usual incentive. Maybe some information would.

"Penelope, just because these drawings are finished and framed, doesn't mean you can't make another one. Everything you need will stay here. After dinner, I'll find you a new model and you can start another drawing." Her body visibly relaxed. When I put out my hand, she took it.

As we walked the path toward her swing, I told her I understood the message in the Marat painting. "If you want to you can finish one of your new puzzles now."

She didn't say anything but squeezed my hand before letting it go.

Jamie was waiting for us on the swing. As we approached, she slipped off and held it steady for Penny. "Did you finish your last drawing, Sweet Pea?"

"It's her third drawing and she's going to start another tonight."

"That's great. I bet the first three look wonderful in their new frames." She gave Penny a push to get her started and joined me on a nearby garden bench. "Still feeling, okay?"

"I hope so." I massaged the back of my neck. "I might be getting a headache."

"Not surprising for someone who was almost ELECTROCUTED!"

"Medical science seems to think I'm fine."

"Almost choking to death on a piece of apple might have something to do with or, wait, isn't there a big reveal happening tonight?"

"A what?" Did she say what I thought she said?

"You know the portrait, the perfect likeness of the Queen B?"

"Oh, that."

"Whatever the cause, I have a pill that might help." Reaching for her purse draped over the back of the bench, she unzipped a side pouch and from a tiny box took two white pills. "Here you go, acetylsalicylic acid. Bet you're impressed I can say that. I know I am." She smacked the side of her head. "Good Lord, I have the early symptoms of logophilia."

I popped the pills into my pocket. "I'll get some water inside. See you later. See you later too, Penelope."

Back in the library, I found Gabe and Caleb had moved the large work table closer to the windows and Penny's drawing table to the far corner of the room. I stowed my paintbox and carryall in my room and returned to relocate the easel to a safe spot between the bookcases. Happy with the placement, I couldn't resist lifting the linen drape from the canvas for a reassuring peek. Yep, still good.

"Hey, Maud," I let the drapery fall back into place. "Since a walk in the woods is off the agenda, I've set up a couple of comfy lounge chairs on the patio. Sound good?"

It certainly did and I wasted no time getting to one. While I nestled into the cushions, Gabe placed a cold glass of lemonade on the small plastic table between us.

"You have to tell me, what's so funny about a walk in the woods?"

"Only if you promise not to repeat any of this to your mother."

He raised his hand in the scout's three-finger salute and I related my tale of trial and error. When I finished, he wagged a finger at me. "I wished you'd told me sooner."

"I would have—if you had called."

"I did call and I left a message."

"Yes, and I called you back."

"You did?" He grabbed for his phone.

"Gabe, never mind. It doesn't matter." I took a deep breath and dissolved into the cushions.

"Maud dear, are you awake?"

My eyes opened to squint at the figure blocking the sun.

"It's time for dinner," Veronica said, before disappearing into the house.

"Holy crap." I sat up and dropped my legs over the side of the recliner. "I have to get changed."

Gabe rose up on one elbow. "No, please don't."

"What?"

"I like you just the way you are." He grinned. "Is formal wear expected?"

Getting to my feet, I felt almost back to normal. "I'm sure you're fine. I, however, have my reputation to maintain."

"Doesn't that mean you can show up in paint-splattered jeans?" he called after me.

Chapter 47

Grateful to have preselected an outfit for the evening, I fussed with my hair, added a little makeup, my best earrings, and exchanged the flip-flops for my second-best sandals. As I descended the grand staircase, Gabe was standing by the fireplace. I approached, and he raised his elbow, ready to escort me to the dining room.

"How very gallant. Did I miss the part where everyone was summoned from the drawing room?" I pictured Caleb in livery.

"Yes, but don't worry you're here now."

We entered the dining room, and Galen rose from his chair. "Here's the artist," he said. I apologized for being late. "Say no more about it, my dear. After the day you've had, we're more than happy to wait."

"Maud," said Veronica, "you're sitting next to Galen, and Gabe, dear, you next to me." We took our places and Veronica introduced the woman sitting opposite and the man to her right. "Maud, I'd like you to meet Dr. Peter Fischer and his wife, Florence. Florence is Galen's daughter. She too is a doctor."

We exchanged the usual greetings, and Galen informed me, with some seriousness, that his daughter married outside the faith. My confusion gave him obvious delight. With a hearty laugh, he said, "Peter is a veterinarian."

Florence raised her eyebrows in response to what must be a familiar joke and introduced me to her son Kurt. A sulky boy of about fifteen, he found a bowl of avocado soup more interesting than a woman who paints faces.

Veronica had seated Penelope between Jamie and me. I knew it was chosen as a spot to ensure the safety of the guests, particularly

Kurt. His adolescent angst made him a likely candidate for Penelope's brand of natural selection.

"Maud," said Florence, "You must find this terribly exciting. I know both Peter and I are truly looking forward to viewing Veronica's portrait." She smiled encouragingly at Veronica.

I thanked her, knowing if all went according to plan she would, no doubt, find it very exciting indeed.

"I've got some exciting news too," Beau said, and Veronica dropped her spoon. "Earlier today I heard from an acting buddy of mine in New York." He paused for dramatic effect. "I've got a lead part in a new play. Rehearsals start next month."

Dinah, busily adding platters and serving bowls to the table, beamed at her boy and as words of congratulation erupted around the table, his mother asked how it was possible to get a lead part in a play without going to an audition. Beau feigned shock at his mother's lack of faith but did not attempt to answer her question. Kurt, now animated and inquisitive, proclaimed that actors were awesome.

Dinah removed the doomed lid from the large serving platter to reveal a roasted chicken, artistically decorated with clementines and surrounded by oven-roasted potatoes. Florence sighed with pleasure and threatened to kidnap Veronica's cook at the first opportunity. Peter agreed, and it occurred to me that I was attending my last supper. Gabe must have read my mind when he said, "We'll be back in the city tomorrow, right, Maud? Looking forward to breathing in the Big Smoke?"

He was referring to one of Toronto's nicknames. A term I was sure my soon to be ex-client would never use. "The air won't be as clean as it is here, but as always, it'll be good to get home."

After the dinner plates were cleared, Veronica invited her "dear family and friends" to the unveiling of a wonderful portrait, an event to be followed by tea, coffee, and Dinah's delectable desserts.

We paraded up the stairs to the library and filed past Caleb, looking uncomfortable in a stiff white shirt and black dress pants. Steady seemed very much at home, resting at his master's feet. It occurred to me he needed to be immortalized in graphite.

Taking centre stage, Veronica directed our attention to the display of her daughter's drawings and almost everyone (Kurt seemed to have found a solitary corner and an interesting book) gathered around to ooze praise and encouragement. Their words would be motivating for most artists, but Penelope was unaffected by the opinion of others and for this, I envied her.

Caleb retrieved a dog bed, as I requested, and led Steady to the small drawing table. Penny followed, ready to begin her next creation. I tagged along, directing the placement of the bed to give the artist the best view of her canine model. As Steady happily hunkered down, Caleb assured me his furry boy had been well-exercised and would appreciate a long nap.

With a clap of her hands, Veronica called for our attention. "We're ready for the unveiling. Select a glass of Dinah's sparkling punch and bring it with you to our seating area." Dinah, standing behind the work table (its utilitarian features now hidden under a fine linen tablecloth) was busy filling the glasses.

The group assembled, and Veronica began a prepared speech. "I'm so glad you could be here on this special occasion. When my children and I decided to surprise my husband with a long-requested gift, we approached our dear friend, the esteemed artists' agent, Evelyn Baer. He recommended Miss Maud Gibbons—an artist who, like Cinderella's shoe, was a perfect fit. In the realization of my portrait, Maud bravely accepted my need for participation. At this point, I invite her to join me at the easel so we may reveal the culmination of our many hours together." The moment I stepped next to the easel, I knew the time I'd spent telling myself there was nothing to be nervous about, was completely wasted. I only had a few prepared sentences, but they evaporated the moment I gazed into the eyes of my small audience. I looked over their heads and saw Penelope. She had paused from her drawing, and her calmness was sending me support. I took a breath and managed to remember most of what I wanted to say. And when I reached up to carefully remove the drapery, it was with a steady hand. The portrait exposed, I forced myself to face the group. Penelope had already returned to her drawing, heedless of the applause that meant so much to me.

"Thank you, everyone," cooed Veronica. "We welcome your comments and questions."

I wasn't entirely sure I agreed with her but I smiled at Gabe and willed him to say something positive. He did. "It's a great portrait, Maud. Congratulations. And you too, Mother." He raised his glass.

Beau geared his comments to what he called the awesome theatrical quality of the painting. "It's an excellent likeness, but there's something else." He paused. "I can't say what it is, Mother, but you look … different." My hope was he meant that in a good way.

Florence's contribution was to say Veronica looked otherworldly. I was grateful she hadn't used the word alien.

Her husband agreed. "Especially with that background, right Flo? It's the sky with stars, yes?"

Veronica explained the reason for the constellation, adding that stars are also symbols of self-fulfilment.

Jamie struggled too. First, she said her employer looked happy, changed it to relaxed, and finally decided neither adjective worked. When Gabe suggested contented, Beau said, "That's it! You're always so busy, Mother. You need to sit down more often and look contented."

"Thank you, Beau. When I have the time, I'll consider it."

Sitting on the floor, his back against one of the bookcases, Kurt lowered the book that held his attention and replaced one awkward moment with another. "Why didn't you just take a photograph?"

"That's a good question, Kurt," said his grandfather. "To answer it properly will require a trip to the Art Gallery of Ontario. Perhaps we can do that soon." His words were a warning and Kurt returned to his book.

Galen turned to me and took my hand. "Fine portrait. Do you know what the name Veronica means?" He winked at our hostess and I admitted I did not. "It's a Latin name meaning *true image.*"

"And now," said Veronica, "it's time for dessert." As the group drifted in the direction of the table, Caleb, no doubt anxious to change into more comfortable clothes, made a furtive exit.

While her guests enjoyed pastries, cakes and creams, Veronica expounded on the rigours of posing for one's portrait. Slipping in next to me, Jamie whispered, "At least you got your name on the painting."

I nodded. "If the artist does a good job, the focus will be on the subject. If the painting is panned, it's on the artist."

"Life isn't fair, is it? And now I suppose you'll be going home."

"Maud, Jamie, forgive me for interrupting." Galen touched my shoulder. "My daughter's family and I have another event to attend. Sorry to rush off." He hugged me. "You take care of yourself and have Gabe bring you back to see me before they close up for the winter."

"Lovely portrait, Maud," called Florence. They waved their goodbyes, even Kurt, though with less enthusiasm.

"I like that idea of Doc Patmore's," said Jamie. "Have Gabe bring you next weekend."

"Where am I bringing you next weekend?" asked Gabe.

"Jamie's kidding but I might consider it in a few weeks."

"Or months," said Gabe, with a wink. Looking at my empty hands he said, "What's this? No dessert for the struggling artist."

"There are far too many to choose from," I told him.

He guided me to the table and with help from Jamie and Beau, my plate was loaded with one of each dessert. "There you go. Do a taste test and pick your favourite."

Jamie laughed. "Bet you can't pick just one."

With the laughter and chatter and clatter of cutlery, no one heard the ring of the doorbell. But then no one was listening for it, except me.

Chapter 48

While enjoying the full chocolate flavour of a creamy piece of fudge, I noticed Caleb arrive at the library door and speak to Veronica. I was tasting a mini éclair when they both left the room and savouring a spoonful of Pineapple Delight when they returned.

They were followed by Inspector Murray and two uniformed officers, and the chatter ceased abruptly. We stood, statue-like waiting for news—hoping it would be good, knowing it wouldn't. One constable remained by the door, the other joined the inspector as he approached Beau.

"Beau Aaron Barrington, I am arresting you for the murder of Cecilia Fox. You have the right to retain and instruct counsel without delay. Do you understand?"

His bright future reduced to a black hole, Beau sought Dinah's eyes. She was the one who had always been there for him. "They're wrong, Nan. I didn't do it. Help me." His chin dropped to his chest, his breathing altered, and a panic attack seemed imminent.

The uniformed officer ignored Gabe's pleas. He grabbed and cuffed each wrist, then placed a hand on Beau's shoulder and walked him toward the door. Before they reached it, Dinah rushed to her boy. Clutching his arm she cooed, "It's okay Sonny. I'm here." Suddenly, she whirled on the officer like a witch ready to unleash her powers. "You get those nasty things off him. Do it now and I'll tell ya what *really* happened."

The officer obliged and my head stopped throbbing.

"That night, the night of your birthday, Sonny, somethin' woke me up." Dinah led Beau to a chair, sat next to him took his hands in her own. "You remember that time your sister started the fire?

When I hear somethin' I have to get outta bed and check to see what's goin' on. It's the right thing to do. Don't you think, Sonny?" Beau nodded. "And what do you think I saw?" She paused, but not long enough for Beau to respond. "I saw that woman who called herself Ceal. I know you said she was your fiancée but Sonny it was never goin' to work. She was a thief. I saw her pilferin' my kitchen. Not only that but when she found what she was lookin' for, she grabbed it and sauntered out like she owned the place."

Beau gently withdrew his hands and asked. "And then what happened?"

Dinah's voice rose in remembered anger. "Sonny, you know thievin' can't be ignored. I followed her and when she stopped near the pool I said, 'I'll have that back, thank you very much.' She almost jumped out of her skin." Dinah smacked her knee. "But did she give it back to me?"

"I don't know, Nan."

"No siree. She thought I was jokin' and giggled like a little girl. As God is my witness, Sonny, she would not return my property." Dinah wagged her finger. "Too much of the devil's brew in that one. There was no reasonin' with her."

"What property are you talking about, Nan?"

"The biscuit tin you bought for me from that British collector. It's a beautiful thing and full of my best cookies."

"What did you do?"

Dinah made a fist with one hand and pounded it into the palm of the other.

Beau's eyes widened. "You hit her?"

"Of course not."

"Then," Beau glanced at the officer standing behind Dinah, "how did Cecilia end up in the swimming pool?"

Dinah pushed her shoulders back and clutched at her hands. "She musta fallen in, Sonny. The way she was staggering. All that drinkin'. Once I had my tin, I went back to the house. I didn't wait to see it happen."

"But someone did." Heads pivoted toward me. "Penelope got up Saturday night, perhaps to work on her new puzzles, and when she did, she saw—"

Dinah interrupted me with a loud guffaw. "Work on her puzzles? That girl works at nothin'."

"As I was saying," I continued, "Penelope saw something that night and the next day she abandoned the jigsaw puzzle of Van Gogh's *Starry Night* and started Botticelli's *Birth of Venus*—the picture of a young woman floating on water."

"That's not proof she saw somethin'." Dinah clicked her tongue. "The kid's not deaf. She knew the girl she stabbed with a fork had an accident." Dinah raised an eye to Inspector Murray. "Besides, it's not uncommon for folks to drown in backyard pools. You'd think the law would know that."

"We do," said the inspector. "We also know Miss Cecilia Fox had been the victim of a violent blow."

Beau jumped to his feet and backed away from Dinah. "You killed her."

"No!" Dinah yelled. "I didn't hit her that hard."

"But you did hit her, Nan. And she died."

"That wasn't my fault. She musta hurt her head fallin' into the pool."

"Penelope says otherwise," I said.

"How can you listen to a kid who won't talk?" Dinah rolled her eyes.

Ignoring her, I looked at the inspector. "Penelope has her way of communicating. After assembling *The Birth of Venus,* a figure on water, she started David Hockney's *A Bigger Splash*—a painting of a swimming pool. She was showing us the scene of the crime. As soon as Jamie and I recognized the puzzle, she abandoned it and moved on to John Everett Millais's painting of the death of Ophelia. This was her way of identifying a drowning victim."

"So what?" mocked Dinah. "She was joining in your conversation. She didn't actually *see* anything."

"I believe the last puzzle she chose proves you wrong." I explained to Inspector Murray that some of the puzzle boxes were labelled with titles, while others had identifying numbers. "Mrs. Barrington saw the number on this particular puzzle box and knew it was originally owned by someone living in the coach house. It depicts a painting by Jacques-Louis David called *The Death of Marat* and by choosing to assemble it, Penelope identified the killer."

"Caleb lives in the coach house," Jamie said, looking at the man standing near his dog.

"He does now," Veronica agreed. "However, for the few years of her marriage, Dinah lived there with her husband."

I turned to the cook. "Dinah, you told me that, the day I arrived. You also said your maiden name was Corday. Since you worked for the family before your marriage, everyone, including Penelope would have known you as Dinah Corday."

Dinah waved a dismissive hand. "Means nothin'. Besides a kid with her issues would never remember that."

I glanced at Penny, absorbed in her drawing of a sleeping dog. "It's precisely those issues, as you call them, that give Penelope a phenomenal memory. At some point, she heard the story behind David's painting of Jean-Paul Marat—a French revolutionary leader, murdered by a woman. That woman was Charlotte Corday. Dinah, you may have even told Penelope the story yourself.

"The day you came to the loft to collect laundry, you recognized the puzzle she was assembling. A couple of days later, I think you lured her to that shed in the woods, locked her in and went back to disassemble the puzzle."

Dinah grabbed for Beau. "I don't know what's goin' on. You know I didn't kill Ceal and I would never lock Penelope away." She dropped her head in her hands. "Help me, Sonny. I can't talk about this anymore."

She started to sob and Beau wrapped a comforting arm around her shoulder. "You don't have to say anything more right now Nan, but the police need you to go with them."

"You'll come with your old Nan, won't you Sonny?"

"I can't Nan, but I will come down to the car with you."

He steered her toward the door and the police escorted them from the room. As soon as they were gone, everyone, except Penny, crossed the room to watch from the window. The police car pulled away, and Jamie said, "What's going to happen to her now?"

Veronica cleared her throat. "She will be questioned and asked to repeat, in greater detail, what she said tonight. For example, she's already admitted to assaulting poor Miss Fox and has made it very clear she believes her actions were justified."

"I think the police will be able to prove Dinah hit Cecilia on the side of the head with a wooden meat mallet," I said.

"How do you know that?" asked Veronica.

I told her Inspector Murray had questioned me about the small wooden mallet I use to bang stretcher bars together. "I think the police found it with the pool equipment and now I'm sure Dinah planted it there to put suspicion on me. I also know the bruise found on Cecilia had a unique pattern and Veronica, I think you've already provided the police with Dinah's own mallet, the actual murder weapon."

"Yes, Maud. It was the first thing they asked for when I went downstairs with Caleb. They also told me what they hoped to accomplish by arresting Beau."

Moments after she said his name, her youngest son walked through the door. "Mother, despite everything, we will help Dinah, won't we? She's going to need a good lawyer."

"Dear, I think Dinah is in far greater need of a good psychiatrist."

Gabe looped his arm into mine. "It seems to me the police had some inside help. What do you say, Maud?"

"I said my uncle was retired, and he is, from the Toronto Police Service. He now runs his own detective agency, and as soon as I realized what Penelope was telling me, I asked for his help. We came up with a plan and he made the arrangements that brought the police here tonight."

"How could you be sure Dinah would confess or even implicate herself?" asked Jamie.

"I couldn't. I knew that if she let the police arrest Beau, he could have been released on a technicality. However, they would still have Penelope's information and Dinah's meat mallet."

Jamie bit into a chocolate eclair. "She was a dictator in the kitchen with old fashioned attitudes but I think we forgot it all when we sat down for a meal. I had no idea she was so … unstable. Do you think she put Penelope in that shed?"

"Yes," said Veronica turning to Jamie, "tell me about that shed."

"Oh, um … I was on the phone with my mother, she's not well, and I lost track of Penelope." She went on to describe her frantic search, my return from the city, and our decision to walk the two paths her daughter recently hiked with Beau.

"And while Jamie searched the more difficult path," I said when it was my turn to continue the story. "I took the easy one and it led me to the shed. I may have found your daughter but she's the one who got us home. And to be honest, I don't know if she wandered there herself or if she was led there by Dinah."

"Which raises another question," said Jamie. "Dinah knew Maud liked to go for a morning swim. Could she have sabotaged the pool?"

"It's possible," said Gabe. "Especially if she thought Maud would figure out the message in the Marat puzzle. Did the electrician get here, Mother?"

"Yes, he found damage to the bonding wire. He thinks it caused electricity to be introduced into the water, though he couldn't be certain how it happened. I mentioned it to the police and expect further investigation."

Collapsing in a chair Beau said, "My God, it's a trail of destruction. And all for a cookie tin."

"I'm not convinced that was her real motive," I said. Beau looked up at me. "I'm sure she wanted the tin back but it was much more than that. Cecilia was doing her best to be unlikable and we all obliged, including Dinah. I've no doubt she saw this orange-hair woman in skimpy clothing a very unsuitable fiancée for her Sonny. She also thought Cecilia was drunk and stealing food from her kitchen. By the time she followed her to the pool, Dinah was carrying a lot of anger and a strong need to protect you."

Beau's voice cracked with emotion. "I told you this was all my fault. I should have taken Dinah into my confidence when we first got here. If only I'd told her the truth about the engagement." He dropped his head into his hands.

His mother gently rubbed Beau's back. "You know Dinah chose to take that mallet to the pool. She also decided how much force to use. And while she may have convinced herself Cecilia's death was an accident, she couldn't hide the truth from your sister."

"That's true Mother, but Penelope isn't going to talk to the authorities."

"Maybe not in her own words," I said. "But she's been precise with her puzzles. Ophelia may have fallen into the water but Charlotte Corday didn't drown Marat, she attacked him. You have a very clever sister."

Beau knelt next to Penelope. "I want you to know I'm sorry for the unkind things I said. I was angry but that doesn't make it right. And despite everything, you came through for me. You saved the day, Penelope. Thank you."

Penny carefully lifted her pencil from the paper. She looked into her brother's eyes and said, "You're welcome."

Acknowledgements

With many thanks to the Medli Committee, Gail Anderson-Dargatz, Constable Clarke of the Ontario Provincial Police, Jane Gutteridge, my editor and my family.

Author Bio

Author of *The Painter's Craft,* editor and contributor for six Hill Spirits anthologies, Susan Statham was born in Toronto and raised Fredericton N.B. and Ottawa. A graduate of Algonquin College she worked in a children's psychiatric hospital. Returning to Toronto, she raised two sons and worked in special education. While attending the National Portrait Academy she travelled to Italy for a workshop at the Cecil Graves studio and by special invitation, to New York to visit the Art Students league. With a major in psychology, and courses in advanced fiction writing, she completed her degree at the University of Waterloo and obtained a job as a school librarian.

Moving to the Cobourg area, Susan taught adult classes in both writing and painting from her home studio, the Cobourg Library and Fleming College. For Canada's sesquicentennial, Susan was commissioned to paint twelve of Canada's prime ministers for a series called The Nation Builders. the 2021 she received Cobourg's Distinguished Civic Award for Arts and Culture. Susan is the president of the Cobourg Art Club, a past president of the Spirit of the Hills Arts Association and Chair of the Spirit of the Hills Writers Group.

Printed in the USA
CPSIA information can be obtained
at www.ICGtesting.com
LVHW010825240924
791916LV00029B/244